BIG
GIRLS

Don't Cry

JOANNE TRACEY

First published in Australia in 2019

by Joanne Tracey

https://joannetracey.com

Copyright © Joanne Tracey 2019

Print ISBN 978-0-9943134-4-7

Kindle ISBN 978-0-9943134-2-3

Epub ISBN 978-0-9943134-3-0

Cover design by Lana Pecherczyk of Author Zoo

A catalogue record for this book is available from the National Library of Australia

For Grant and Sarah...

Always

CHAPTER ONE

'For God's sake, Abby, let's just get married.'

Brad wasn't even looking at me. Instead he was gazing into the dark beyond my balcony door. His dog, Bert, raised his head briefly from his position on the rug and wagged his tail once.

'Was that supposed to be a proposal?' I asked.

If it was, it was obvious that he hadn't made any effort with it. He still carried his usual distinctive end-of-day aroma – eau de cow shit – and hadn't even bothered to wash the dirt properly from under his fingernails. Even the way he'd just blurted it out in the middle of an argument indicated that it wasn't something he'd been planning.

He thought for just a second too long. 'Actually, yes. We've been together for long enough – we should make it legal.'

'You want to marry me to make it legal?'

He finally turned to face me, a little pulse beating in his cheek. 'Don't twist my words, Ab. I want to marry you because I've loved you almost my whole life.'

'See, that's your problem. If you'd told me that at the start, I might have said yes.'

'So, you're saying no because I didn't ask you the right way?'

'No, I'm saying no because you don't really mean it. If you did, you would have made it special.' I felt my chin begin to poke out, and made an effort to tuck it back where it normally lived.

'What the fuck?'

Brad had never been good at arguments – they exasperated him. He'd told me once that most things weren't worth fighting over, and that arguments should be saved for things that were worth fighting for. He'd said there was a difference. I'd told him that if we never argued, we could never have makeup sex. He'd said we could skip the argument and go straight to the sex.

'Well, you could have made it sound a bit better than "I'm going to Austria to check out enviro-friendly garden design, so we may as well get married",' I said. 'You could have made it romantic.'

'It's Denmark,' he corrected me. 'Is this because I'm going to Denmark, or because I asked you to marry me?'

'I don't care if you want to go to Denmark, or Austria, or Poland, or … wherever for three months. It's your business. Whatever. I just said that if that was a proposal, I would have liked it to be special, and it wasn't.'

Brad and I had been together for about three and a half years. Although we hadn't talked about it, although I wasn't keen on the idea of marriage at all, I couldn't think of anyone else I would even consider marrying. I'd always figured that at some point we'd take the plunge and schedule in a date, book a celebrant, a restaurant and a holiday, and I'd buy something vaguely bride-like to wear. But right now things were great between us, so why mess with it? We had plenty of time for all that. Brad had a landscaping business, so he was used to waiting patiently for things to happen – like grass to grow, and bulbs to bloom, and hedges to do whatever it was that hedges did … Screen things? It stood to reason that with all that practice at waiting, he'd be happy to wait until I was ready. He was also the romantic one of the two of us – again, also because of the gardens. Seeing flowers every day, and using nature to make things look beautiful, tended to bring out the romance in a person. So even though I hadn't really thought about it, even though I wasn't really keen on the idea, I probably would have said yes if he'd asked me properly.

'Well, there's absolutely no chance of that now, is there?' He gripped the edge of the kitchen counter, leaving dirty smudge marks that I (rather generously) ignored. 'No, Abby, this is about Denmark. You're picking an argument because I asked you to come with me and you don't want to make the decision. What's happened to you? There was a time when you would have jumped at the chance of an adventure – you'd have been on that plane before I finished the sentence. Once upon a time, you would have jumped out of the plane!'

'You know I can't just walk away from my job. You might be able to come and go as you want, but I've worked long and hard to get to where I am, and I'm not going to throw it away just because my boyfriend wants to waltz off to fucking Sweden to look at fucking gardens. I've got responsibilities. I want to make partner. I'm *this* close.' I demonstrated with my thumb and finger just how close I was.

'It's Denmark, and I'm a landscape architect – looking at fucking gardens is what I do. You know that's the direction I want to take the business in. We've talked about it.' Had we? I mustn't have been listening. 'I was excited about the opportunity and I thought you might be too.'

He looked hurt, and beneath my anger something that in someone else could be guilt began to stir. I pretended not to feel it.

'How many hours do you put in at that firm now?' he went on. 'There aren't any more billable hours you can physically clock. We haven't taken holidays for ages because you've been "this close".' He used his fingers to make quotation marks. He knew that gesture pissed me off. 'I can't even remember the last time you had a whole weekend off. You've got so much leave owing – just take it!'

'Hello, we've booked a holiday to Bali next month, remember? So I am taking leave. We've been looking forward to that for ages. And I've got heaps to do before we go. I've got the due diligence for Warner Enterprises that has to be supervised, the contracts and financials for Simcorp to be finalised, and then there's the –'

'Okay, I get the picture.' He rubbed at the dirty marks on the counter with a kitchen cloth. It smeared them further across the benchtop, but gave him something to do other than look at me. 'You don't want to come.'

'It's not that I don't want to go with you. I can't just up and leave town for the winter. That would put me behind a couple of years, and I'm not prepared to take that risk. I thought you'd understood that.'

'Seriously, Ab? Taking a couple of months' leave would put you behind a couple of years? That's ridiculous. What happened to the work/life balance the partners were prattling on about at last year's Christmas party?'

'We've talked about this before – work/life balance doesn't apply to people trying to make partner, and it especially doesn't apply to women trying to make partner. You only get to take holidays when you are a partner, or don't want to be a partner, or have dangly bits that have been dangled at the same school or golf club as the partners.'

He gave up on the smudges on the benchtop and paced the room. 'Jesus, Abby, I love you, but sometimes you make things so hard.'

'I'm too hard, or this, us, is too hard?' My hands were on my hips and I could feel my chin jutting out from the rest of my face.

Brad squeezed his eyes shut and took a deep breath. 'Look, I know there are so many reasons why you don't want to come with me, and so many reasons why you aren't into getting married … I get that.' He paused and ran his fingers through his hair, pushing the cowlick the wrong way so his hair sat up in all different directions. Then he said it.

'This is about your family. That's the real reason you don't want to take a risk on us, isn't it?' He looked deep into my eyes. 'I want to be with you, Abby. I want to live with you, and I want to grow old with you. If it makes you feel better, let's forget about getting married, but say you'll come to Denmark. Just for a month? You need the break – it'll do you good. It will do us good. Don't you think?' He attempted a smile.

I wanted to tell him that I loved him too, and there was no one on earth who I'd rather be old with, but those words couldn't get past the lump that had made its way into my throat.

Instead, I said, 'This has nothing to do with my family. How dare you bring them into it?'

'Why shouldn't I bring them into it? Don't you

think it's about time you let all of that go? Don't you think it's time that you trusted me? Trusted in us? Everything else was yesterday.'

'It's got nothing to do with you, Brad.' Even I could hear the huffiness in my voice.

He half-laughed, but there was no amusement in it. 'Nothing to do with me? At this moment it has plenty to do with me.'

I was silent for a moment. Then I said, 'What about Bali? We've had that booked for so long, and you know how hard it was for me to get time off work. You said it had to be April or May because it's quiet for you, and before the end-of-financial-year rush for me. Didn't you say you wanted to check out some of those tropical landscapes, and new ways to use water in your designs?' See, I had been listening.

'I know, but this type of fellowship rarely comes up. We have the rest of our lives to lounge around a pool in Bali. I don't see why it has to be now.'

'It just does. It has to be now.'

It was important. Surely he knew that? If he really knew me, really loved me, he'd know that.

'Well, Europe has to be now too.' Brad could also be the stubborn one. 'This chance to spend a few months in Denmark with all expenses paid? I can't turn that down. You can't expect me to turn it down. Besides, I'll be away for the winter when business is quiet, so I have nothing to lose.'

'Except me.' Wow, that came out loud.

In his eyes was something I'd never seen before: nothing.

Something watery and hot was prickling behind my eyes. I gripped the soft, webby bit between my forefinger and thumb and pretended I couldn't feel it. I pinched hard.

Brad was the first to break the silence.

'I truly hope it doesn't come to that,' he said quietly, 'but I guess that's your decision too. Call me when you've made up your mind, but don't wait too long. I leave in a few weeks. I'd like for you to come with me, but …'

He left the rest of the sentence unsaid, pulled his boots on, grabbed his keys, whistled for Bert, and left, slamming the door hard behind him.

CHAPTER TWO

'Do you agree, Abby?'

Mark, my managing partner, was waiting for a response. I flicked the screen on my phone back to idle. The bloody thing wasn't working anyway. Now, what had Mark been saying? Aaah yes, something about the Singapore tender we were preparing.

'I hear what you're saying, Mark, but I'm concerned about the potential impact of the Asian market on our costs. If the run-off is greater than five per cent over our estimates, because of the volume clause, it will reduce our projected profit margins to unacceptable levels. We can't lose sight of that.'

'Perhaps,' he conceded to the room. 'But the sensitivity analysis you've completed covers us against a complete collapse of the Asian volumes, plus a quadruple dip in the Global Financial Crisis.'

Everyone around the table laughed and I tilted my head in acknowledgement. Mark was right – there weren't any possible scenarios I hadn't considered. I'd spent all of last Sunday making sure our margins were completely covered.

I was a finance manager for one of those large publicly listed firms that handled everyday business processes for companies who really didn't want the hassle of them. If it moved, we could work out how to do it better … or cheaper. It was part of my job to make sure that not only did we win the business but we also made money out of it. I was usually working on a few contracts at various stages of development at any one time: some at the feasibility study stage where I looked into what-ifs; some at the bidding stage where I tried to put together a deal that proved we could do the job better and cheaper than anyone else; some at contract negotiation stage where we were fighting over conditions, inclusions and penalties; and some at actual implementation stage. I did my best work when I was juggling.

'With the additional work you've done on these numbers, I don't suppose you've had a chance to look through the Warner contract?' Mark asked me.

'Actually, I have. I'll pop the proposed alterations onto your desk after we finish here. I think we need to tighten up the earn-back clauses, and some of the service levels they've proposed might work with their other suppliers, but they're not what we're used to here. I'm particularly keen to talk through items …' I referred to my paperwork, 'twenty-three and twenty-nine. It worries me that these are "get out" clauses in disguise.'

Sophie Martella, our senior project manager, was impressed. 'That's great work – thanks, Abby. That wasn't due for another week. I know you always get things to me on time, but it's usually *just* in time. Sometimes I think you do it deliberately to keep me on my toes.' She grinned to let me know there was no malice in her statement.

Sophie's job was to make sure that all the balls that I (and my fellow associates) were juggling landed in the right place at the right time. It was a running joke between us: how she hassled me for whatever it was I was due to deliver to her; and how I told her it was all under control, even though both of us knew I hadn't started whatever it was I had to get to her; and how I always managed to meet my deadline.

'Was it ever in doubt?' I asked her as we walked back to my office.

She smiled. 'Somehow you always seem to pull a rabbit out of a hat.'

'You're back.' My assistant, Paula, stated the obvious. 'There's a message for you.'

I knew Brad would crack first. He'd said I was the one who had to make the decision, but deep down I knew that he'd call first. He'd always been the one to ring first – he was reliable, like rain on Melbourne Cup Day. He'd held out longer than I'd thought he would though – over a week longer. I could have called him, but this whole thing wasn't my fault, so why should

I be the one to blink? He was the one who'd blurted out a marriage proposal like a projectile vomit. Sure, I was the one who'd rejected it, but technically it had been a non-starter in the proposal stakes. Of course he'd cracked first. Not that I'd tell him that. I'd simply call him back and we'd pretend that none of this had happened. We'd be back to normal in no time.

Paula interrupted my thoughts. 'Andi called.'

Oh. 'Is that the only call?'

'Yes. Were you expecting anyone else?'

I didn't want to think about what her look could mean. 'No. I think my phone's playing up – I don't seem to be receiving calls.'

The same expression as before crossed her face. 'Andi said to tell you that she's in meetings this morning so not to ring back, but she'll see you at the usual place for lunch. She also said to tell you not to even think about cancelling.'

I smiled my thanks to Paula, and opened my laptop, scanning quickly through the emails that had come in over the last hour or so. It didn't take long. My inbox was the emptiest it had been in years and my to-do list was completely done. I'd even completed those tasks I'd always said I'd do when there was nothing income-producing to take care of. My desk was spotless, and my drawers had been tidied. Even my stapler was where it should be, and it was full of staples.

When Paula had opened my top drawer yesterday

to top it up with the pens I was always losing, she'd actually gasped out loud. Then she'd raised her eyebrows at me. Then she'd added up the clean desk, the empty inbox, the ticked-off to-do list, the stapler with staples in it, and the fact that I asked her a million times a day if there'd been any messages, and had drawn her own conclusions. Ever since she'd been watching me closely, and I was pretty sure that strange expression I'd seen on her face before was pity.

I checked my phone again. Bloody thing.

Andi was a picture of concentration as she teetered her way across the restaurant to our table. She greeted me with a sigh and the kind of smile that had every straight male in the place wishing it had been directed at him.

'Honestly, A, I have no idea why I order this every time – it takes an age to prepare, and I always end up with half of it sloshed across my tray.'

I smiled as she began the production of loading her lunch onto the table. Andi did everything with drama. She might be short in stature, but she was larger than life. She rested her handbag on her chair, balanced the tray on the table beside us, and sent its occupant an apologetic grin. First off was her bowl of teriyaki chicken and rice, followed by the remains of her miso soup, and finally the bottle of water that had caused her woes by tipping over into the soup. She cursed mildly, retrieved some tissues from her handbag, and apologised again to our neighbour before finally settling into her chair.

The man sitting directly behind us seemed particularly enraptured by her performance. He was cute – if you liked the type – with blond curly hair, blue eyes, a dimple in each cheek, and dressed in a navy blue pin-striped suit. He looked too pretty and polished for my liking, but all he needed to be perfect for Andi was a wedding ring. I suppressed a giggle.

'You'd think I'd learn to lie the water bottle on its side, or at least put it into my handbag,' she said. 'I'm just always so concerned about my heels on this floor.' She looked at the sticky floorboards with distaste.

At just a few inches over five feet tall, Andi was a regular pocket Venus and rarely left the house without heels that added at least three inches to her tiny frame. She was the only woman I knew who could duck out for a carton of milk and come back with another pair of divine shoes and no milk. Where I was all legs and long lines, she was a Botticellian vision of defined black curls, smooth pale skin and traffic-stopping curves. Today those curves were barely restrained in a tight black pencil skirt and an emerald green silk blouse with the buttons done up far enough to be decent yet undone enough to offer a tantalising glimpse of creamy cleavage. Sheer black tights and patent black peep-toe stilettos completed a picture whose whole effect was sexy smart. The look worked a treat for her in her job as a lawyer –

men in particular tended to completely under-estimate her.

'Tell me again why we always come here?' she said.

'Because it's exactly three doors from your office and just over a block from mine. Given that my legs are twice as long as yours, that makes it roughly halfway for both of us. And I love the dumplings.'

Piled in front of me were three little bamboo steamers containing an assortment of the delectable, soup-filled morsels. I was hoping they'd stimulate my appetite.

'How can you eat like that and never put on any weight?' she complained. 'I'll only be allowing myself half of this rice today. It doesn't seem fair.'

'Aaaah, but my weight has further to stretch. Besides, I'd love your boobs.'

It was a common theme between us.

Andi and I met in a law lecture – a compulsory unit in my economics/law degree – during the first week of our first year at Sydney Uni. She spilt coffee over my notebook and offered to buy me a replacement. We'd been friends ever since. The other members of our group used to call us Big A and Little A, for fairly obvious reasons. After uni, the two of us spent six months backpacking our way around Europe, although Andi seemed to find plenty of men willing to carry her pack for her. I was kept busy getting her out of scrapes and making excuses to whoever was making puppy-dog eyes at her. I still remembered the night in Munich when she'd popped some toast and cheese under the grill at the hostel and forgot about it when a cute American boy turned up. It was fortunate that I was good at fire-fighting.

On our return to Sydney we'd flatted together for a couple of years before Andi scored an associate role with one of Melbourne's leading law firms. When I followed her to Melbourne just a few years later, we shared again while I looked around for something to buy. Even though we each now had our own apartments, we still talked on the phone at least once a day, caught up for lunch a few times a week, and did the occasional wine-bar session after work on a Thursday or Friday evening. She was my best friend in the world – yet I still hadn't told her about Brad.

'So,' she said, once she'd arranged herself and her food, 'Jason called me this morning. He said he's going to tell her this weekend.'

'That he's leaving her for you?'

'Uh huh. I really think he will this time, Ab.'

For a brilliant woman, Andi had a dreadful habit of choosing the wrong men – she tended to fall in love first, and ask questions later. Her latest obsession was Jason, a married executive at an advertising firm in her Collins Street office building. Her previous mistake had been a two-year affair with a married general manager of an IT company, also in the same building. That one had ended when the holiday to Phuket, during which he'd intended to finally tell his wife that it was over, resulted instead in a renewal of their wedding vows.

'He's not going to leave her,' I said.

'I think you're wrong. This time it feels different.'

One of the things I loved most about Andi was her ability to hope for the best, even though deep down she knew she'd have her heart broken again.

'I think Brad and I broke up,' I said, concentrating a little too closely on my dumplings.

She stopped mid-slurp and looked at me. 'When?'

'Umm, a week or so ago.' I couldn't meet her eyes.

'What the fuck?' Andi never swore.

'Actually, it'll be two weeks tomorrow.'

'Why didn't you say anything?' she asked gently.

'I don't know. I guess I thought that it wasn't really happening. That he'd call or something, and we'd both laugh about it, and everything would be back to normal.'

She nodded. 'That sounds like the way you would think. And he hasn't called?'

'No.' I prodded at the dumpling with my chopstick. The juicy stock leaked out and pooled in my bowl.

'Are you eating?'

I shook my head. 'I don't feel like it.'

'What about exercise? Are you still running?'

'Every morning, even on weekends.'

'Hmmm. You look tired – have you been sleeping?'

'I can't. I feel like shit.'

I hadn't felt like this in years. It felt like it did when Dad died.

'I have this pain, right here,' I punched at my chest, 'that I'm trying to run through, but it won't go away.' I attempted to lighten the discussion. 'Maybe we should pop my symptoms into that cyber-chondria app of yours – the one where every symptom you key in comes out as cancer? I have a blister on my big toe – cancer. I have a sore throat – definitely cancer. A strange little twitch in the eyelid – you guessed it, cancer, or an eyebrow stroke. A headache – I must be having an aneurism.' I forced a laugh, but she didn't smile.

'I don't need to enter the symptoms – you're suffering from a broken heart,' she said. 'I know the signs too well.'

'Well, whatever it's called, it stinks.'

She cradled her chin in her hand as she looked at me. 'What happened?'

'Brad sort of proposed and, well … you know how I feel about marriage?' She nodded. 'I thought he knew how I felt about it too.'

'Why now?'

'He's got this fellowship or grant or something … to go to Denmark or Poland or Austria … somewhere like that … to look at gardens and watering systems. It's to do with them being on the cutting edge of water-wise and compact and vertical growth systems – I think I've got that right? Anyway, he's going for the winter so he just assumed that I'd be happy to drop everything and follow him.'

'Really? But he knows you're on the partner track. You can't afford to just get off that path.'

'Thank you.' I acknowledged the obvious. 'Just how long have I been working towards that? It's not as if that would come as any great surprise to him. It was like he was asking me to give up my ambitions so he can go running off after his.'

'That doesn't sound like Brad,' she said. 'He's always been respectful of what you're trying to achieve.' She sipped at what was left of her soup. 'Nor does it sound like Brad to do something on the spur of the moment. Are you sure he hadn't mentioned anything about it before? These trips take a bit of organising – there's a rigorous application and approval process to go through.'

She watched me as I replayed in my head conversations of the last few months. 'He did mention it … didn't he?'

'Okay,' I conceded. 'He might have said something a few months ago about applying, but I'm pretty sure he didn't talk about it again.'

'And you didn't bother to ask,' she accused.

'We booked Bali, so I figured he hadn't been successful. Don't look at me like that. Maybe I should have asked him about it, shown an interest, but the last few months have been mad at work – he knows how busy I am with this proposal. I am *this* close to finally getting partnership. There's no way I can hang up my business suits and back out of the race just yet. He knows that.' Another thought occurred to me. 'Maybe that's why he's angry with me – because I didn't take an interest in his application. He's not a child, and I'm not a mind-reader. If he'd wanted to talk to me about it he could have.'

Andi raised her eyebrows at me. 'Would you have stopped to listen?'

I shrugged, and poked some more at the dumplings.

'I still don't get why he proposed. It's not as if anything's changed between you guys … has it?'

'I have no idea. I thought things were fine as they were. Anyway, the whole proposal thing seemed like an after-thought. It's not like he had a speech or a ring or anything. He just blurted it out mid-argument.'

'What did you say?'

I contemplated pushing away the remains of my dumplings. Things were serious when I left soupy dumplings in the steamer. 'Well, I didn't say yes. I'm not romantic like you – you know I've never wanted to get married. You spend the equivalent of a tropical holiday on a white dress that'll probably end up stained with red wine by the end of the night and that you'll never wear again, and the equivalent of a mortgage payment on underwear – sorry, lingerie – that holds you in so tightly your internal organs will never be the same again, and the equivalent of a house deposit on a party with people who you don't care if you never see again. Then you have kids – and never have sex, sleep or tropical holidays again. Don't get me started on the promises you make that, let's be honest, you have no intention of keeping. Who really knows how they'll be feeling in five years, let alone fifty?'

'As evidenced by the men I end up with.'

I acknowledged her comment with a rueful smile. 'Exactly. God knows I've got no reason to want to do the whole wedding palaver, but I always thought that if I married anyone it would probably be Brad. I just thought it would be a little more special than it was. You know, at that rooftop bar where we had our first date … or maybe even when we were on holiday. I don't need the whole bended knee, months worth of salary on a ring in a blue box, love, honour and cherish thing. I just would have liked it to be a little bit special.'

She was silent for a moment, studying me over her chopsticks. 'Would you have said yes if it was?'

I lifted one shoulder. 'Maybe … I guess … probably … I'd sort of decided that if he did propose – properly propose – I'd say yes. But he didn't ask properly, so … Okay, maybe I freaked out.'

'What caused that?'

'Oh, I don't know. It's a big thing – saying yes to something like that with someone … you have to be sure, you know? You're not just saying yes to a big meringue dress, you're saying yes to never having sex with anyone else. Ever. Your whole life.'

'Try again, Ab. You've always said that Brad is the best sex of your life.'

'Yeah, well, what if he isn't?'

She was shaking her head. 'Don't make me laugh, sweetie. What's the real deal?'

I screwed my face up into a don't-know look, and pushed the now cold dumplings around a bit more.

She watched me poke at them. 'Are you going to eat those?'

'Probably not.'

'So when does he leave? For Denmark or Austria or Poland or wherever it is?'

'I don't know … soon. I don't think he's already gone. Surely he wouldn't go without saying goodbye … would he?'

'You did reject his marriage proposal,' Andi pointed out. 'That's got to have hurt. How long is he away?'

'He'll be gone all winter – he said he'd be back in time for spring landscaping. This whole thing is designed to work around his business and to hell with what I've got on.'

Andi ignored that last dig. 'Aren't you guys supposed to be going to Bali next month?'

'Yep.'

'What are you doing about that?'

'I'm still going.'

She raised a single eyebrow. 'On your own?'

'Sure. The peace and quiet will be nice. He knows where I'll be if he wants to find me.'

'Have you talked at all?'

'Nope. He hasn't rung me, and I don't see why I should be the first to ring him.'

I didn't tell her that I checked my phone for messages every five minutes. I figured she'd know.

'He's a Taurus – you know he can be really stubborn when he wants to be,' she said.

Andi, the eternal romantic, was into all of that. She was a Pisces, and told me that was why she loved inappropriate shoes, hopeless causes, the possibility of a happy ending, and unattainable men. I told her she was just deluded and lost in her fantasy world and that had nothing to do with astrology. She said it had everything to do with it.

'Well, he's certainly being stubborn now,' I said.

'So are you. You're doing that wilful Aries thing you do. You don't have to win every battle. If you're not careful, you'll take it too far and be left with nothing.'

'I think he's already decided that. Nothing I say now will make it right.'

It used to be so easy to come back from an argument when we were kids. All that was required was Brad leaving one of his mum's cupcakes on my front step, and me getting to it before the dog did. If he left a cupcake on my doorstep now, I'd be happy to call him.

'You could always tell him that you love him, you

miss him and you need him,' she suggested gently.

'But I can't need him, Andi, I can't need anyone. It's bad enough that I think I love him more than he loves me.'

'What the fuck?'

'You've got quite a potty mouth on you today,' I said.

'You're driving me to it. I've never heard such drivel in my life. Love isn't a competition, and there's no equation for who loves more – you just love. It's that simple.'

It wasn't. It never had been. If you were the one who loved the most, you were also the one who was most vulnerable and exposed.

'It's not that simple,' I explained. 'When it comes to relationships, there's always someone who loves more, and I never wanted it to be me. I've seen what happens when you love more than the other person does. I saw it when Mum fell apart after Dad died. She obviously loved him more than he loved her, otherwise he would never have gone away. And if he hadn't gone away, he wouldn't have died. If she'd played it cooler, he would have wanted her more and stayed. She drove him away by clinging too tightly.' I'd vowed back then that I'd never let myself be that dependent on another person. Not even Brad, the only man I'd ever really loved. 'She's done exactly the same in her second marriage, with Peter. She's loved him more than he loves her, and he treats her like she's household staff.'

'Ab, that's your mother's choice – you're a different person. I didn't know your father, but I do know Peter – and I know that Brad is very different to him. There's nothing wrong with admitting that you need him. Brad wouldn't let you down – he adores you.'

'I needed him once before, and Mum married Peter and dragged me away from him. I needed my dad, and he died.'

Andi was silent for a few seconds. 'Sweetie, you have to trust Brad – he's never given you a reason not to. I don't know the whole story, but maybe it's time to let the past go.'

'That's what Brad said. I told him that there's nothing to let go of.'

'Are you sure?'

'Yep. Nothing more to see here.'

'Ab,' she said gently, laying her hand on my forearm, 'you've been in love with Brad for most of your life. It took you over fifteen years to find each other again – you owe it to each other to take a little longer than fifteen minutes to break up.'

CHAPTER THREE

The first time I fell in love with Brad Ingram, I was eight and he was nine.

My family had recently moved to a red-brick paradise. Our house was red brick, matching the red-brick stepped wall that ran across our front yard. Most of the houses in the street were red brick – except the Ingrams'. They lived at the top of the cul-de-sac and their house was blond brick, with a bay window my mum coveted. I could see it from the highest balancing point (just four red bricks high) on our wall. I'd sit on our red-brick mailbox and watch Brad and his brothers freewheeling down the road on their dragster bikes. They'd skid around in front of our place before standing in their pedals to head back up the short hill.

Even though Brad was a year older than me, he was in the same class at school. Mum said it was something to do with him being a May baby and me being April, and boys not being as mature as girls. Although I'd seen him around, I didn't talk to him until the afternoon he helped me stand up to the infamous Scott Gang.

Every school had a group like the Scotts: Debbie, Sharleen and Kylee (Mrs Scott liked the effect of a double 'e'). They ruled the girls, and a good proportion of the boys, in our school through a combination of fear and popularity. Debbie was Brad's age and also in our class, Sharleen was eleven and in fifth grade, and Kylee, a very well-developed thirteen, was still in sixth grade. At school the Scotts decreed who was allowed to play handball in the centre quadrangle and who was relegated to the outer squares. At the public pool they'd lounge around on the best part of the grass. No one else was allowed to sit there, even if the Scotts weren't present. Kylee had this little white crocheted bikini, which I thought looked so sophisticated but had Mum muttering about how Mrs Scott was going to have problems with those girls if she didn't make them dress a little more modestly. Kylee, and some of her friends who were already in high school, would rub baby oil into their long limbs and stretch out on their towels in the sun while the boys buzzed around them. Sharleen and Debbie were allowed to sit with them as long as they kept everyone supplied with Redskins, Chupa Chups, and Splices.

The Scotts had an inner circle of chosen ones – girls who aspired to their particular brand of cruel popularity and would do whatever it took to be accepted. On this particular afternoon, Debbie, Sharleen and a few of their entourage had bailed up Lisa McMullen. Lisa was one of those girls every class had: she wore glasses and was even skinnier than me. Worse than that, she was smart. All of which made her a target. When I came across the gang that afternoon after school, they'd finished emptying Lisa's bag and were running around and tossing its contents between them. Without thinking, I hurled myself into the middle of them, grabbed at Lisa's bag, and yelled at Sharleen to 'rack off and leave her alone'. Everything went quiet. The friends I was with ran off – everyone knew it wasn't wise to take on the Scotts. Which left me – hands on narrow hips, pointy chin stuck out, and wispy, dirty blonde ponytail coming out of its elastic – to finish what I'd started.

'Rack off yourself,' said Sharleen, her vocabulary still recovering from the shock of being challenged.

'Whaddyathinkyadoin, mollface?' growled Debbie, also with hands on hips.

'Stopping this,' I declared, pointing my chin out further and holding my ground.

'Youse and what army? You're just an ugly scrag.' Sharleen grinned in the universal way of bullies everywhere.

'Like I need an army?' I sneered back. 'You're piss-weak, you are.' I didn't really know what piss-weak meant, but it sounded appropriate.

Lisa had finished gathering her stuff and was watching me with her mouth open.

Sharleen looked around for support from her

disciples, but they seemed lost for words too. No one had ever stood up to a Scott before.

'You think you're so brave picking on someone who can't stand up to you. But do you want to know what I think?' I said.

'Nope.'

'Tough, because I'm going to tell you. I think you're all gutless wonders. Too scared to try it on your own without all your piss-weak crew. That's what you are. Gutless. Wonders.' My elbows pointed forwards and back in time with my words.

Debbie moved forward to take her place beside Sharleen. At her signal the others moved to join her.

'Ya reckon we should tell Kylee 'bout this moll?' Sharleen asked Debbie.

I'd begun to realise what I'd got myself into, but pride wouldn't allow me to back down. My hands stayed on my hips, my chin didn't waver, and I stuck a see-if-I-care look on my face. A stare-off commenced, but I wasn't blinking. I was never the first to blink.

'Are you just going to stand there and stare at me, or are you going to do something about it?' I taunted.

Sharleen stepped into my space. 'Shut your mouth, moll. I'll give ya ten seconds to get out of here so no one gets hurt and Kylee doesn't need to know.'

I stepped forward as well, looking up into her face. 'Can you count to ten? Good to see that three years in kindergarten wasn't wasted.'

And that's when all hell broke loose. Sharleen leapt forward and knocked me to the ground. Debbie joined her, and the others stood around cheering. My little fists flew and I gave as good as I was getting, but the numbers were very much against me.

And that's how Brad found me.

Later I discovered that Lisa had run for help, and found Brad, his best mate Todd and his older brother Ricky kicking a football around on the oval. They got straight on their bikes and pedalled back to help me. Once the cavalry arrived, it was over pretty quickly, with the Scotts muttering threats about telling Kylee and then I'd be sorry.

'I'm not scared of Kylee,' I yelled at their retreating backs.

'Ya should be,' one of their followers screamed back.

Lisa went home, and Ricky and Todd took off. Brad helped me to my feet and watched as I tried to dust myself down.

'Why'd you have to interfere?' I said indignantly. 'I was doing all right. Another few minutes and I would've had them.'

'You've got a lot of guts for a girl,' he said, ignoring the error in my bravado.

'You ride your bike pretty good for a boy,' I said. 'But I reckon I could beat you home.'

After that, the Scotts never bothered me again, and

they left Lisa McMullen alone too. Actually, they left anyone who was associated with me alone. It enhanced my popularity no end – not that that was ever a major concern for me. I didn't care much about things like that. I still didn't.

I fell in love with Brad Ingram for the second time three and a half years ago. It was a Saturday afternoon, one of those rare bright days that Melbourne got in September when the warmth of the sun and the flash of fresh new green on the trees tricked us briefly into thinking that winter was over. Fashion retailers fell for it every year, stocking the stores with light floral confections and pastel heels that offered no protection against the likely event of a southerly change. I'd spent the morning breakfasting with Andi at a cafe near her apartment in Albert Park. Over eggs benedict (me) and fruit salad with low-fat yoghurt (Andi), we'd compared dating disasters from the previous night.

'So,' she said, once I'd conceded that her date had indeed been the worst, 'what's on the agenda for this afternoon?'

'I was thinking I might wander over to the garden centre.'

'You in a garden centre? That's too funny. Didn't you kill that cactus they gave you for Secret Santa last year?'

It was true, I had. The same happened with the

one I'd got the previous year too. What was it with people buying me cacti?

'I thought the point of those things is that they don't need water.'

She smiled knowingly. 'They may be prickly, but even cactuses need some love.'

'I think you'll find that the plural is cacti.'

She laughed and ordered another coffee from the waiter who'd been loitering, hoping for a smile from her. 'They still need water every so often.'

'Okay, I get that plants and I don't have a great record together, but I've decided the time has come for me to take on the commitment of caring for another living thing. As long as I get something that just needs me to wave some moisture in its general direction, I should be right. What about you?'

'A manicure, a little general maintenance, maybe some shopping … I have another date tonight and I really feel this one could be it.'

'Who is he?'

'A guy I met at the wine bar last night.'

'I thought you were on a date last night?'

'I was, but I had a quick couple of glasses with the team from work first.'

'So this guy's someone from work?'

'No, we started talking when I went to the bar, and we made a date for tonight. Somewhere in Hardware Lane, but I have expectations.'

'You always do.' I threw some cash on the table, and my handbag over my shoulder, and stood. 'It's been lovely as always. Have a great time tonight, and make sure you text me in the morning and let me know the gory details.'

I bent down to kiss her goodbye. As I left, I noticed the man at the next table moving to take my seat.

An hour later I'd almost given up on the instant garden idea. Why did plant shops like to prove they were smarter than me? Those little signs on each row of plants saying things like 'herbs', 'seedlings', 'cordylines' (just what exactly was a cordyline?) told me absolutely nothing. Surely a more appropriate system of labelling would have been something like:

- Plants that need a lot of water.
- Plants that don't need much water.
- Plants that are hard to kill.
- Plants that are high maintenance.
- Plants that would work well on a balcony.
- Plants that grow fast.

That was another problem with plants – aside from needing water and sometimes clipping, they seemed to take so long to grow. Who had time for that? If you weren't prepared to wait (which I wasn't) you could buy what they called a 'mature plant'. I took that to mean it no longer had tantrums.

I'd once seen a gardening show where this couple was considering moving because their neighbours were noisy and annoying. The landscaping guy suggested they grow some hedges to act as both a separator and noise insulation. They lapped it up, smiling and nodding, followed by a boring few minutes while the presenter produced some knee-high plants with Latin names in black pots, and dug a few holes. I'd felt like reaching into the screen and saying, 'Look at the size of those things. It's going to be twenty years before they're big enough to screen out anything!' Honestly, they'd have been better off growing a pair of bollocks and marching next door and telling their neighbours to keep the noise down. Just saying.

And why did pots and plants have to be so … dirty? After picking up yet another pot filled with something I'd probably kill before I got it home, I wiped my hands impatiently on my jeans and decided that I had no choice but to ask for help from someone who looked like they did things with dirt. Up ahead I saw some dirty jeans covering what looked from this distance to be a very nicely formed male bum. Its owner straightened to a perfect-for-me height of just over six foot, and put a pot holding some mottled greenery back on its stand. Hmmm, nice shoulders too, under one of those rough cotton shirts that guys who did things with dirt, plants and spades wore. They looked like shoulders that could wield an axe with ease, and hold a power tool. I bet he even knew what a cordyline was.

He turned and saw me watching him, grinned and

came towards me. The front view was as nice as the rear. A mostly blue, mostly cattle dog trotted at his side.

'Can I help you?' he asked.

'Do you work here?'

'No, but I've been watching you wandering around for the last half-hour looking more and more confused.' His mouth had curled up into a smile, and he pushed his sunglasses onto his head.

'Do you know anything about this stuff?' I waved my arm to indicate the plants.

'You mean do I know my way around plants and dirt?'

Nice eyes too, and, if I wasn't mistaken, they were twinkling at me.

'Yeah.' I twinkled back.

'Well, yes, I do know about this stuff. What do you need?'

What would he say, I wondered, if I answered 'you'? Thankfully that didn't come out loud. 'Something for my balcony. It needs to be hard to kill – I killed a cactus last year.'

'No one kills cactuses.'

'Who'd know they need to be looked after? It didn't come with any instructions.'

The dog sniffed around my feet.

'You'd be surprised,' he said. 'Even prickly things need some nurturing.'

I grinned. 'That's what Andi said.'

'He's a smart man.'

'He's a she.'

He raised his eyebrows. 'Really?'

'Yeah, my best friend.'

'Oh.' He laughed. 'Not that it's any of my business.'

I smiled to let him know I hadn't taken offence. I was sure Andi had been the subject of just as many female fantasies as male.

'Were you looking for shrubs or some kitchen herbs?'

'Kitchen herbs? Now you're getting technical and showing off.'

'So you're not a cook then?'

I screwed up my nose and shook my head. 'That would be a no.'

'What about some herbs that look like shrubs, so you can use them if you change your mind about cooking?'

'Cooking isn't something I'm likely to change my mind about, but does that mean they'd smell nice?'

'They would. I'm thinking of lavenders or rosemary. They grow easily in pots, smell nice, and flower in spring.'

'Do they need much care?'

'No. Just a decent-sized pot, a little light pruning after flowering and the occasional watering. Even you won't be able to kill them.'

His dog nudged my hand so I'd pat him.

'Bert likes you,' he said.

Bert? Really? I ruffled behind the dog's ears. His tail wagged harder.

'What do you mean "even me"?' I said. Cheeky bugger.

The smile grew wider and his eyes in his tanned face were dancing. For some reason, it felt really familiar. He felt familiar. In that I-know-you-from-somewhere way. Weird. I wondered briefly if I'd dated him over the years, and discounted it just as quickly. I was pretty sure that if I'd slept with him I would have remembered, and I was also pretty sure that if I'd dated him I wouldn't have been able to resist sleeping with him – at least once.

'You're the one who said you weren't good with plants,' he said. 'What direction does your balcony face?'

'Why do people ask questions like that? As if I'd know what direction my balcony faces. It faces into the street.'

'Yeah, it's like in those western movies where the dude rides up on his horse and says something like "Howdy, pardner, which way to the McKillop ranch?" And the other dude says "It's five miles due north", and the first dude turns his horse around and rides in the right direction, without a GPS. How do they know that?'

He watched me very closely, a little smile playing around his mouth.

The breath caught in my throat, and in my chest

my heart was doing a weird dance. Someone had said the same thing to me a long time ago – a kid, with freckles and grazed knees, on a bike that was really a horse in disguise. I was there too, and we were both ready to ride off into the sunset. Towards the McKillop ranch – or rather his mum's house for cupcakes, from where we'd plan our escape.

Could it be?

He was still looking in my eyes. Oh. My. God. Goose pimples ran up my arms and back down again.

'What's wrong? Is it my poor American accent?' he asked.

I couldn't speak.

'I've never known you to be lost for words before, Abby.'

It *was* him. After all this time. And he'd recognised me. How had he recognised me?

I tried to swallow, but nothing happened.

'How do you know my name?' I managed.

He was still smiling, his eyes crinkled up at the sides.

'It's you, isn't it?' I asked.

'Yes, Abby, it's me.'

'Brad Ingram?'

'In the flesh.'

'But you got so tall and …' And cute! When did that happen? Had he always been cute?

'So did you. But I'd still know you anywhere, even

without those god-awful plaits you used to wear.' He leant forward and flipped at the ends of my hair.

'It's been … how many years?' I still couldn't believe this was happening.

'A lot. You left the year I turned fifteen.'

'Wow. Brad Ingram.'

'Wow. Abby Brentnall.'

We stood there grinning at each other, until a kid pushed his metal trolley into the back of my leg. His mother smiled apologetically, and Brad pulled me off the path. Bert followed.

'Are you okay?' he asked as I rubbed at the sharp pain.

I nodded. 'I'm fine, thanks. So … what do we do now?'

'Now? We swap numbers and we meet tonight – somewhere we can talk and catch up properly. Are you free, or is there someone you've already promised your Saturday night to?'

'Umm, yeah, sure. When … I mean, I'm free. Where do you want to meet?' I busied myself ruffling Bert's head.

'Do you know that new rooftop bar in Swanston St? Right near Little Bourke, upstairs from the pie place?'

'Yeah, I know it.' I straightened and met his smile.

'How about I meet you there at eight?'

I managed to nod. 'Sounds good. I'll see you then.'

I wiped my palms against my jeans and held one

out for him to shake. He took it and pulled me close enough to kiss my cheek.

'Well, bye then.' I pulled away and walked backwards a few metres. He grinned and waved. I waved back and forced myself to move forward.

Brad Ingram … here … and so cute. He'd asked – well, virtually asked – if I was single, but I didn't know if he was. Maybe he intended bringing a girlfriend tonight? Surely not.

I turned back. He and Bert hadn't moved and were still watching me. He grinned and waved once more. Shaking my head at my predictability, I smiled too and walked back down the path.

CHAPTER FOUR

Melbourne, September 2010

The contents of my wardrobe were now on my bedroom floor, and I'd changed my clothes three times. Jeans felt too casual, and a dress too dressy. Finally I settled on a pair of tight, black, flat-fronted pants, tucked into black high-heeled boots. I unbuttoned my top just far enough so the lace trim of my add-a-cup-size bra could be seen if I leant forward in the right way. Not that I would be leaning forward in that way tonight. After all, this wasn't a real date, just a catch-up with the childhood buddy I hadn't seen since I was fourteen. A childhood buddy who'd grown into the most shaggable man I'd seen in a long time.

One of the advantages of living in the city was the proximity to everything. I could be fashionably late to any appointment in a three-block radius just by walking out of my front door on time. As a result, when I arrived just a few minutes late, Brad was already there, leaning against the bar and watching the stairs for my entrance. He'd replaced the dirty denims with a cleaner, darker pair, and the muddy work boots with black riding boots. A black button-down shirt and leather jacket completed his look. He didn't look at all like someone who'd spent his day playing in dirt.

He crossed the floor to meet me and kissed me on the cheek in greeting, before looking me up and down. In my heels, we were at eye level.

'Wow, Abby, you've grown up nice!'

'So have you.'

'It's funny, whenever I thought about you, I always thought you'd be like this – tall, slim and gorgeous.'

It was nice to know that when I'd thought about him, he'd been somewhere out there giving me the occasional thought too.

'Now you're embarrassing me.'

'Impossible.' He grinned. 'The Abby Brentnall I remember doesn't embarrass that easily.'

He led me across to a bar stool, took my drink order, grinned again, and disappeared to the bar. Over drinks we chatted idly, looking for subjects that would help us get to know each other again, to fill in the gaps between then and now. Inevitably, after a short but not uncomfortable silence, we strayed into the past.

'I remember the last time I saw you,' he said. 'Your pale face with those skinny plaits looking back at me through the window.'

I swallowed. 'I waved, but you put your head down and your hands in your pockets and trudged back home.'

I'd tried not to remember that day, that last view of him walking home. I'd watched out the back window of the car until I couldn't see any more, but he didn't turn around.

'You were being so brave,' he said, 'and I didn't want you to see me cry.'

'Boys don't cry.'

'They do when they're really sad – and I was really sad that day. My best friend was leaving.'

'It wasn't like I was going to the other side of the world, just the north shore.' Peter, my new stepfather, was a government minister, and we were moving across the city to his home. 'If it was now, we'd have been able to stay in touch on Facebook or by email.'

'It felt like the other side of the world,' he said.

'You still had Todd.'

'I know. I was lucky.'

I focused on the light reflected from the copper planters onto the exposed brick wall we were sitting beside. The planters acted as a separate, softer light source for this corner. Clever.

'That day we left I wasn't feeling brave,' I said. 'I wanted to cry so badly, but there was no way I was showing it in front of Mum and Peter, and I didn't want you to feel sad for me. So I bit the inside of my gum with my braces, so hard that it bled. Then Mum got mad because I wiped my sleeve in the blood and it was my good cardigan.'

He laughed. 'Your mother never did appreciate some of your more charming habits.'

I grinned back as flashes of scuffed shoes, grazed knees and blood-curdling calls to action rolled through my brain.

'You know, except for when your dad died, I never saw you cry,' he said. 'And even then I'm not sure I saw it. I remember once asking you what you thought had happened to your father and you threw a rock at me. I knew you were really upset because you missed and your aim was usually better than that. You always used to grit your teeth and charge on. You never ran away from anything.' He took a contemplative mouthful of beer. 'I always thought that if you could run headlong into whatever it was, you wouldn't have time to think about being scared or sad.

'I kept up with you for a while. Every time Peter was re-elected, they'd have a photo of your family. You were always in the background, sort of blurred, but it's how I recognised you today. I used to rip the pages out of the newspaper and try and make you bigger with the magnifying glass – you know, the one I got when we were going to be private investigators, like Nancy Drew and Ned?'

'Oh. My. God. I'd forgotten about that! The only case we ever got was the Mystery of the Missing Beetle – when someone found our car bonnet and took it away.'

'We never did find out who'd taken that. I bet it was someone from the council.'

I giggled at the memory of us sitting in the bonnet at the top of the hill and sliding down into the creek. Brad would be at the pointy end, steering, while Todd and I would be keeping the back balanced.

'Ned and Nancy came up at a trivia thing I was at with Todd a couple of years back. I thought of you immediately.'

He smiled and something warm flushed through me. They really needed to do something about the heating in here.

'You're still in touch with Todd?'

'Sure am. We went our separate ways for a few years – you know how it is, what with uni, backpacking, jobs – but he's in Melbourne now too. I rang him this afternoon and told him I'd met you – he said to say hi. He's looking forward to seeing you again.'

I didn't reply, concentrating instead on the patterns I was drawing on my wine glass from the condensation that had settled.

He reached forward and, using one finger, lifted my chin slightly. 'You still have the scar from the day you pranged into Mum's washing line on your bike. I don't think I'd ever seen that much blood before.'

'There was a lot,' I said, remembering.

He ran a finger lightly along the roughened skin on the underside of my chin, dragging it tantalisingly close to my lips. Then he raised his eyes to meet mine, smiled, and the bottom fell out of my world.

I went to Luna Park once with Brad and the Ingrams. It must have been a special event – a birthday maybe. It wasn't that long before we left, so I would probably have been thirteen. Brad and I had whirled our way through the roller coaster and the pirate ship, screaming and laughing at the adrenaline rush, eager for more. Then we found the Gravitron. You stood flat against its wall and the speed of the spin held you there, even when the floor dropped away and you were looking into terrifying black space. It was the only ride that really scared me – that feeling that I had no control, and there was only that black space. I'd wondered if it was like that when you died. I'd wondered if that was how it had been for Dad, as if he'd been hurtled out of life into the dark with nothing below him but an empty black space. When we staggered out of the ride that day, I wasn't laughing. All the laughter had been ripped out of me. Brad had started to tease me, until he realised that it wasn't fear but rather terror I felt. Fear was something you could laugh at, could stare into the face of. Terror was not. Then he punched me on the arm and said, 'Hey, Abs, race you to the hotdog stand.' And we were off and running.

That's how I felt now – as if I was on the Gravitron and the floor had fallen away. For a brief moment, I experienced that same terror. Something told me that this time Brad wouldn't be punching me on the arm and challenging me to a race. I scrambled to bring the conversation, and my tummy, onto safer ground.

'What do you do? I remember you used to say you wanted to build gardens for people to live in. I always thought that sounded so cool. And now you know about plants and dirt and things.'

'I sure do. I have my own business as a landscape architect. This bar was one of my creations.'

'Really?'

He nodded, the pride of what he'd done on his face.

I'd been in here a number of times before, but knowing that Brad created it, I saw it differently, as if for the first time. Snaking through the timber floor like a stylised snail was a narrow planting of something herbal – so I assumed from the fragrance. Mismatching tables and chairs were scattered throughout the area, along with corrugated-iron planters containing plants … of some description. On a square of synthetic grass sat beanbags and sun lounges. It felt like somebody's backyard – with an open invitation to a barbecue that required you to bring your own seating. Like the copper planters reflecting light onto the brick wall near us, everything decorative had a purpose, or two. It all mixed functionality with style, and Brad had made it.

'It's great,' I said. 'Perfect really. How did you learn to do this?'

'Thanks. I did a degree in horticulture and environmental management, and then spent a northern summer in Austria looking at what was happening over there. Rooftop bars are quite big in Europe, but they were only just starting here, so the time was right. I've done a few now, each with a different brief. The one further up Swanston, near Little Lon, is one of mine too. They wanted an English spring garden-party feel – without the rain.'

'I know the one – it has a different, more formal feel than this place. I always feel as though I should be wearing something pastel and floaty when I go there, and I don't do either.'

He laughed. 'I know what you mean. These guys wanted a mix of Aussie backyard and functionality – something more laidback.'

'Well, you certainly got that right. I'm impressed. Not only are you creating gardens to live in, but also gardens to drink in.' I raised my glass to that. 'You must do something other than rooftop bars though?'

'I do some domestic work, but mostly corporate accounts – where the client wants the landscaping to bring the outside in. It helps with creativity.' He paused for a mouthful of beer. 'I recently finished a breakout space for one of the big banks. They wanted an indoor area with enough raised seating for all staff – to feel like the outdoor seating at a sports ground. Right now, I'm working on a pop-up allotment for one of the malls here in town.'

'Pop-up?'

'Yeah. Something that can be assembled and disassembled quickly. Fashion designers are jumping on the idea as a way of having an outlet without the cost of a permanent footprint – I see no reason why it can't work for gardens too.'

'Aaah yes, the constant challenge to maximise sales against fixed costs. Clever.' My brain began searching through my files for opportunities to put the idea into practice from a corporate viewpoint.

'What about you, Abby? What do you do? No, hang on, let me guess … After the Nancy and Ned discussion, I'm thinking private investigator is off the list?'

'Sure is.'

I leant back in my chair as he ran through options. His 'thinking' expression hadn't changed over the years. He still raised his eyes to the sky, screwed up his nose and frowned a little.

'There was the time you wanted to be a explorer and find somewhere no one else had ever found, but you didn't have the patience.'

I nodded. 'Too true. Who has time to waste discovering something only to find out you're the second person to get there?'

'Minor, but inconvenient detail.' He grinned. 'Speaking of getting lost, I could see you leading a travel expedition through a tropical forest.'

I didn't think he realised what he'd said, or its significance. I felt the grin start to slip from my face and tried to catch it before he noticed. 'I wanted to be a war reporter or a travel writer – does that count?'

'Absolutely. You'd be wearing dirty combat pants, the type with lots of pockets for things like water flasks and cameras and spare film canisters, and you'd be presenting news stories with the wind in your hair, and gunfire and bombs going off in the background. You'd be embedded with troops and parachute into the places other reporters wouldn't dare venture.'

I smiled. 'That's a very descriptive picture.'

'I'm sorry, Ab …'

'What for?'

'The comment before. You know, the tropical forest, your dad and all … For a minute there I forgot.'

Our eyes met, and in his was something I hadn't seen in years – sympathy. I didn't do sympathy.

'I'm a finance manager,' I said, deflecting the whole Dad thing.

He looked surprised. 'Really? Sorry, that probably came out wrong. I guess I'm just surprised. If you'd asked me, the last place I'd expect to see you would be in an office. Do you enjoy it?'

'Who really likes what they do?'

'I do.'

'You're one of the lucky ones. Numbers make sense to me. I can make them do what I want them to do, and I'm great at putting together deals – finding the chink in my competitors' armour, exploiting their weakness to get the business and the win. When there's a takeover or a deal on the table and the adrenaline starts to flow – yes, I enjoy that. Then it's like a competition, a race to have the customer choose you, to be first past the post, to beat the others. The money's good, and when I'm made partner it will all have been worth it. I'm *this* close.' I held my forefinger and thumb together to show him just how close.

'What about your family? How old is Tyler now?'

I smiled. 'Nearly seventeen. He looks very like Peter. I know Peter has expectations of him taking a seat in Federal Parliament some day too.'

'You sound fond of him.'

'Yeah, I am. He's a good kid. I don't see him that much, just a few times a year. We talk a lot though.'

'And your sister, Zoe? I see her on the front cover of magazines from time to time. She was always going to be pretty special.'

My smile slipped again. 'Yes, Zoe's life is about being special. So,' I said, in a clumsy effort to change the subject, 'why didn't you write to me?'

He paused for a few seconds. 'I did, but you never wrote back.'

'Did you? I never got your letters. I wrote to you too. I gave them to Mum to post for me. But then you didn't write back and I figured that you'd forgotten me.

I didn't have the luxury of keeping up with you from news reports.'

I smiled, but I didn't think he was fooled by my attempt to lighten the discussion. His eyes bored into mine. I broke the stare first – a thought had just occurred to me. And, by the look in his eyes, I think it had occurred to Brad too. It wasn't a nice thought. I made a mental note to ask Mum about the letters I hadn't received the next time I saw her.

'Whoa! Abby Brentnall blinked first,' Brad said. 'That's gotta be a fist-pump moment. You must be out of practice, girl! Either that or you need another drink …'

We ordered some tasting plates and more drinks, and spent the next few hours bantering and laughing. It was if the last seventeen years had melted away. We chatted about the Ingrams, Brad's nephews (it appeared the Ingram pattern of boys had extended into the next generation), and how Mrs Ingram was concerned that Brad was still single.

'I tell her that I'm waiting for the right woman.'

As he said it, he looked directly at me and a delightful fizz ran through my veins. My eyes dropped to his hands. Work-roughened, capable and strong. Then I started wondering what his hands would feel like on my body. Then I couldn't swallow.

'What about you? Are you seeing anyone?' he asked.

'No. I'm not.' I raised my eyes, but that meant I had to look into his, and that also meant looking at his mouth and wondering what it would feel like to kiss it. So I leant forward (in that way), looked into his eyes once more, and found that I couldn't look away.

He was smiling at me, his eyes were crinkling around the edges. His gaze dropped to my enhanced cleavage, then moved back up to my lips. I could feel my chest rising and falling, just a little too fast. He swallowed, and leaned in towards me, close, but not close enough. His hand moved to mine, and he idly stroked the back of it with one finger. I could feel the circles of heat in my tummy moving lower.

'Umm, I think I'll go to the bathroom.' I pulled my hand away and clambered off the stool.

His grin told me that he knew exactly what was going through my head, and between my legs.

In the stall I took some time to clear my head – and the other parts of me that were over-reacting. I couldn't remember the last time I'd wanted someone this badly and so quickly. I wasn't sure that I ever had. Every cell in my body was screaming for him. Maybe it was the alcohol. Maybe I should have eaten more.

I went back to our table. 'You know, I really feel like dancing – somewhere dark and loud. Do you want to come?'

He looked surprised. 'Dancing? Seriously?'

'Sure, why not? Let's go to the Basement. Come

on … it'll be fun.'

The activity would clear my head of the rubbish that was taking it over, and, with luck, distract the rest of me too.

We drank some more and hit the dance floor. It felt good. It was also a mistake. We moved in and out of each other's space, his eyes holding mine, the music winding around us, pulling us so close that there was barely a goose bump between us – until someone knocked into me and forced me against Brad. He placed his hands on my waist to steady me and I could feel that he was feeling it too. My heart was racing and I knew I should pull away, but I wiggled my hips a little closer. He half-closed his eyes and groaned. As his mouth moved towards mine, I stepped back and shook my head to clear the fog that had gathered there. This was getting out of control.

'You know, it's getting late, and I've had a big week, so I might head off,' I said, moving away from him. I was almost shouting over the music.

'What's the matter, Abs?' he asked, adjusting his jeans. 'Surely you're not scared?'

'No,' I lied, 'it's just that it's late.'

'I'll see you home.'

He reached out and stroked my cheek, letting the middle finger wander to graze my lips. I bit my lower lip lightly where his finger had been. I opened my eyes to find him smiling into them.

'I'll walk,' I said. 'I'm just up in Flinders Lane, in one of those apartments behind the cathedral.'

'Well, I'll walk you home then.'

We left the club without speaking. All around us Saturday night in Melbourne was bustling. While we were waiting for the lights at Collins Street to change, Brad took my hand in his and held it tightly. I turned to look in his eyes, and left my hand where it was.

We walked up Collins Street and, at the corner where the Westin Hotel stood, Brad gently pushed me to the shop window and, with both hands lightly cradling my head, finally kissed me. It felt like I'd been waiting for him to kiss me my whole life. It felt like no one else had ever kissed me before.

He pulled his head back, unsmiling, and searched my eyes, then tucked an arm around my waist and we started to walk again, cutting through the lane that ran down to Flinders Lane and my apartment.

'Well, this is me,' I said, all too soon.

'Already?'

'Uh huh.'

We stood in the dark looking at each other.

'Do you want to come up?' I asked. So what if the contents of my wardrobe were on the floor of my bedroom?

'For coffee?'

'No.' I didn't want coffee and I didn't want to play games. I just wanted him. 'Do you want to come up?'

I asked again.

He thought about it, then shook his head. 'No.'

I was confused. I rarely got those signals wrong. I could have sworn he wanted me just as much as I wanted him.

My bewilderment must have been showing.

'I want to kiss you again, Ab, but out here, not up there. It's too soon for me to go up there. We have plenty of time for that.'

'Oh.'

This time the kiss was longer and deeper. I hadn't read the signals wrong.

He pulled back and rested his forehead against mine. We were both having difficulty breathing. He brushed his thumb across my lips and I nipped the side of it gently.

'Are you sure you don't want to come up?'

'No,' he said, shaking his head again. 'I'm sure I do want to come up, but not tonight. Not yet. But soon.'

'Yes … please. Soon.'

He grinned again. 'What number are you?'

'Eight … that balcony up there. Why?'

'So I know for next time.'

He kissed me again.

This time when we separated, he stepped away. 'Now go,' he ordered, 'upstairs. While I can still let you.'

'What if I don't want you to let me go?'

'Abby,' he warned.

'Okay.'

'I'll call you tomorrow,' he said, and I knew that he would. With Brad there'd be no games, no waiting for calls, no manipulation.

I opened the security door and looked back. He hadn't moved.

Once I was inside, I stepped out onto the balcony and looked down. He was still there, watching. He waved, I waved back, and he turned and walked back up Flinders Lane. I watched in the dark until I couldn't see him any more.

Morning found me up and out the door for a run around the Tan – a picturesque, almost four-kilometre track around the Botanic Gardens. By the time I got there and back and did a couple of loops, my ten ks were done and dusted. I just didn't normally do them on a weekend – running was part of my working week. The thing about running in the morning was, no matter what type of shit your day descended into, you'd started it with an achievement. In my job, that was an important thing to remember. Weekends were for more pleasurable activities, like sleeping. But this morning, the morning after my first date with Brad, I had certain energies that needed to be burnt off. I wasn't used to not getting my own way, and I certainly wasn't used to going to bed unsatisfied when an offer had been made – especially not when I was damn sure he felt the same way.

I didn't know whether I'd actually slept or just thought I'd slept, but I certainly didn't feel rested, which was why I was up and pounding the paths at a time I'd normally set aside for snuggling under my doona. I was finished and back home for a shower by 9 am. Less than an hour later I was sitting cross-legged on the rug in front of my lounge, dressed for a morning of not a lot in navy and white stripy man-style pyjama pants, a tight-fitting white T-shirt with no bra, bare feet and my hair tied in a short ponytail. I had the Sunday papers spread out in front of me, and the Sunday morning current affairs programs on the TV. I liked to get my news and current affairs fix for the week in one intense burst. It was my version of multi-tasking.

When the door buzzer rang, I cursed and scrambled to my feet to check out the image in the intercom. It was Brad. Mentally shrugging, I let him in. He may as well see me in my natural state now rather than later.

He gave me a disappointingly brief kiss on the lips, and looked me up and down. 'Nice look.'

I did a little twirl.

He grinned at me. 'Here, take these.' He shoved a tray of coffees and bags of what I hoped were croissants into my hands. 'I've got some more to bring up.'

What the …?

I propped the front door open as he disappeared back down in the lift, and took the opportunity to fluff my hair and pack away the newspapers. I didn't have time to do anything about the pyjama pants and no-bra situation.

He reappeared a few minutes later with some pots. 'I remembered that you didn't end up buying anything at the garden centre yesterday, so I figured I'd bring the garden to you. And …' he tilted his head a little to the side as he grinned, 'I couldn't wait to see you again.'

'So you brought breakfast.'

'So I brought breakfast.'

'And plants and dirt?'

'Yep, those too.'

'Thank you. But what are they?'

'The breakfast or the plants and dirt? The breakfast is pastry and caffeine, and the plants are rosemary and lavender – they'll grow well on your balcony, despite your best efforts.'

'What if I'm one of those women who doesn't eat breakfast?'

'Abby, you'll never be one of those women who doesn't eat breakfast. You always had a good appetite as a kid, although the way your mother used to carry on I'm surprised you don't have hang-ups around food. She used to get into you about it all the time.'

Mum was so afraid that I'd grow out rather than up. Actually she was mortified that I'd got this tall. Apparently men didn't like to see women eat, and they didn't like tall women. I was both, and made it worse by wearing heels. Zoe was tall too, but her height was okay because she was an international model. Also, she was delicate and didn't eat. I ate, and there was nothing remotely delicate about me.

'I know,' I said. 'She didn't understand that I always burnt it off. Why do you think I was at your place as much as I was? Your mum knew the way to a growing girl's heart. She was always baking.'

I opened the first bag of croissants and set them and the coffees on my kitchen bench, and motioned him towards the stools.

'And,' I said, tearing into a croissant, 'it appears you know the way to a growing girl's heart as well.'

'You always did say what you were thinking.'

'I don't see a lot of point in playing games.'

'Some games can be fun though.'

His eyes were doing that twinkling thing and he leant in towards me. And then it was like it was last night. Except this wasn't a dark nightclub. It was broad daylight and we were approximately ten fast steps to my bedroom.

'Did you sleep last night?' he asked.

There was barely a breath space between us.

I licked a croissant crumb from my bottom lip, chasing it around with my tongue. 'I don't think so. Did you?'

He watched the movement. 'No. I couldn't. Every time I closed my eyes I thought of you and how amazing it is that I've found you again.'

He brushed the buttery crumb from the corner of my mouth. I could feel my nipples hardening under my T-shirt. He looked in that direction and then back into my eyes. One large hand cradled my head, while the other cupped my breast through the fabric.

'And how I couldn't wait to kiss you again.'

As his thumb played with my nipple, his breath came a little faster, but his eyes continued to hold mine. I felt my eyes glazing over and swallowed hard. Somehow I was still holding onto the pastry.

He kissed my lips lightly and drew back, taking the croissant from my hand and placing it back on the paper bag. My nipples missed the attention.

I put both hands into his hair and pulled his mouth back to mine, giggling when I realised that I'd transferred those buttery crumbs to his hair. He moved his head to nuzzle his way down my neck and, in one quick move, pulled my T-shirt over my head. He looked at me for a few seconds, then lowered his head to trace one breast with his tongue. Oh.

He lifted his head and smiled, his other hand still at play. 'What are you thinking now?'

I couldn't think about anything other than how he was making me feel.

'How much I don't want you to stop what you're doing,' I managed to say.

'Anything else?'

'How much I want you in my bed.'

'Then how about you take me there?'

'It's not too soon?' I teased.

'It's not soon enough,' he growled into my mouth.

'You're the one who chose to go home last night,' I reminded him.

'I'm not going anywhere now. I'm not sure I'll be going anywhere again.'

CHAPTER FIVE

Back in the office after lunch with Andi, I checked with Paula for messages, ignored the look in her eyes, and settled down to look for problems in the contract that Mark was about to sign with Warner Enterprises, a Perth-based company that provided IT and engineering support to the mining industry. It was a deal unlike anything we'd done in the past, so I was keen to make sure all of our bases had been covered. We were developing and implementing a new accounts receivable and workflow management system, and Mark had asked me to sponsor the project. Effectively that meant its success or failure would be on my shoulders. This was my first time taking charge of a deal this important and I was sure it was the final step in the partner process, so I needed to get the right team together. I'd already engaged Sophie as project manager, and commenced the planning stage of the project so we could get the scope signed off very soon after the contract was executed. The developer's schedules had been freed up from the end of April, and all systems were go. We just needed signatures on paper, and that was scheduled to occur when I was on holiday.

Two hours, three major discrepancies and some clause issues later, my phone rang. It was my mother. I grimaced and answered.

'I'm just phoning, Abigail, to let you know that we're all alright up here.' Mum rarely wasted time on pleasantries.

'Why, what's happened?'

'Nothing. But you haven't phoned for a while, so something could easily have happened in that time.'

Right … she was being sarcastic.

'I'm sorry, Mum. Things have been a little chaotic down here. How are you? How's Peter … and Tyler?'

'Too busy to phone your family? Peter's fine, and Tyler's doing very well at university. I have the usual concerns, but I'm sure you don't want to hear about those.'

I sighed heavily and rolled my eyes. If there were such a thing as the guilt Olympics, my mother would be a gold medallist. She took passive-aggressive and raised it to a new art form.

'I know that you'll probably be too busy to care, but Zoe will be in Melbourne in a few weeks. She's style ambassador for that British store opening in Chapel Street. I'm sure she'd like to see you.'

'Yes, she texted me a few weeks ago. I'm going on holidays around that time, so told her to send me her dates.'

I heard her sniff of disapproval down the line. 'Can't you be a little more flexible? It's not every day that Zoe comes to town.'

I muttered something about how my plans couldn't be changed at this late stage, and she responded with a meaningful silence.

'She'll probably be out later in the year for Fashion Week, so she can call me then and maybe we can catch up,' I suggested, making a mental note to plan a business trip somewhere, anywhere, to coincide with Fashion Week.

'Why don't you call her? She's too busy to be dropping everything to fit in with you. It doesn't always have to be about you. I don't think it would hurt you to put yourself out once in a while for her.'

I sighed again. 'Anyway, Mum, I'm in the middle of something here. I'll call soon.'

Despite Mum saying that everything was always about me, it had really always been all about Zoe. She'd been special since the day she was born – the day after our father died. I was nine. Mum had channelled her grief into caring for the new baby, leaving me mostly in the care of Dad's mother, Grandma Brentnall. As Zoe grew up, despite always getting what she wanted on account of her being so special, she also wanted whatever I had too. When I was a teenager, she'd sneak into my room and steal whatever it was that was special to me, returning it broken or damaged in some way. And as soon as she was old enough, her focus moved from my things to my boyfriends. Zoe had been stealing my boyfriends since she was sixteen. My last three serious boyfriends before Brad had ended up preferring my sister's bed to mine. She returned them to me when she'd tired of them. She didn't want to keep any of them, just liked to toy with them, like a cat with a mouse, for long enough to ruin any relationship I could possibly have had with them.

Brad was the only one who hadn't been dazzled by Zoe, despite her best efforts. She only ever wanted to see me if Brad was around, then she'd spend the whole night shamelessly flirting with him. He'd smile and laugh along with her, his hand on my leg, or his arm draped protectively around me. The one time he came to Sydney with me and Zoe contrived to be home, she paraded around the house in an assortment of skimpy lingerie. A lesser man would have quickly melted, but he ignored her resolutely, until the day she deliberately took her top off while bra-less, ostensibly to change her outfit. She'd kept it off long enough for him to notice, and smiled seductively in his direction.

He'd laughed and said, 'Zoe, you're wasting your time, energy and talent on me. There's nothing about you that would interest me. There never has been.'

She was stunned, more so when he'd turned his back on her to finish telling me whatever it was he was telling me. I couldn't even remember what it was we were talking about. It wasn't important. What was important was that he'd ignored her. On the few occasions we'd met up in the intervening years, she'd tried harder. He'd remained immune. Why hadn't I remembered that?

I attempted to bring my attention back to the contract in front of me. Where was I?

Maybe I should take Andi's advice and call Brad. If I called now, he'd be more likely to be at a job site and less likely to hear the phone. If I called from the work phone, it would show up as an unknown number, and if he did happen to hear it, he'd be less likely to pick up if he didn't know the caller. Both these scenarios meant I'd get to hear his voice – and oh, how I missed hearing his voice. He had one of those voices that was rich and just deep enough. In the right mood, it curled around you and warmed you to the core. I'd learnt from extended business trips that it could warm other body parts effectively too. Best not to think about that now.

My plan also meant that he would listen to his messages and call me back before I left work. That way, I rationalised, it would be as if he'd called me, not the other way around. In other words, it wouldn't *really* seem as if I was chasing him … would it? In fact, if I tried hard enough, I could convince myself that he was the one phoning me.

Counting to three, I called his number. Once

his voicemail clicked in I'd say something cool and nonchalant like:

'Oh, hi, Brad. I'm sure you're busy packing, but I've bundled up some of your things.'

Or, 'Brad, I'm just wanting to check that you're okay. All's fine here. Anyway, have a great trip … Maybe give me a call when you get back?'

Both were good options.

What I hadn't bargained for was him answering the phone on the second ring.

'Hello? … Who's there?' he said in response to my silence.

I cursed under my breath. I didn't have a script prepared for this scenario.

'Umm … hi …' I finally managed.

There was a short silence, then, 'Abby, is that you?'

'Umm … yes.'

More silence. This was going surprisingly well. Not.

'How are you?' I asked. Good question.

'Fine. You?'

'All good.'

More silence.

'Was there a reason you rang?'

'Umm … yes.'

'Well?'

'I … I was wondering when you're leaving … and … umm … and I wanted to know if you're okay.'

'I leave at the end of the week, and I've already

answered your other question.'

He wasn't going to make this easy.

'Oh. Well, who's looking after Bert while you're gone?'

'Todd.'

'Okay … Is there anything at my house that you need?'

'Do you want me to get my stuff?'

'Umm, I guess it's up to you. I don't mind. You can either get it now or later, or when you get back maybe.'

Shit, shit, shit, shit. That just sounded like I wanted him to move his things out.

'I need to give you your key back too,' he said, sending a fresh wave of pain through my middle.

More silence.

'Abby? Are you still there?'

I wanted to tell him how I felt, how everything reminded me of him. I wanted to tell him that I couldn't eat or sleep, that I was exhausted, that I wasn't alright, and nothing felt right any more. I wanted to tell him that I needed him to hold me against his chest and say it was all a big mistake and he wasn't really going. I wanted to ask him to stay, but I couldn't say any of it. There was something lodged in my throat, and the words were stuck in my chest.

'Yes.'

'I take it that you haven't changed your mind about coming with me?'

I shook my head and bit the inside of my mouth, tasting the salty blood on my tongue.

'Ab?' he asked again, more softly this time.

'I can't.'

'I guess that's all we need to say then.'

More silence.

'For Christ's sake, Abby!'

'I'm sorry,' I managed. And then I said it first – I couldn't help it. 'I love you, Brad.' And then, 'I miss you.'

Finally, he replied. 'And I love you too, but it's not enough any more. I want more of you than you're prepared to give me. I'm tired of separate houses and separate beds and freak-outs every time the subject of commitment comes up. I'm nearly thirty-five years old, and if you don't want a proper family, I need to find someone who does.'

'Oh.'

It was what I wanted too – to be a family with him and Bert, to grow old with him, to feel safe and loved and everything else that went with being with Brad. But I couldn't tell him.

'I know what I want, but, Ab, I'm sick of dealing with whatever it is that holds you back. Maybe these few months apart will help you decide what you want.'

I couldn't speak. If I did, I'd cry, and if I cried, he'd know – even over the phone – and I couldn't bear that. Besides, I'd never cried at work and wasn't about to start now. I bit the other side of my gum. It bled too.

'Okay,' I said.

'Okay,' he said. And then he hung up.

Sophie ducked her head around my door. 'Hey, have you had a chance to review those service levels yet?'

'What?' I had no idea what she was talking about. I had no idea about anything except the things I should have told Brad.

'In the contract … on the desk in front of you?' She started to laugh and stopped when she saw my face. 'Are you okay?'

I gave myself a mental shakedown. Head in the game, Abby.

'Sorry, my brain's a little foggy from going through these clauses. I've finished the review of the service levels, and I'll be done with the rest later this afternoon. Do you want part of it now, or would you prefer to wait until I'm completely done?'

'There's no hurry – I just wanted to check you were on track.' She was still watching me with what I thought was concern in her eyes. 'Are you sure you're okay? You're looking a little peaky.'

'I'm fine, thanks.' I plastered on a smile and waved her concern away. 'It's nothing that an early night and a decent sleep won't fix.'

'Okay, well, don't work too late tonight then. We're ahead of schedule so there's no pressure.'

I nodded and she left.

And I let my smile slip to join the other broken pieces of me on the desk.

That night when I got home, I found my spare key pushed into my mailbox. I supposed that made it official – we'd broken up.

I wandered through the rooms looking for things he might have left, evidence that he was coming back, that this wasn't really the end. More a little blip. Something we could find our way back from when he returned from Denmark or Poland or Austria or wherever it was he was going. His side of the bathroom cabinet was empty. His toothbrush, razor and that aftershave he wore that always made me want to burrow into him had gone.

I remembered nuzzling into that point below his jaw, closing my eyes and knowing that no matter what shit had gone down during the day, he was my safety net. The truth was, I'd never loved anyone the way I loved Brad. There were a few times in the past when I'd thought I might almost be there, in love, but it had never been like it was with Brad. Besides, Zoe put paid to those relationships. With Brad I felt it right from the start, but I didn't say it – I love you – not until he did.

The first time he said it we were making love. It was about a month or so after we'd found each other again. He stopped what he was doing, looked right into my eyes and said, 'I love you.' Just like that. We were at a crucial point in proceedings so I probably moaned or something equally encouraging. I didn't say it back in case it was the orgasm talking.

The next morning we were having breakfast at an inner city cafe, and he rested his toast on the plate, picked up his coffee, took a sip, looked deeply into my eyes and said, 'I meant what I said last night, Abby. I love you.' Then he picked up his toast and took another bite. It was that casual. There was nothing casual about the feeling of pure joy that rushed through my veins, but I nibbled at my own toast and said it back to him. 'I love you too.'

Then we smiled at each other like idiots, paid the bill, and broke all land-speed records to get back home to bed, where we each said it again.

Ever since, I'd been careful not to go overboard in telling him too often – just in case anyone was keeping score on the relationship spreadsheet. Maybe I didn't tell him enough.

In the bedroom, the book he'd been reading before that last night had gone from the bedside table. So had the little pile of clothes on the floor, and the few things he'd hung in the wardrobe. The bowl I kept outside on the balcony for Bert had been washed and left to drain on the sink. He'd taken Bert's dinner dish, and the spare bag of dog biscuits was missing from the pantry. If I concentrated really hard I could see Bert lying on his mat beside the door, his tail wagging every so often as he heard us talk or move about the room. I straightened the edges of the mat and blinked my eyes a few times until I couldn't see his doggy grin any more.

There was an empty space on the fridge where a photo of the two of us used to be. I couldn't remember who'd taken it – Todd probably … or maybe Andi. The four of us had been in the Yarra Valley and had bought some bread and cheese and a bottle of wine to share for a picnic lunch. It had been a magical late spring day – the sky was blue, the lavender was purple and the buds had burst to life on the grapevines. And, for a change, Todd and Andi weren't arguing. Brad and I had always harboured a secret hope that Todd and Andi would get together, but instead they'd always clashed. This particular day they'd been playing nicely. Brad had pushed me onto my back on the rug and was tickling me. In the photo we were looking into each other's eyes and laughing. Just a few minutes later the laugh had turned into something else – as it so often did with us – and I'd forced myself away from him and poured another glass of wine. He'd rolled onto his tummy and grinned at me. 'Later,' he'd mouthed.

He'd taken the photo with him. There was nothing left of us on display.

I rummaged through the drawers in my bedside table and found another photo. It was from a different time and place, but it was us, and we were happy in it. I took it out of the frame and popped it under the magnet on the fridge. I found another lying behind a stack of books, and placed it beside the TV.

Hidden underneath the throw on the couch I found a wool jumper he'd missed. I remembered taking it off him only a few weeks ago when we didn't quite make it into the bedroom. I pulled it on over my work clothes and inhaled him.

The saddest thing of all was that I knew exactly what I could have said to make it all better. It wouldn't have been hard. Something like 'I need you', or 'I'll come with you', would have been enough … yet I couldn't do it.

CHAPTER SIX

Brad had been due to leave two weeks ago. I assumed that he had. I'd hoped, rather than expected, he might call me before he left, but he didn't.

The two weeks had passed quickly. I was up each morning at six for a run, at my office by eight thirty; lunch a few times a week with Andi; and the usual fire-fighting at work. Weeknights found me balancing cheese on toast on my lap in front of the television, or throwing something pre-packed and frozen into the microwave. The way I was going, I'd be able to publish a cookbook on microwave delicacies. I'd call it *A La Ding*.

I certainly ate better when Brad was around. He liked to cook, spending hours on the weekend preparing meals for us – meals that often went cold when we got distracted by other appetites. Even during the week he'd make sure that we had something quick, fresh and nutritious to eat together when I got home – the benefit of having a boyfriend who finished work while it was still daylight.

The due diligence with Warner Enterprises had

kept me busy enough to justify some distractingly long hours. Often I didn't walk through my front door until after 9 pm. The contract had more service level agreements, SLAs, than I'd seen before. Warner were used to getting things their own way, so it had been a matter of choosing which SLAs were deal-breakers and worth fighting for, and which we could live with. I'd relished the battle. It took my mind off Brad not being there.

It was my birthday today. Brad hadn't called. Maybe it wasn't yet my birthday wherever he was. As I'd done so often since he'd left, I called his home answer machine just to hear his voice. 'Hi, you've rung Brad. I'm not here – I guess you know that – but your call is important. You know what to do.' His voice curled around me in a virtual hug. It was the closest I'd get to the real thing this year.

Mum and Peter had sent the usual card containing the usual overly generous cheque, and Tyler had called when I was on my way to work. I almost told him about Brad and me breaking up, but couldn't – not even when he closed with his usual 'say hi to Brad for me'. Naturally, there was nothing from Zoe. I couldn't remember the last time she'd acknowledged my birthday, but heaven help me if I ever forgot hers.

Andi had dropped by this morning with a gift – a brightly patterned sarong for beside the pool in Bali – and an invitation to drinks tonight.

'It'll just be a few quiet ones with Tiff and Lisa,' she said. 'Tiff's always good fun, and we haven't caught up with Lisa in months.'

'Okay,' I agreed, 'but let's not make it a big one – we're flying out tomorrow.'

Andi had convinced me that it would be a good idea if she came to Bali with me. 'I'm just thinking of you, love. It's an awful lot of money to waste,' she'd said.

'Not really,' I'd countered. 'The price of the room won't change, and I bought the airfares using frequent flyer points. It would actually cost me more to change the details.'

'Even so,' she argued, 'you don't want to waste them. Also, I'm worried about you … you know, drinking on your own … You need me there, and I'm happy to drop everything to be with you.'

'You're such a good friend,' I'd simpered. 'So selfless.'

She'd shrugged. 'Well, I'm happy to make the sacrifice.'

I knew I'd be glad of her easy company.

'You know there'll be some things I want to do that you won't,' I warned.

'Trust me, Abs, all I want is a week or so on a deckchair by the pool. Besides, it doesn't look like Jason is going to leave his wife after all, so me being out of town will give him the opportunity to miss me.'

'Of course he's not going to leave her,' I'd said.

'I really thought it would be different this time.'

'You always do.'

Now she said, 'Trust me – you'll be tucked up in bed nice and early.' Her smile told a different story.

We started on sparkling wine, but moved on to martinis – as you do. The conversation moved too – from work and general catch-up to men. Andi had obviously filled the others in on the break-up, so everyone was side-stepping Brad's name and avoiding any reference to anything we'd all done together. This was a difficult feat considering Brad and I had rarely strayed from each other's side for over three years.

Andi was upset because she'd just broken up (apparently for the last time) from Jason. 'He was never going to leave his wife,' she wailed.

'Not even for you, love.' I patted her back in sympathy.

'They never do,' said Lisa.

'Why did you think he would?' asked Tiffany.

'Because they'd grown apart,' Andi explained. 'She hasn't understood him for years.'

'Dickheads,' said Lisa. 'They're all dickheads.' Lisa had been single for the last few years.

'Let's have another drink.' Tiffany, called over a cute Italian waiter who looked to be somewhere in his mid-twenties. His biceps were obvious under the white T-shirt he wore.

Andi brightened, dimpled, smiled at him and pushed her enviable cleavage ever so slightly forward. I looked at her and laughed. She was incorrigible.

'Way too young for you,' I said.

'But so cute, and he'd take my mind off Jason for a few delightful minutes. Did you see his guns? And he had abs I wouldn't mind sipping a martini off.'

'Gay,' said Lisa.

'Oh, you think? But he's so cute.' Andi sighed. 'If I was a cute gay man, I'd have my pick of cute gay men.'

We all laughed, and when the cute waiter came back with our martinis, we laughed some more.

'Do you think he'd turn for me?' Andi said, watching his tight bum disappear through the crowd.

'Why did you believe Jason would leave his wife?' I asked, bringing Andi's focus back to us.

'Why do I ever believe it? I don't know … He made sense, and he seemed really sad. They'd been together for years and she hadn't changed, but he had. He was ambitious and she held him back.'

Despite the martinis and the laughter, I felt sudden empathy for Jason's wife who had no idea how close she'd come to having her world ripped apart by my best friend. As dearly as I loved her, sometimes Andi's refusal to accept the consequences of her behaviour irritated me.

'I feel sorry for her,' I said.

'What about him, being in a loveless marriage?'

asked Lisa.

'Is it though – loveless? Or is it just that she's become a little too much like the kitchen furniture and he's taken her for granted? He's looking for something more exciting, or burying himself in work and telling the world that she doesn't understand him. One day soon she's going to decide that while she still loves him, she needs him to tell her more often how he feels about her. She needs him to show her how he feels and to tell him what she really wants, not just have him assume that she'll always be there to come home to. Because one day she won't be there. She'll have buggered off to Denmark or Austria or Poland or somewhere to look at fucking gardens, and he'll be left here with his heart broken, not knowing what the fuck just happened, and living with every single thing reminding him of her. And then he'll know that despite all the efforts he's made to the contrary, he'll have to admit that he loved her more than she loved him.'

I finished my rant to silence and stares from the others.

'I don't think we're talking about Jason any more,' said Tiffany.

I drained my drink and stood. 'I need to pee.'

'Do you want me to come with you, sweetie?' Andi said.

'No, I can manage on my own. I've gotten quite good at it over the years. Can someone get that waiter back? I need another drink.'

In the bathroom I straightened my dress and touched up my makeup. We'd all dressed up for the evening and I was wearing a black strapless sheath dress that fell tightly to just below my knees. A split at the back allowed me to walk rather than shuffle. I'd teamed it with my highest black heels, a red velvet wrap for my shoulders, black chandelier-style earrings and red lipstick. I'd had my hair cut and the colour updated last weekend and it fell to my shoulders in feathery layers. Making the effort was supposed to make me feel better and a little celebratory – but it wasn't working. I tucked the longest layer behind my left ear, took a deep breath and went out to face the girls. There were bound to be questions after my little outburst. I hoped that Andi had answered some of them for me.

The waiter was back with our fresh drinks, and we toasted each other again. Tiffany opened her mouth to say something, but closed it quickly when Andi nudged her. Instead she moved on to discuss her theory on break-ups. Tiff had an opinion on every aspect of the mating game, and a checklist and set of rules that any man would need to be super-powered to jump over. Andi and I joked that one day she'd wake up with someone who was the exact opposite of her version of Mr Right – he'd have completely the wrong job, wrong look, wrong income, wrong car, live in the wrong suburb, come from the wrong family, have gone to the wrong school and support the wrong football team. That would be the day she'd fall hopelessly in love.

'When it comes to break-ups, you should take the same number of months as the years you were together before moving on to someone else,' she said.

'That means Abby won't be able to look at anyone for nearly three months. That won't work – she'll need a rebound shag before that.' Lisa looked across at me. 'You know you need a rebound shag, right?'

'You girls are all assuming this is a forever break-up.' Andi was eternally optimistic and romantic. 'I don't think we should write them off yet. Maybe they need the break to make them both realise that they're meant to be together.'

I looked around the room for distractions. Leaning against a tall bench in the opposite corner I saw Todd. He raised an eyebrow at me and, without smiling, tilted his glass in my direction in a silent toast. I shrugged a velvety shoulder and toasted him back.

Todd and Brad were like Andi and me, but for longer. Todd was the only person Brad would have spoken to about me, and it pained me to think he could be thinking badly of me for the way that I'd treated his friend. I looked down at the table and gave the drink coaster more attention than it deserved. Lisa and Tiffany were arguing good-naturedly about break-up do's and don'ts, but I felt like I'd hit a wall and wanted to go home.

When I raised my eyes it was to see concern in Andi's, and Todd standing at the table beside me. I scowled at Andi (she knew I didn't do concern) and smiled at Todd.

'Hey, you.' He greeted me with his usual kiss and hug. 'Happy birthday, sweetheart.'

'Thanks. I'm surprised you remembered.'

He half-smiled. 'I can't take all the credit for it – I remember that yours is near mine, but always get the dates mixed up. I was talking to Brad this afternoon and he mentioned it.'

Yet he hadn't called me.

'Happy birthday to you for last week,' I said. 'Sorry, I forgot.'

'It's okay, Ab. I'm sure you've got other things on your mind.'

I wanted to ask how Brad was, and if he'd settled in, and if he was missing me, but when I opened my mouth nothing came out. Todd raised his eyebrows as if anticipating my questions. I shook my head – I couldn't ask.

He gave me a sad little smile and gripped my shoulder reassuringly. 'I know,' he said.

I swallowed hard, nodded and plastered on a smile that I was sure wouldn't fool him for a second. 'It's lovely to see you, Todd. You know the girls, don't you?'

'Sure do. It's good to see you all. Andi …'

They greeted each other warily. The last time we

were all out together, Todd and Andi had ended up in a heated argument about Andi's choice of men. Todd had challenged her when she'd said that it wasn't her fault that the men she fell for belonged to other women. Todd told her that he didn't believe it, and asked her how she'd feel if the man she loved went off and did that with someone who looked and behaved like her. He told her that she was scared to fall for someone who would actually love her the way she wanted to be loved. She told him to shut the fuck up. Brad told them to play nicely and use other, nicer words.

'Do you want to stay and have a drink with us?' I asked him.

'No, thanks. I'm out with some friends from work so I'd better be getting back. I just wanted to wish you a happy birthday.' He paused. 'When are you flying out to Bali?'

'Tomorrow. I'm looking forward to lying by the pool. Andi's coming with me.'

'So you have nothing else planned?' His eyes didn't leave mine.

'No … why?'

'It's just that I thought you might take the opportunity to … Look, don't worry about it – I shouldn't think too hard. Anyway,' he changed the subject, 'it doesn't seem a year ago that we were all out celebrating our last birthdays.'

'Sometimes I think the time goes too quickly.'

'And then it's gone,' he observed.

I didn't think he was referring to time. In just a few short minutes he'd managed to do what I'd been avoiding all night – taking me back to this time last year.

That night, Brad and I had been all loved up, catching and holding each other's eyes during dinner. As we sat and chatted with the others, his calf was resting against mine under the table and every so often he would reach out with his little finger and run it gently against my hand. I'd spent the previous two weeks in Singapore for work and, aside from a quick detour to drop my bag and change, had come out straight from the airport. Both of us were anxious to spend some time alone. Skype sex was a very poor substitute for the real thing, no matter how inventive we'd tried to be. We'd drunk a lot, talked a lot, danced a little, and kissed some more. Behind every glance, touch and kiss was the promise of what would happen when we got back to my place.

Late in the evening, he'd pulled me into one of the dark corners and kissed me in a way that made everything and everybody else go away. I could feel his erection through the thin material of my wrap dress and pressed myself against it. It felt so good to feel his warmth and inhale his smell after two weeks away.

'Brad,' I finally said, 'let's get out of here – I need you inside me. Now.'

He felt rock hard as he kissed me once more. 'I can't wait either, but you'd better give me a few moments to make myself presentable.'

In answer I moved my hand down to his jeans and held him through the denim.

'Shit, Abby, you're going to get us both arrested.'

I kissed him again, made sure that my dress was appropriately arranged, and made my way to the bathroom.

I passed Andi at the edge of the dance floor, dancing with someone who, by the way she was looking at him, was likely to get very lucky later that night. She winked at me and mouthed, 'Naughty, naughty girl'. I smiled wickedly and mouthed back, 'We're out of here'. She grinned a 'Have fun' at me, and turned her attention back to her partner.

On my return, I found a more composed Brad chatting idly with Todd. They both smiled at my approach and I felt myself blush a little. Brad laughed and pulled me to him, kissing me hard on the mouth. Todd ruffled my hair, kissed my cheek and said, 'Have fun you two … Happy birthday, Ab.'

Brad leered. 'I'm about to give her something special to unwrap, so it will be a happy birthday.'

I thumped him lightly and we left. We barely made it into my apartment before our clothes were off and he was driving into me against the door. He slowed his pace and kept me on the edge as he looked deeply into my eyes. I moaned my frustration. He smiled and I pleaded with him not to stop, please don't stop. So he didn't, not even when I cried out.

This year, I went home alone, to an empty apartment and a half-packed suitcase. Things couldn't be more different. As I'd done every night since he'd taken his things, I pulled on his jumper and put myself to bed. Alone.

Just as I turned out the light a text came through. It was from Brad and I couldn't help the little flip that my heart did.

Hey Ab. Hope you've had a great day. Wish you were here x

What was that? And the single kiss at the end. It was the sort of message a friend would send to another friend.

Before I could stop myself, I replied: *Me too x*

Then I pulled his jumper over my face so I could pretend it was last year and he was snoring softly beside me.

CHAPTER SEVEN

I stretched out my legs on the pool lounge, admired my freshly painted toenails and, sighing contentedly, reached across to the table beside my chair to take a sip of the cocktail that had just been delivered.

Over the last few days Andi and I had been busy soaking up everything the island had to offer. We started our days at the buffet by the pool, indulging in pastries and a cooked breakfast. Each morning Andi said that she shouldn't, she really shouldn't, but was unable to resist. I didn't even try. My appetite was back – at least for now. Purely for health reasons we made sure that we finished off each breakfast with a plate of fresh rambutans and mangosteens. As we peeled the fruit and sipped at our coffee, we watched the squirrels dart across the pavers and up the trees. Sometimes they'd steal the fruit or crackers from the offerings in the small palm-leaf baskets left (seemingly) randomly on pavements, outside doors, and on the special altar in the resort's grounds. They'd sit back on their haunches to nibble at their prize, their little whiskers twitching, then skip off as quickly as they'd arrived, the palm trees forming some sort of squirrel super-highway.

Yesterday as we were eating breakfast, the rain came down suddenly and hard. It hit the thatched roof of the breakfast pavilion and flowed over the edge, cascading like a watery wall. We waited it out before heading back to our room, and I snapped a photo with my phone, making a mental note to tell Brad about it – if I ever got the chance.

Andi watched me with a question in her eyes.

'I was just thinking how impressive this would look as part of a water feature in a landscape design,' I said.

She nodded in understanding. 'Brad would love it.'

Back in Melbourne, the idea of having so much 'me' time had sounded wonderful – nothing to do but lie by the pool, bliss out and pretend that I was getting over Brad. The reality was different. Five days in and I was restless. The days were fine – there was plenty to keep us busy and distracted. It was the nights that were the problem. Even though Andi was here, after sunset the loneliness hit. Hours and hours of darkness punctuated only by the noise of firecrackers on the beach. I'd tried to hide it, but every so often I caught Andi looking at me with a combination of concern and pity.

Given that she was busy getting over Jason, we'd have made a fine maudlin pair if it weren't for the fact that we were both determined not to. Each night we'd pop a sarong over our bikinis and find a different beach bar from which to watch the sunset and engage in a little light flirting with other visitors.

The other night we'd found a bar a little further up the beach towards Seminyak. It had beanbags, paper lanterns, cheap beer and watered-down cocktails. I'd tried not to think about how much Brad would have loved it.

'Brad would love it here,' said Andi, who'd had one more happy-hour Bintang than I had. 'He'd be making notes about how he could translate the experience into a bar back home. There's no way that he'd be able to replicate that sunset though.'

'Thanks for that,' I said, determinedly turning my attention to a group of Aussies who'd flown over for a few days' R&R from the mines in Western Australia. A few people lit little paper balloons and let them go into the sky with loud whoops. We watched the flames getting smaller and smaller until they disappeared.

'Make a wish, make a wish,' they urged each other. One of the group turned to Andi and me. 'You guys have a go,' she encouraged. 'The locals say that your wish is bound to come true.'

I looked into my watered-down margarita and pretended not to hear them.

Andi jumped out of her beanbag and ran down to the water to launch hers. 'Come on,' she called back to me. 'You can share mine.'

I watched her shut her eyes and silently mouth

her wish as the balloon drifted away. The only thing I wished for was on the other side of the world.

I couldn't help it … I closed my eyes too and pretended he was on the beach with me, his arms pulling me back into his warmth. When I opened my eyes again, the balloon was just a dot in the sky, like a faraway star.

Ignoring my protests, Andi had booked us into a cooking class. 'It says here that it's one of the must-do activities,' she'd said, referring to the pocket-sized guidebook that had been her constant companion since we arrived.

'Really? Neither of us cook, which makes it a waste of our time and our money. Wouldn't you rather spend the day looking through some of these shops? Didn't you say there were some designers that you wanted to check out?'

I didn't tell her that when Brad and I first booked this trip, a cooking class was one of the things that Brad had really been looking forward to. 'You can't really understand a country until you understand the food and its ingredients,' he'd said.

Andi wasn't budging. 'You can't really understand a place or its people until you see where they shop and what they eat,' she'd argued.

Great.

'Do you think he knows where he's going?' she

asked me now, as we followed the class leader through the maze that led into Ubud markets.

'I hope so. I'm not sure I'd be able to find my way back out without him,' I said.

The entrance to the market was crowded with stalls selling the same products available in Kuta and Legian – dresses, Bintang-branded singlets, wooden penis bottle-openers in all colours and sizes, one to match every kitchen or bar.

'What do you reckon the plural of penises is?' asked Andi. 'Peni? And what do you call a cluster of them? A collective? Maybe it's a handful?' She picked up one of the larger models. 'This is definitely more than a handful.' She raised her eyebrows. 'And it looks painful.'

'Can you imagine declaring them to Australian Customs? "Excuse me, madam, do you have any wooden products to declare?"' I grabbed one by the shaft and waved it about. '"Why, yes, Officer. I have some wood."'

Andi giggled, and had to turn away when the stall-holder brought me a selection he thought I might be interested in.

Groups of women sat alongside the path, preparing the daily prayer offerings and chatting. We'd seen the offering baskets everywhere. Some held just a couple of water crackers or a few grains of rice and a cigarette, while others were filled with petals, fruits and incense. A few of the women were weaving palm leaves into tiny baskets, while others filled already-made ones from larger wicker vessels holding flower petals of all different colours.

I snapped photos, filling the screen of my phone with layers of colour.

Opposite the flower women, a man was grilling satay sticks on a charcoal burner, and dogs of disputed parentage wandered in and out of the crowd. It had been a while since breakfast and I looked longingly towards the smells coming from the satay grill. Andi shook her head in warning and I kept walking.

Once inside the market walls, we followed the group downstairs to where stalls selling raw ingredients of all types flowed into each other. There were vendors with baskets filled with aromatic raw spices, more selling vegetables, sometimes just a single product, sometimes an array of earthy goodness. Some specialised in root vegetables, some in green leafy vegetables, others in ginger, galangal, candlenuts and garlic. There were baskets full of red chillis, green chillis, long chillis and bird's-eye chillis. Although the ingredients were foreign to some of the group, I'd seen many of them before in Brad's kitchen.

Brad loved to cook and kept a well-stocked kitchen garden, but the Melbourne weather wasn't conducive to growing the ingredients he used in his Asian recipes. Often we'd take a Saturday morning drive to one of the farmers' markets, and wander the produce aisles hand in hand. Brad would stop and chat to growers, and I'd pick up herbs and marvel at the way their fragrance remained on my hands. These days I knew the difference between rosemary and lavender, and could even be trusted to pick oregano or thyme from the wall of pots Brad had hanging outside his kitchen. On those Saturday afternoons, Brad would chop, stir and do food-preparation-type things, while I'd sit opposite him with a glass of wine, reading the lift-outs from the weekend papers and sharing snippets of useless information. Sometimes he'd push across a board, a knife and an onion and order me about a bit. Sometimes there'd be a word or a glance, and he'd abandon the chopping, take the glass out of my hand and lift me onto the kitchen bench. Those nights we'd eat late.

Andi and I staggered out of class with full bellies a few hours later, and collapsed into the air-conditioned comfort of the car our driver, Wayan, had brought around to the front door.

Wayan wound through some narrow side streets to avoid a procession, but despite his efforts we still hit traffic. I leant back in my seat and looked around. The problem appeared to be a minibus unloading a group of tourists. They waited at the back of the bus for their backpacks, then left in groups, chatting in a dozen different languages, or so it seemed. It was the words on the side of the bus that made me sit up and take notice: *Extremity – Adventure Tours*. Across the road was a shopfront of the same name.

I watched as an older man came out and greeted the bus driver. They exchanged a few words, and the man from the shop handed the driver an envelope – presumably his salary for the day. They shook hands and the driver climbed back into the bus and drove off, clearing the road for the rest of us. Just as the traffic was about to move, and us with it, I flung open the car door. It was now or never.

'What are you doing?' Andi asked, following me out of the car. Behind us, horns blared as this time it was us blocking the road.

I hesitated before pointing to the *Extremity* sign. 'I just want to see what these guys have to offer.'

She looked at the shopfront and laughed. 'I wondered how long it would take for Adventure Abby to come out to play. Okay, while you're in there I'll duck into that jewellery store across the road.' To Wayan she said, 'You may as well find a park. We shouldn't be long.'

As I turned to walk into the shop, she yelled across the road, 'Do not, I repeat, do not book me on anything more strenuous than a deckchair.'

I grinned at her. 'Why not? I did a cooking class with you. It's only fair that you push your boundaries too.'

She smiled and waved. I took a deep breath and, straightening my top, opened the door. A wall of cool air hit me. Bliss.

'Can I help you?'

The man behind the counter was the man I'd seen paying the driver. I put his age at about fiftyish, although from a distance he could pass for someone much younger. I couldn't think of anything to say, so I pulled a random brochure from the stand in the corner and pretended to read it. He shrugged and turned his attention to paperwork.

'Are you interested in that tour?' he said eventually.

His smile was wide and bright in his tanned face, the lines around his eyes indicating a life filled with sun and laughter. Everyone in the pictures looked young, fit, happy, brave and vital too.

'We have plenty to choose from. Depending on your adventure appetite you might want to try canyoning or white-water rafting? Maybe you're into trekking or mountain biking?'

Still concentrating on the pamphlet, I said, 'No. I don't think so. I was just wondering …' I took another deep breath. 'Did you work here about twenty-five years ago?'

He narrowed his eyes and frowned.

'I'm sorry,' I said, 'forget it.' I turned to walk out. It was a ridiculous idea anyway.

'Wait a minute,' he called.

I stopped.

'I was here twenty-five years ago. This is my

business, I started it back in the early eighties.' He held out his hand. 'Hamish Munroe.'

I shook his hand. 'Abigail Brentnall ... but please call me Abby.'

'I'm pleased to meet you, Abby, but I'm not sure how I can help you.'

'So,' I managed, 'if you were here then ... all those years ago ...'

'Yes,' he still looked confused, 'I was here.'

'You were here then ... when my father, Roger Brentnall ... died on one of your tours.'

CHAPTER EIGHT

It happened in October 1989. I was nine years old, and Mum was heavily pregnant with Zoe.

It was a pregnancy that had seemed to go on forever. I remembered her sitting on the lounge with her hands on her belly and a strange smile on her face, which was unusual as my mother never really smiled much. At other times I'd catch her crying quietly to herself. If it wasn't for that smile when she thought she was alone, I'd have thought it was the pregnancy that had upset her so much.

I figured Dad must have seen some of those smiles and thought that she was happy enough – not that they ever talked about anything like that in front of me. Mum and Dad didn't really talk very much at all, not like Brad's mum and dad. The Ingrams were always talking. Mr Ingram would come home and grab Mrs Ingram in a hug and plant a kiss on her lips. Then he'd get a beer and they'd talk about the day. Mrs Ingram even laughed at his bad jokes. My mother never laughed. When my father came home each night, he'd move to kiss Mum hello and she'd turn her face so the kiss landed on her cheek. Dad would get a beer and ask her about her day, but she always brushed him aside and suggested he put his feet up in front of the television while she finished dinner.

He'd come into the lounge room, where I'd be sprawled in front of the TV, and ask me about my day instead. We'd laugh and chat about whatever it was that Brad and I had been up to, until Mum came in and told me not to annoy Dad, that he'd had a busy day and needed some quiet time. When she'd gone, he'd raise his eyebrows at me and we'd giggle some more.

Dad worked in advertising, so if one of his ads came on telly I'd be quiet until it was over, then he'd talk me through the idea. Mum hated that too. She said it was bad enough that we had one person in the family who made things up for a living without him teaching me how to do it. He'd say that she mightn't like his job but it kept a very nice roof over her head. Then she'd do the huffy thing she did and disappear back into the kitchen.

Instead of bedtime stories, Dad used to talk to me about different countries and the adventures we'd share one day. Mum would get mad at him and tell him not to fill my head with rubbish, that we had perfectly good children's books he could be reading to me. Once she was pregnant she seemed to stop worrying about it. And it didn't bother her any more what Brad and I were getting up to. She even stopped making me go to those infernal dance classes that were supposed to turn me into a lady. Who knew a dancer's bun was about hair not food? It was as if nothing else mattered except the baby she was carrying.

One night after I'd gone to bed, there was shouting downstairs, lots of it. Mum and Dad didn't usually shout. Or Dad did sometimes, but Mum would purse her lips in disapproval and either say nothing or leave the room. This time Dad was shouting and Mum was crying.

The next morning Dad came into my room, kissed me on the forehead the same as he did before going to work every day, and told me that he had to go away for a few weeks. 'I'll be back before you know it, my magic girl.' He called me that because of abracadabra – it sounded like Abby.

'Where are you going?' I asked.

'A place called Bali. It's in Indonesia. They have beautiful beaches and rainforests. It's a good place for me to have a rest.'

'Can I come too?'

'No, sweetie. You need to stay here and look after your mother. I won't be gone for long. I'll be back before the baby comes, and I'll bring you some great presents.'

'If it's a good place can you take me there one day?'

'Of course I will. I promise.' He hugged me and kissed my forehead again. 'Love you, my magic girl.'

'Love you too, Dad,' I'd said, and smiled sleepily. I didn't know that was the last time I'd see him.

A week later, the phone rang in the middle of the night. Mum got up and I heard her talking softly. The next morning she packed me off to school as normal, so I thought I'd dreamt the call.

Brad grabbed me at morning tea and took me to one side. 'I heard on the news this morning that some Australian man died in Bali yesterday. Have you heard from your father?'

I hadn't heard from him, not a word. Yet somehow I knew that it was my father they were talking about in that story. I connected the news with the phone call that Mum had received the night before. I ran out of school and all the way home, hating that she'd acted so normally that morning, hating that she hadn't told me.

Mum wasn't at home; Grandma Brentnall was. She told me Mum had gone into labour and was in the hospital having the baby. She told me that there'd been some bad news, an accident, and she took me in her arms and held me tight. And I knew that my father had died in the jungle and was never coming home.

'Do you remember the accident?' I asked.

Hamish paused before replying. 'How could I forget?' He shook his head. 'You don't forget things like that.'

'No, I don't imagine you do.'

We were both silent for a minute, and then he turned the open sign on the door to closed. 'Perhaps you'd better sit down. You've gone a little pale.'

I did as he suggested. He disappeared into the back of the office and returned with a bottle of water and a small glass containing something that I assumed was alcoholic.

'You'll need this,' he offered.

I swallowed the spirit in one go, wincing as the alcohol burnt on the way down. I followed with the water.

He waited until my colour and my composure had returned. 'How old were you when he died?'

I shrugged. 'Nine. I didn't really understand what had happened until I was much older.' I laughed ruefully. 'Not that I know much even now. No one talks about it, you see. No one talks about him. All I knew then was that Dad hadn't come home.'

I was babbling, but Hamish seemed to understand.

'There wasn't anything we could have done, you know,' he said. 'I've beaten myself up over the years, wondering whether there was a way I could have predicted the surge that came down the valley that afternoon. These days, with computer forecasting, we absolutely could have, but not back then. Back then I don't think there was a computer on the island. There certainly weren't any cell phones.'

'I don't blame anyone,' I said. 'I just wanted to

know … to see where it happened. Maybe even talk to someone. I haven't been told much and I wanted to know.' I lifted the glass and drained the last couple of drops from it.

He nodded in understanding. 'I can help you there. Are you free tomorrow?'

'I am.'

'Okay, let's swap details and I'll collect you tomorrow morning at nine. I'll take you to the spot I last saw him alive.'

In the car on the way back to Legian, I was quiet. Andi commented on it, but I told her that I was tired and headachy.

'It must have been all that cooking,' I joked.

I closed my eyes and leant my head against the headrest and pretended to sleep.

CHAPTER NINE

That evening I headed straight to the Sunset Bar in the resort. Andi had received a text from Jason, so stayed in the room to talk to him, muttering something about absence and hearts and how when you put them together it produced fondness. Apparently he'd just needed some time.

Sipping at what I suspected would be the first of many cocktails, I admitted to myself that the encounter I'd had today and the trip I would be taking tomorrow were exactly the reasons that I was here in Bali. The reason why I'd insisted on still coming, even though it meant I wouldn't be going to Denmark or Austria or Poland or wherever it was that Brad had gone.

It had started just before my birthday last year, when a random comment from someone reminded me that I was about to turn thirty-three. It didn't seem that old, but it was four years older than my father had been when he died. It occurred to me that I didn't know how he'd died, not really. I didn't know what the yelling and crying had been about that night before he left. I had my memories and those stories of adventures we'd never had, but I didn't know him – not really.

I didn't know how to answer any of those questions – and asking Mum wasn't an option – so I pushed them way deep inside, took on more responsibility in the office and worked even longer and later than I'd always done. Part of it was a genuine push for that elusive partnership (*this* close), and part of it was to make sure I was way too busy to think about whatever it was I was using work to run from. I supposed I'd been aware of a distance growing between Brad and me, and that it was all coming from me. He'd say nothing when I cancelled yet another date or weekend outing so I could go into the office to finish something that absolutely couldn't wait until Monday. Sometimes, though, I'd catch him looking at me with something that was either concern or confusion in his eyes.

A few times he asked if everything was okay, and I always snapped, 'I'm busy. Can't you see that?'

'You're always busy.'

'Yeah, it goes with the job. Besides, I'm covering for Mark at the moment.'

'You're always covering for Mark. He's either up in Asia, interstate, or on one of those golf trips he goes on with his friends. He takes you for granted, and you're taking more and more on.'

'I have to. If I drop the ball now, I'll be proving that I can't handle the pressure.'

'I understand that, but all I'm asking is for you to take one night off so we can go out for dinner. It's been ages since we went out and really talked.'

'Sure, but it doesn't need to be this night.'

His eyes would look hurt, but I'd have already moved on to the next task.

Then, a few months ago, he decided that we needed a holiday. 'We both need a break, Ab. You haven't had more than a four-day stretch off in at least two years, and I'm going to be exhausted by the time autumn comes.'

'I guess. It's just that there's always so much on the go, and I'm *this* close.'

He'd laughed. 'I know, but you and me – we need to be together. Just us. No ducking into work, no late-night teleconferences. Just us. There are things we need to talk about. The next steps.'

I didn't pretend to misunderstand. I hadn't been easy to live with, and he'd been very patient with me. 'Okay. Where did you have in mind?'

'I've heard good things about Bali. There are some resorts up there doing some really cool work amalgamating the views, the rice paddies and the culture into the garden. Plus, it's far enough away that you can't be called back for a last-minute meeting.'

I didn't think he remembered that Dad had died there. He certainly never made the connection between Bali, my father's death and my growing detachment. Why would he? We didn't talk about my father. No one did.

At first it was because Mum seemed to be in such emotional pain. There she was, twenty-nine, with no husband and two children, one who would never know her father. As a result, Mum became completely wound up in Zoe. It was as if she was some sort of miracle that represented everything that had been lost.

Thankfully Dad's life insurance had paid the mortgage on the house and given Mum a little something to live on, but the fact remained: she was on her own. Until she met Peter Lockhart. He was the lawyer acting for her at the inquest, and he made sure she didn't need to wait too long for Dad's life insurance. They must have hit it off, because a few years later, when their paths crossed again, apparently it was love at second sight. Peter was just getting over the tragic death of his wife from breast cancer, so the timing couldn't have been any more convenient. They were married not long after. Their wedding made the newspapers, as by this time Peter was a shadow minister in Federal Parliament and had been identified by the party leaders as one to watch. He'd earned the sympathy of the nation while he cared for his wife in those last months; and as Mum had lost her husband in particularly tragic circumstances, made more dramatic by the birth of Zoe, it was the perfect fairytale ending for both of them.

After this, my father's death became media fodder each time Peter was campaigning. No one ever stopped to consider how I felt about it. It was as if he'd never existed in my life, only in Zoe's. Mrs Ingram and Grandma Brentnall were the only grown-ups who seemed to remember that I'd lost someone too. I knew how he'd died – that was in the papers – but no one talked to me about it. I didn't even know what he was doing there on that river in Bali that day.

I asked Grandma Brentnall, and she sat me down and told me as much as she knew. 'Your mother told me that he was at a conference for the advertising company your father worked for, dear. She said your father had opted to take a white-water rafting tour. It was supposed to be an exercise for team bonding, to help them all get along with each other and be more creative. There was a storm to the west of where he was that caused some flash flooding and sent a huge amount of water down the river to where your father and his tour were. Your father helped some of the others, but was caught when he tried to get out. He was swept away.'

They'd never found his body. It was a freakish, completely unpredictable accident that had never happened before, or since. That was all I knew.

There hadn't been a funeral, just an odd little memorial service that Mum wouldn't let me go to, and a coronial inquiry with the dispassionate pronouncement of 'death in absentia' or 'missing presumed dead'. I read about that in the newspaper in the school library.

And that was it. Once Mum married Peter and we

moved to the other side of Sydney, it was as if, outside of election time, my father had never existed. The kids at my new expensive girls' school only knew about Peter. He'd adopted Zoe, but I refused – my father's name was all I had left of him.

I hardly saw Grandma Brentnall after we moved. She died not long after. If it wasn't for Todd's comment last week, I could easily have believed I was the only person who remembered that Peter wasn't really my father. Dad and the circumstances of his death weren't something I talked about. Why would I? It was all yesterday's news.

Andi had asked me about it once. I didn't go into details. I didn't need to – all I knew was freely available in the newspapers.

Perhaps it was because Brad and I were on the threshold of formalising our relationship. Perhaps it was because I was at that age when I should be thinking about settling down properly and having my own children. Whatever it was, those questions that had been lurking below the surface decided to poke their heads up. Why did Dad leave? Was he planning on coming back? What had gone so badly wrong that he had to go and die in a jungle? If he wasn't intending to come back, what did that say about me? This holiday could be the opportunity I needed to have some of those questions answered. Even if I found nothing, just being in the place where it had happened would help me understand – wouldn't it? There was a part of me that felt I wouldn't be able to commit to anyone, not even Brad, until I'd faced my personal demons. So I'd agreed and we booked it.

Why hadn't I told Brad? I didn't think it was a conscious choice to exclude him, but once the idea was in my head, it seemed like something I needed to do alone. As they say: be careful what you wish for. I guessed part of me was disappointed that he hadn't put two and two together. Surely if he really loved me, he would have?

My memories were interrupted by a shadow and a voice. 'I have the feeling you're not appreciating this sunset in the way you should be.'

The man standing in front of me looked vaguely familiar. It was the blond hair and dimples. I squinted into the dying light. 'Do I know you?'

'I'm not sure. I've been sitting over there trying to place your face too.' He looked intently at me and then shook his head. 'Give me time- it will come to me.'

He pulled a chair out and sat down, beckoning a waiter over. I raised my eyebrows at the presumption.

'This is okay, isn't it?' he asked.

'Yeah, sure … I guess. If you're going to sit there, you may as well tell me your name.'

'It's Clinton – Clinton Barclay.'

'Well, Clinton, seeing as how you're sharing my sunset – I'm Abby Brentnall. But I'm warning you, I'm not great company this evening.'

'I'll take my chances.'

We sat in silence and watched the sun go down, dipping into the ocean with one last burst of orange. The lights in the trees came on and I snuck a look at his profile. He was quite cute, and I did need a distraction …

'So, Clinton, what brings you to Bali?'

I felt him smile in the darkness. 'Oh, you know – the usual reasons: over-worked, need a break, a few days somewhere with the phone turned off. It was one of those last-minute bookings. And you?'

'Much the same, but I'm here for longer than a few days. It's such a long way – surely you could have found somewhere closer to home?'

'I know, but as I said, I really needed the break, and there were some cheap airfares. Tell me, Abby, are you travelling alone?'

Someone must have told him once that girls liked men to lean in and maintain eye contact. I normally didn't like it – it was a personal space thing – but I was feeling just a tad on the reckless side tonight, so decided to let him practise his flirting. In any case, he seemed much more Andi's type than mine, although there was no wedding ring in sight.

'No, I'm here with my friend.'

'Where is she?'

I smiled over the top of my cocktail glass, and beckoned to the waiter for a fresh drink. As if on cue,

Andi arrived. She'd changed into a short, strappy, black beach-dress that highlighted her creamy skin and made the most of her considerable assets.

'God, I need a drink after that!' she exclaimed. 'Would you believe – oh … hello.' And just like that, her dimples appeared. Great – two sets at the same table. 'I know you, don't I?' Andi echoed my line. 'Hang on … I rarely forget a pretty face …' She squinted in the half-dark. 'I know! I've seen you at Noodelicious.'

I saw the light bulb moment hit him too. 'Of course! I've noticed you too – it always takes you longer to set your lunch out than it does to eat it. You know, you should lay your water down on the tray so it doesn't topple into your soup.' At our raised eyebrows he added, 'I eat there a lot, and you're pretty hard to miss.'

Andi and I were silent for a minute before I laughed. 'That is the lamest pick-up line I've heard in … well, a very long time.'

'You think? I thought it was pretty good.'

'Umm, no. It was lame. Does it usually work?'

He laughed. 'Actually, yes, I have a pretty good success rate with it.'

'I'm sure you do,' simpered Andi.

I sighed heavily.

One drink led to another and then another. The three of us shared a meal in a restaurant outside the resort, and had a few more drinks after that in a bar around the corner. I wasn't sure whether it was the cocktails or the beers, but I had a good time. As well as being good-looking, Clinton was a charming and attentive companion – and a diversion from what I suspected I'd be facing tomorrow.

Andi made arrangements to do some shopping with him in Seminyak the following day. He was keen to know how I was spending the day, and hinted a number of times that I should join them. I avoided the questions and ignored the hints, but agreed to meet them both later in the afternoon to go and take photos of some temple or other. Sure he was attractive, but I had the feeling that, just like an overly sweet dessert, he would be more palatable in small doses. Andi was welcome to him. With them it was the battle of the dimples.

When we got back to our room, Andi was full of questions. 'Where are you off to tomorrow that you're so secretive about?'

'Nowhere special. I just didn't want Clinton knowing all of my business.' I busied myself putting clothes away. 'What did Jason have to say for himself?'

'Oh, the usual.' She waved it away. 'Just how he misses me, and it's a delicate time right now, but he will tell her soon. Blah blah blah. I've heard it all before.'

'And you've fallen for it all before,' I reminded her.

She sighed. 'Yes. And I've also fallen for your attempts to avoid the subject. What's this about? Is it something to do with that Extremity place from this afternoon? Is it something to do with your father?'

The speed of Andi's brain constantly surprised me, although after all these years it shouldn't have. 'How did you know?'

She shrugged. 'I overheard something Todd said to you in the club the other night. And this afternoon when you came out of that shop, you looked like you'd seen a ghost, so I put two and two together. I figured you'd tell me when you were ready.' She chanced a look at me. 'I'm right, aren't I?'

'Yes.'

'Do you want to talk about it?'

'There's not a lot to talk about,' I said. 'Extremity is the company that ran the tour Dad was on when he was killed. The guy who owns it, Hamish, is still there and he's going to take me tomorrow to show me where it happened.'

'This is why, isn't it?'

'Yes.' I didn't pretend to misunderstand her. She was too smart for that.

'Did Brad know?'

I shook my head. 'I hoped he might have worked it out, but I don't think he did.'

'And you didn't say.'

I shook my head again. 'It's not something I talk about. It's not something we talked about. He was there when it all happened, so we never needed to.'

'Oh, Abby,' she hugged me, 'that's tough. I'll cancel Clinton and come with you.'

'No, don't do that.' I gently removed myself from her grip. 'I'm okay, really. I just have to get my head around it.'

'But –'

'Thanks, love, but I've come this far. I have to do this on my own.'

CHAPTER TEN

Hamish was waiting for me in the lobby when I emerged – more than just a little worse for wear – the next morning.

We made small talk for most of the drive. He told me how he'd come to Bali back in the early eighties to surf, and joined a group doing some trekking through the country around Klungkung. It was the dry season so the rapids were beginner level and quite tame, but having seen similar operations when backpacking in Europe, he'd been able to see the possibilities.

'I went home to Brisbane and tried to settle back into the office, but couldn't get the idea out of my head. I did a bit of research and was back here within twelve months. We started with the white-water stuff, and moved into trekking. Now we've added canyoning, horse riding and another couple of locations into the mix.'

'It sounds like you've done well,' I said.

'Yeah – I needed to. I fell for more than the island, and now have a wife, four children and six grandchildren to support.'

I laughed. 'You *have* been busy. Have any of them followed you into the business?'

He nodded. 'Two of my three sons. The youngest boy is travelling, and my daughter went to Australia to study and has stayed there.'

'You must be proud.'

'I am.' He paused for a minute. 'After your father died, I nearly gave it up and went home.'

There was nothing I could say to that.

Before too long we reached the point from where the tour had departed and, after an easy walk, found ourselves at the bank of the river. Being the dry season, the rapids were picturesque but benign. I guessed that was the way they'd probably looked the day it happened.

I said as much to Hamish. He nodded. 'The conditions that day were much like they are today. October is the end of the dry, and although you can get the occasional storm or downpour, there was certainly nothing that indicated that would be the case.' He had his hands on his hips as he surveyed the landscape. 'In fact, we didn't even feel the storm here that caused the surge – it was further up there.' He pointed to the mountains. 'It was freakish. The coroner said it was a one-in-a-million chance ... or even less. These days, with cell phones and computer forecasting, we know about inland storms and can cancel trips if there's even a hint of a risk, but back then? No way of knowing, mate. No way.'

He squatted, his gaze focused on something twenty-five years ago. 'You know, I can still picture him sitting by the edge of the river before we went out. Your father was one of those men you can't help but notice. So tall, so fit, and so cheerful.' He let out a short laugh. 'There were a few Japanese tourists on that trip who were really nervous and your father was calming them down. He was telling them to concentrate on how beautiful it would be to raft through the rice fields after the canyon.'

I smiled. 'Yes, my memories are of him always looking at the brighter side of life. To Dad, life was an adventure and there was always a silver lining to be found. He said to me once, "Abby, the glass is half-full, and the other half was bloody delicious."' I could picture him there on the bank, moving between the others with a reassuring pat on the shoulder or a 'good on you' slap on the back. 'It was always the possibility of more to come that motivated Dad. I didn't understand it as a kid, but now …'

'That's a nice memory to have,' he said. 'So happy they were … and so much in love. They couldn't keep their eyes, or their hands, off each other.'

What? Who couldn't?

'What are you talking about?'

Hamish paused. 'I'm sorry, I didn't think.' He walked off a few paces.

I called after him, 'Hamish, what did you mean by

that? That "in love" comment?'

He stopped, and seemed to be carefully considering his answer. 'I'm sorry, Abby, I thought they were together. I wouldn't have known any different if it wasn't for the inquest. I wouldn't have known he had a family back in Oz.'

I waited for him to explain.

'Are you sure you want to hear this?' he asked.

'Please. I feel like there's so much I don't know.'

He gazed into the green. 'It's just the way he was with the woman he was with – well, it was like there was no one else in the world for either of them. It wasn't just in the way they looked at each other, it was more than that. They had … a force field around them, as though nothing could come between them … That probably doesn't make sense to you. It didn't feel like it was what you'd call a hook-up or a holiday romance – it was more than that. It was like they gravitated towards each other.'

Like in the Gravitron … I was taken back to thoughts of Brad, and how we were together, as if there was no one else in the world for either of us. But my father and someone who wasn't my mother … like that?

'Yes,' I said, 'it makes sense.' Then a thought occurred to me. 'But what about the others?'

'The Japanese tourists?'

'No, the other participants in the conference. Wasn't there a group of them? Dad's workmates?'

A look of genuine surprise crossed his face.

'Workmates? No … we do conferences, but your father wasn't here as part of one. It was just him and … well, and his …'

'It's okay,' I said, 'you can say it.'

'His girlfriend.'

I walked down to the riverbank and knelt to trail my fingers in the water. I felt Hamish's eyes watching me. Gathering my thoughts, I stood, wiping my hands against my shorts. So there was no conference, but there was a woman. Was any of what I'd been told true?

'Do you know who she was?' I asked. 'The woman he was with?'

'Not off-hand, no. I'd have the records somewhere though if you wanted to try to look her up. She's probably married or something by now.'

I suddenly felt drained. 'No, that's okay. You know what, Hamish? I think I've seen enough … Thanks so much … but I'm ready to go back now.'

We didn't talk much on the way back to Legian. I had a lot that I needed to process.

The idea that my father was having an affair was beyond my comprehension. Had he met her here, or was it something that had been going on for a while back in Sydney? Had he left Mum and me to come here with her?

Then I wondered whether Mum knew about it. Of course she must have – it would have come out at the inquest. Then came the worst thought of all: what if I'd been blaming the wrong parent all these years? What if my dad, who I'd idolised, hadn't been deserving of that? What if Mum had been trying to protect me? What if he'd never intended to come back?

Mum had always told me that I was too like my father. She used to say it as if it was a bad thing. Perhaps it was a bad thing. If I really was like my father, would it follow that I too would have a problem committing to one person? That the minute things got tough or too close or too hard, I'd back out, run off to Bali and fall in love with a complete stranger?

Maybe Brad had had a lucky escape. Maybe he was better off without me.

Back at the resort, our room was in darkness. Andi had a migraine and had taken a sedative. Knowing her, it was one of those that could keep a good horse down for twenty-four hours.

'I'm sorry, A,' she mumbled in the dark. 'You know what I'm like when one of these hits – I just need dark and quiet to sleep it off. You go out with Clinton as planned, and we'll talk in the morning.'

'Is there anything I should know about – between you and him?'

'No, but he's exactly my type.'

'You mean married?'

'Don't make me laugh – it hurts too much. No, he says he's not – I asked. He's all yours … if you want him. He's pretty enough to play with for a little while. He's the opposite of Brad – that's a good thing. Don't make me talk, it hurts my head.'

I smiled at her in the darkness and headed out to meet him.

Clinton was waiting for me in the lobby. As I approached, his dimples burst into action, and he kissed my cheek. 'No Andi?'

'Sorry, she's got a migraine. I hope you're not too disappointed.'

'With you? Absolutely not.' He leaned closer. 'Don't tell Andi, but I'm looking forward to getting to know you better.'

I forced a smile.

'Our driver's here, so let's go.' He guided me towards the car.

Once inside I asked, 'Where are we going?'

'Tanah Lot.' At my blank look he added, 'It's a sea temple. The views and silhouettes at sunset are incredible. It's probably one of the most photographed spots in Bali.'

'Does that mean we'll be sharing the sunset this evening with a thousand other like-minded souls?'

He laughed. 'I expect so. Is that a problem?'

I shook my head. 'No.'

Like yesterday, I wasn't really in the mood for crowds and traffic, but I was in the mood for forgetting.

'You don't seem very relaxed after your day out.

Where did you say you went again?'

'I didn't say.' I concentrated on looking out the window.

'So,' he tried again, 'did you have a good day?'

'Yes, thanks. And you?'

'Very relaxing. Wow, your girl can shop! Then we spent some time down by the pool this afternoon – I thought we might have seen you.'

'Unlucky.'

'It's such a pity I have to go home tomorrow – I could do with another couple of days of this. We'd have more time to get to know each other properly.'

I turned from the window to face him. The poor guy wasn't to blame for what I'd learnt today. I was sure that he meant well, and it wouldn't hurt to be nicer to him. He was very pretty, it was just one night, and then I never had to see him again. Except perhaps at Noodelicious, and Andi and I could always find somewhere new to eat if necessary.

'It seems a long way to come for just a few days. You must have needed the break very badly,' I said.

'I did. We've been working on an outsourcing deal that's taken a lot of energy, so as soon as the contract was signed I figured I could get away for a few days.'

'Once those contracts are executed the really hard work starts, so it's probably a good thing you got away when you did. I'll be going back to a similar situation.'

I understood exactly where he was coming from.

We'd been due to sign Warner the week I flew out. Even now Sophie would be working through the project documentation I'd left with her. That partnership was so close I could taste it.

'What is it that you do, Abby?'

'Is it important?'

'Not really, it's just that I don't know very much about you – other than you like noodles, you have a hot friend, and you're a fabulous piece of woman.'

Seriously? He was incorrigible. It was no wonder he and Andi had gotten along so well.

I let out a short laugh. 'True, but I'm on holidays and don't really want to have to think or talk about work. I'm trying to switch off completely.'

'It's just that most people exchange little pieces of information. You know – I tell you something and then you tell me something.' He flashed his dimples at me and managed to make his eyes twinkle at the same time. This guy could multi-task.

I shrugged, but had to concede he was right. Clinton had been trying to get to know me and I'd been blocking him at every turn. Even last night over dinner I'd managed to avoid giving away any personal information. Not that it had mattered. After a conversation with Jason, Andi had enough personal information to share for both of us.

'Okay,' I said, 'I'm in finance.'

'Really?' He seemed surprised.

'Is that a "really" as in "you're kidding"? Or a "really" as in "how interesting"?'

'Surely it's not as simple as just finance?'

'No, of course it's not that simple. It's much more than spreadsheets and numbers. It's about finding a way to make the numbers do what you want them to do, and it's also about the thrill of the chase when it comes to negotiations.'

'Definitely not as simple as I thought.'

I smiled a little and looked out the window again.

'Don't you want to know what I do?'

'Not really.'

He laughed. 'Do you always say what you think?'

'Most of the time.'

'But what about flirting and the game?'

I shrugged. 'I don't normally see the point, and I only like games that I'm interested in winning.'

'Ouch!' He collapsed back into his seat, dramatically clutching at his chest.

I couldn't help but giggle.

Tanah Lot – or Pura Tanah Lot, as Clinton corrected me – was more impressive than I'd expected, and just as crowded. More than a simple sea temple, the site was also a temple to mass tourism and hawkers. Perched on a rocky outcrop, the temple itself provided a silhouette well worth photographing at sunset – once you'd passed the rows and rows of shops selling the same dresses,

T-shirts, wooden penises and bootleg DVDs that you could buy everywhere else. Snappers from all around the world were pointing and shooting cameras of all levels of sophistication at the sight. I made a mental note to come back sometime when the tide was low and earlier in the day. It would be quite something to walk across the rock platform without the bus-loads of people.

The cliff and coastline were dramatic and rugged, and I leant against the wall and watched the waves crash below what I had to admit was an impressive sunset.

Clinton took a large SLR camera from his backpack, mucked around fitting a lens, fiddled with the controls, and set to work. A few times he called me over to pose, but I declined.

'Come on,' he urged, 'you look so beautiful against the silhouette.'

I raised my eyebrows.

'It would be something to remind us of our time together.'

Our time together? I looked across at him and he was smiling, so I assumed he was joking and replied in kind. 'So it would, but the answer is still no. I'm no cover girl.'

He pouted a little and flashed his dimples, but I'd never responded well to pouting to get your own way. Hello, Zoe had been doing it since she was a baby. I was immune. Maybe I should introduce them — they could practise their dimply pouting on each other.

Once Mother Nature's light show had finished, Clinton announced that he'd let our driver go for an hour or so and we'd be eating in the open-air seafood restaurant high above the rocks. Even as I acknowledged the practicality of the plan, I swallowed my annoyance. It sounded a little date-ish and contrived to me, and I'd have liked him to ask me before he made the arrangement.

We were led to a table near the cliff edge. Candles flickered inside glass jars on the white paper cloth, serving a dual purpose of providing gentle light and anchoring the cloth to the table. Clinton beamed and held out my chair, before settling in his and commenting with a sigh just how romantic it was.

It was very romantic. Yet all it did was remind me that my father had been having an affair, and my boyfriend had left me for plants and dirt in Scandinavia … or somewhere.

On the upside, I was here with a very attractive man who, for whatever reason (possibly just because Andi wasn't around), seemed to be interested in me. So when Clinton ordered fruity cocktails, despite the fact that I didn't like umbrellas and plastic animals in my drink or alcohol that tasted of cordial, and would have preferred beer, I smiled sweetly and clinked glasses as he toasted the coincidence that had brought us together.

One of my pet hates was men who arrogantly assumed that they knew better than I did what I felt like eating. I didn't find that whole 'let me look after you' caper at all sexy and masterful – except in the bedroom. That kind of man might have thought it made him look commanding, but I thought it made him look like a wanker who didn't care about what I wanted. Yet I said nothing when Clinton declared he would take over the ordering of the seafood, and even resisted the impulse to raise my eyebrows.

The scampi and grilled fish, when they arrived, were absolutely perfect and, I had to admit, exactly what I would have felt like eating if I'd been asked.

Once I'd made the conscious effort to relax, the conversation flowed as easily as it had last night when Andi was with us. When a troop of musicians came past to sing cheesy songs, we both laughed and joined in. I posed happily beside the lead guitarist as Clinton snapped a photo on his phone, then handed them a handful of rupiah.

'I have a confession to make,' he said, sometime between the end of the cocktails and the first beer. 'I really feel like we were meant to meet like this. I know you think that it's Andi I'm attracted to, but it's really you.'

I laughed. 'I think you've had too much to drink.'

'So you don't like compliments either?'

'Either?'

'As well as talking about yourself.'

I took a swig of beer. 'No.'

'No to the compliments or the talking about yourself?'

'Both, I guess. I don't see the point in talking about things that don't matter to anyone, and as for the compliments – it's been a while.'

'Do you have a boyfriend at home? Is that why you're keeping me at a distance?'

I sidestepped the question. 'I don't think I'm keeping you at a distance, I just don't think we need to get too close. After all, we're not going to see each other again after this.'

'You'd be surprised,' he said, raising his beer bottle to mine. 'Stranger things have happened.'

'True … just not usually to me.' I was glad for the darkness. 'I don't let them.'

'Are you always in control?'

'Mostly. I find it best.'

He studied me in the candlelight. 'You didn't answer the question.'

'What question?'

'The one about your boyfriend.'

'That one …' I shook my head slowly. 'No, I didn't answer it, nor do I intend to.'

'But I thought –'

I leant forward and kissed him. It seemed the nicest and most effective way to shut him up.

CHAPTER ELEVEN

Clinton flew out the day after our dinner on the cliff. Thankfully he hadn't tried to contact me, but he did leave a message at reception saying goodbye, thanking me for 'everything' (and, yes, he used the inverted commas) and closing with a hope that we might meet again soon back in Melbourne.

Not if I had anything to do with it. I didn't feel good about what had happened between us; I didn't feel good about using him. What Clinton had offered me was simple when everything else was complex. That didn't mean I wanted to see him again.

Andi slept through breakfast, finally surfacing in time to venture down the road with me for lunch.

'How was last night?' she asked. 'I didn't hear you come in … Did you come in? Please tell me you didn't come in.'

'You were out cold,' I said.

'Yeah, those things could put an elephant to sleep. Speaking of which, if I only eat half of this rice, it isn't exactly like eating carbs, is it? God, I wish I had your metabolism.'

'I wish I had your boobs.'

She smiled. 'You've got to know how to use them too.'

I'd ordered a chicken curry that came served in a coconut shell. It was a bit on the watery side, but looked impressive. I forked through it, picking out and eating the vegetables separately.

'Why do they crinkle-cut the carrots and zucchinis? I hate crinkle-cuts. The only vegetables that should be crinkle-cut are chips, and then just so they can hold gravy.'

'The crinkle-cut holds the sauce better.' She looked at the beer in front of her with disdain, and reached instead for a bottle of water. 'So, tell me about last night.'

'It was fine. We ate at this fresh seafood place on a cliff. Yeah, it was nice.'

'Nice?' She stopped eating. 'It had to be more than nice. He was really into you. You know how we went shopping yesterday? All he wanted to know was information about you. I was a bit insulted at first, then I figured you needed the distraction more than me.'

'Gee, thanks. What was he asking?'

She ignored my sarcasm. 'Umm, mostly general stuff – what you do, who you work for, whether you've got a boyfriend ... that sort of stuff.'

'What did you tell him?'

'Nothing really. I know what you're like about your

privacy. It felt weird though.'

'Hmmm, he questioned me a bit last night too. That's why I kissed him – to shut him up.'

'You kissed him? Anything else?'

'No. I couldn't go through with it. It was stupid – I shouldn't have done it. In any case, he didn't push the point, so I think I got lucky.'

'Why did you pull back?'

'He's a little prettier than I'd normally go for.'

'You mean he wasn't Brad.'

I shrugged, and picked through my curry. 'Perhaps.'

We ate in silence for a few minutes.

'So,' she asked, 'what happened? With Clinton?'

'We made out a bit in the car. I went back to his room and then I changed my mind.'

'Why?'

'I don't know … I tried … I thought I could, you know, get the first one since Brad over and done with, but when it came down to it, I couldn't.' I mock-shuddered and she laughed.

'Was he a good kisser?'

'Not my cup of tea. He forced his tongue in as if it was the main event. Some girls might find it a turn-on. I just felt like it was a domination and got the hell out of there.'

'And we all know how you are about control and domination … You could have used your safe word, you know.'

'Oh, ha ha.' I laid down my fork. 'It wasn't just that. The truth was … you're right – he wasn't Brad. I'm not ready to be with anyone else. I thought I could be, but I'm not.' I drained my beer and held my hand up to signal for another. 'What if not going with Brad was the biggest mistake of my life? What if I'd asked him not to go? I should have told him why I had to come here.' There, I'd said it. 'I don't know why I didn't tell him … I shouldn't have assumed that he'd know.'

Andi considered her response. 'Perhaps, but think about it, A, it's not something you ever talk about. You never have. It wouldn't even occur to him. It only occurred to me because of what Todd said the other night … and I only know what I know from googling it.'

'Up until yesterday, I didn't know much more than that myself.'

'I get that, but my point is, after all these years of not talking about it, there's no reason why Brad would have put two and two together. That's all I'm saying.'

I acknowledged what she'd said with a half-shrug. 'There's not a lot I can do about it now.'

'Are you changing your mind about not marrying him?'

'No, but I'm wondering whether I should have gone with him.'

Andi wasn't smiling. I shouldn't have said anything.

'Are you okay, Ab?' she asked.

'Sure.'

'I'm serious. I'm worried about you. Did something else happen yesterday? How did that go? Did Hamish tell you anything about what happened with your father?'

I nearly told her then. I nearly told her what Hamish had told me yesterday, about Dad and his … whatever it was that woman was to him. I nearly told her that it felt as if everything in my world was imploding. As if everything I'd thought I knew about my parents, about their relationship, and everything I'd thought I knew about Brad and me, was wrong. I nearly told her that I missed Brad with every single fibre of my being. But I couldn't. Not yet. Not until I'd figured at least some of it out for myself. Besides, to Andi I was always in control, always together. She was the one who was usually in turmoil. That was the way things were with us.

'No, everything was fine yesterday. Hamish took me to where it happened – it was such a gorgeous spot too. He said it was a freak one-in-a-million thing. That's what the coroner said too.'

'Did he remember your father?' She corrected herself. 'That's a stupid question – how could he not?'

'Exactly. His recollection was pretty good – he was able to tell me how Dad had been reassuring some of the other tourists. It sounded like something Dad would do.'

'And you're fine with it?'

I nodded. 'Yes, I did what I wanted to do, what

I came here to do. It brought it all back, but I'm okay with it now.'

I smiled, and thought I'd convinced her.

Aside from a few shopping excursions to Seminyak, and the occasional massage or manicure, we rarely strayed far from the resort during our last few days. As a result I felt completely rested yet also more than a little stir crazy by the time we boarded the flight for home.

Andi had a short fling with a Swedish backpacker she met at the beach bar one sunset. He didn't speak English and she couldn't speak Swedish. His friend seemed to be interested in me, but after the episode with Clinton I wasn't in the mood for pretty young men.

Hamish sent me a message to check whether he could be of any more help to me. I thanked him, and told him the same as I'd told Andi – that I thought I was finally ready to move past it all. Part of me even believed me.

Autumn had well and truly arrived in Melbourne. There was a definite chill in the air, and the trees were turning the same colour as a Bali sunset. I usually loved this time of year. The days were shorter, so Brad would be home earlier; and the nights colder, giving us more reason to snuggle under the covers on weekends. It wouldn't be like that this year. I'd thought that being away might have helped me miss him less, but that plan hadn't worked.

The last time I flew home from a business trip, Brad and Bert had been at my flat waiting for me. Brad had something wonderful-smelling on the stove, fresh flowers in a jug on the kitchen counter, and the heating on. He and Bert fought over who would be first to greet me. Brad won, folding me into his warmth, while Bert pushed his way between us, his tail beating against our legs.

This time, the apartment was cold and empty. I unpacked, loaded my clothes into the washing machine, and heated up something that tasted like the box it came in. Then I dialled his number so I could listen to his message, wrapped myself in his jumper, and lay in the darkness wishing he was here or I was there.

Back in the office, I reviewed the project charter and task list that Sophie had prepared for Warner Enterprises while I was away. We had our first executive team meeting this afternoon, and I wanted to make sure that I'd double-checked every section, every milestone, every scope inclusion and exclusion. Successful implementation of this contract would guarantee my partnership, or so Mark kept telling me.

'Get this right, Abby,' he'd said, 'and the promotions team won't have an excuse this year.'

I'd restrained the urge to tell him that there had been no real excuse for the last three years. There was the year my billing hours were substantially higher than anyone else's (sorry, Troy's been promised this year's spot); the year I'd brought in more new business than anyone else (I'd give it to you except that Rhys went to school with the managing partner's son); and last year when both my billing hours and my new client introductions were higher than everyone else's (it's such a tough call, Abby – it's a pity you don't play golf).

I called Sophie in. 'This requirements register – I know I'm being niggly, but can you please make sure that each section is labelled with the same numbering system as in the charter and the project plan?'

'I'm not sure what you're asking?'

I opened out the plan. 'See how we have facilities as a separate listing with sub-tasks in the project plan, and a separate line item in the scope section of the charter? I'd like it to have its own section in the requirements register, using the same numbering as in the plan.'

'Okay, I get you.' Sophie was nodding her head. 'So where I have facilities tasks starting at section 3 in the charter and the plan, and scope inclusion number 4, and included in the requirements register under item 2, you'd like them to have the same number across all the documents?'

'Yes, please.'

'And the same for training, development, testing and process documentation?'

'Absolutely. Let's keep it all consistent. Every item included in scope should have its own section. We'll manage the risks in the same way.'

'Okay.' Sophie had always been quick on the uptake. 'I'll get the changes made in time for this afternoon's meeting.'

'Thanks Soph.'

I was lucky: not only was she an amazing project manager, she was also easy to deal with.

A couple of hours later, Sophie and I were walking into the conference room. Already present were Mark, his assistant Lisa, and a number of others from Warner Enterprises. I sat at the top of the table next to Mark and busied myself arranging the documents Sophie had prepared for us.

Mark began the introductions. 'I'd like to welcome Andrew Warner and the team from Warner Enterprises here today. I'll let Andrew introduce his team shortly, but for now I'll just say how thrilled we are that Warner chose us as the successful tender. I think it goes without saying, but my team know that I'll say it anyway,' he paused for polite laughter, 'that I'm sure the two teams will work together in order to achieve the outcomes we've agreed upon. So, without further adieu, I'll introduce our team.'

Mark had a dreadful habit of getting certain words and phrases wrong. Mixing up 'adieu' and 'ado' was probably the one that set my teeth on edge the most. Don't get me started on the metaphors he insisted on mixing.

'On my left we have Abigail Brentnall. Abigail is a senior associate on our finance team, and will be acting as project sponsor. Beside her is Sophie Martella, our senior project manager. Andrew, could you please introduce your team?'

Behind me the door opened and someone else entered the room. I hoped this wasn't a sign of how Warner were going to be on this project. I hated lateness.

'Sure.' Andrew Warner moved to the front of the room.

He was taller than Mark by a good few inches, and substantially slimmer and fitter. He was also much younger than I'd expected. Mark, in his early fifties, was greying and had long given up the battle of the bulge. Andrew, on the other hand, appeared to be in his mid-forties and obviously worked hard to keep himself looking good.

'Firstly, I'd like to echo Mark's comments and say how much we're looking forward to working with you. As you probably know, I'm based in Perth, but will try to get over here as often as possible. In the meantime, I'll be leaving you in the safe hands of our Melbourne-based team. I'm sure there'll be the ceremonial swapping of business cards shortly, but for now, going around the room, we have …'

I turned my head for the first time to acknowledge the Warner team at the other end of the table as Andrew introduced them one by one. I stopped breathing.

Surely not.

'And our late-comer is Clinton Barclay. Clinton will be our project sponsor. Abigail,' Andrew turned to me, 'Clinton is very much looking forward to working closely with you.'

At the other end of the table, Clinton was beaming at me. I felt sick.

CHAPTER TWELVE

'You knew, didn't you?' I accused.

Clinton and I were in the coffee shop in the lobby of my Collins Street building.

Somehow I'd got through the executive meeting with my composure intact. Clinton, on the other hand, hadn't seemed at all surprised to see me.

Mark had closed the meeting with a thinly veiled request for Clinton and me to 'get to know each other a little better over a coffee'. I'd pleaded a schedule clash and the need to catch up after being away on holiday, but Mark had waved my protests away. 'Don't worry about that, Abby. Go have coffee with Clinton – the rest can wait.'

So here we were, having coffee.

He smiled at me. 'Yes, I knew. I've known who you are for a long time – I've seen your name and profile on the bid documents. I couldn't believe the coincidence when I saw your bio photo and realised you were the same woman I'd seen around town. It's tough to miss you and Andi – you have no idea how striking you are together. You're tall, blonde and toned, and she's like a mini Victoria's Secret model. Of course you attract attention.'

'Is that why you approached me in Bali?'

'No. I approached you in Bali because I'm attracted to you and because I couldn't ignore the coincidence. I've thought for a while that we'd be very good together. I was right too, wasn't I? Under that controlled exterior lies a woman just needing to let go and be taken care of.'

'I'm sorry? I don't need to be taken care of by anyone.'

'You know you do. You desperately want someone to break through that hard outer shell, and you've seemed so lonely since your boyfriend left.'

I paused with my coffee cup raised to my lips. 'What do you know about my boyfriend?'

'Only what you've told me,' he replied, both dimples on show.

I slowly put my cup down and looked around the cafe before speaking. 'The thing is, I haven't said anything to you about my boyfriend.'

'Really? I thought you did … over drinks perhaps? It's easy to lose track of the conversation when you're having a good time.'

I shook my head. 'No, Clinton, I never lose track of my conversations, and I certainly didn't talk to you about my boyfriend. You asked me, but I didn't tell you.'

He shrugged.

'I'll ask again, what do you know about my boyfriend?'

'Enough to know that there is no boyfriend – well, not any more …' He held both hands up to signal his surrender, and gave those dimples of his some more airtime. 'Okay, I'll admit it, I may have happened to overhear you and Andi talking about him at lunch one day.'

Of course. I wondered how long he'd been sitting there and how long he'd been listening to us. I hated the thought that he might have overheard some deeply personal stuff. Not that there was anything I could do about that now.

I sat back in my chair and studied him. When I'd played with him the other night, it had been for my own amusement. I certainly hadn't planned on anything like this happening. In Bali, he'd been a cute distraction I never had to see again. Now he was someone I needed to work with effectively if I was to satisfy the terms of this contract and, more importantly, achieve my partnership. Okay, logically speaking, this was no more than a series of unfortunate coincidences. It could still be salvaged.

'You don't seem happy to see me,' he said.

I smiled. 'It's not that … I just didn't expect to see you again, that's all. You've surprised me.'

'You said the other night that very little surprises you, that you're usually in control.'

In Bali that smile of his had seemed cute. Now it was just plain arrogant.

'True, but there's a first time for everything … and you had the unfair advantage of knowing you'd be seeing me again.'

'I did, didn't I?' He didn't appear at all repentant as he leant forward and attempted to hold my gaze. 'Are we okay, or do we need to talk about the other night?'

'We're fine.' I forced my eyes to his. 'Nothing happened the other night.'

'You don't mean that, Abby. We had a connection. You know that – that's why you kissed me. You felt it too. I let you leave my room when you did because I figured it was a little too soon for you – you were still thinking about him. That's okay, I can wait. Besides, we have plenty of time to get to know each other now.'

He reached for my hand. I moved it away.

'Please don't do that. We have to work together so I suggest we keep this strictly business.'

He was still smiling. 'What if I don't want to keep things strictly business? What if I want to start up where we left off the other night?'

He reached for my hand again, and again I moved it away.

'But I don't. The other night was a mistake. It was unfair of me to take it as far as I did. I shouldn't have done that.'

'Why did you?'

'I don't know. I think I was feeling lonely maybe? I don't know. It wasn't right of me to lead you on like that and then leave you. I'm sorry.' I couldn't afford to upset him – he was a client and my promotion depended upon his business. I softened my tone. 'I know it sounds a little silly, and it's nothing personal, but I have a policy about not dating anyone I work with. I'm sure you understand.'

'Perhaps you're right, we do need to work together.' He did the dimple thing again. 'Strictly business it is.'

That coffee meeting set the tone for the next couple of weeks. Clinton was friendly, but not overly familiar. We spoke most days, and met at least twice a week when issues critical to the project needed to be sorted through.

Warner Enterprises had their head office in Perth, but this project was being managed by the Melbourne team, so Clinton was on-site a little too often. He had an uncanny ability to predict exactly when I was about to sit down at my desk in the morning, and when I was about to leave each afternoon. I tried mixing up my arrival at work – just five minutes here, fifteen minutes there – yet still the phone would ring as soon as I sat down. I was initially suspicious of his motives, but he always kept the calls professional, so as the days went by I decided that my radar was faulty and allowed myself to relax.

Andi and I had changed our regular lunch catch-ups and destination, and, to date, I'd managed to avoid Clinton outside of work. He and Mark had become quite friendly, lunching a couple of times a week and meeting for the occasional after-work drinks. I thought Clinton dazzled Mark – he dazzled most people. The men wanted to be him, the younger women wanted to sleep with him, and the older women wanted to mother him. He breezed into the office with his designer suits, flashy ties and wide smile, and within record time had everyone eating out of his manicured hands. That was another thing I didn't like about him – his manicures. Brad had work-roughened hands that felt amazing when they … Best not to think about that.

After we'd been working together for a few weeks, Clinton asked Sophie out, phoning me first to make sure I had no objections.

'I know Sophie works for you, and I know you have your policy about not mixing work with play. I don't want me dating her to make you feel uncomfortable,' he said. 'If it's going to impact the job we have to do, I'd respect that.'

I assured him that I was fine with it. 'Sophie's a professional; she knows where her boundaries need to be.'

At least I hoped she knew. Clinton could be very persuasive.

Later that day Sophie pulled me aside after our

regular teleconference to tell me about it. 'Clinton's asked me out for dinner. I'm not sure of the protocol here – you know, dating a client … What do you think?'

'Do you like him?'

She smiled, her gaze dreamy. 'Oh yes. There's something about him that's difficult to resist. I can't describe it.'

How could I say no? 'As long as it doesn't affect your work, I don't see a problem with it. We've already won the tender, so if you want to see him outside of the office, that's fine with me. Is he taking you somewhere nice?'

'The courtyard bar in Little Lonsdale. It's quite new … do you know it?'

I did. Brad had designed the exterior so we'd gone to the opening. It was one of the last events we'd attended together. He'd made a feature of the street art on one of the walls, lighting it as if it were a gallery piece. He'd been so proud of it, but my head had been full of the tender I was putting together for Warner and I didn't give it the appreciation and attention it deserved. He must have known I was distracted, it must have disappointed him, but he'd said nothing to me.

'I know it,' I said. 'You'll like it. The mural is incredible.'

The following day, Sophie couldn't stop talking about Clinton, the date, and how attentive he was. 'Oh, Abby, I really think this could be it. He's not like anyone else I've been out with in the past. Not only is he totally gorgeous, he holds the door open for me, orders my meals, and doesn't let me pay for anything. And when he smiles at me with those dimples – oh my God, he makes me feel as though I'm the only girl in the world.'

Paula wasn't convinced. I'd heard her muttering phrases like 'handsome is as handsome does' or words to that effect.

She told me she'd caught Clinton going through things on my desk the other day. He was early for a status meeting, and I was still in the conference room on a previous call. Paula said that he didn't look at all uncomfortable when she'd opened the door, but gave her one of his wide smiles and said, 'Abby likes me to wait for her in here.' Paula had held her ground and told him that she'd prefer him to wait on one of the chairs near her desk.

'I don't trust that man,' she'd told me.

I'd attempted to reassure her. 'He's fine, Paula. Besides, there's nothing on my desk except a few personal bills I was paying before I went to that last meeting. See,' I'd held them up, 'my landline and electricity accounts.'

'Even so,' she'd grumbled, 'he has no right to be in there when you're not, and he's got that girl of yours not thinking straight. Mark my words, that will end in tears.'

•

Zoe and I finally caught up. She was in town for another promotional something or other. I was trying to put the finishing touches to some numbers I was re-casting for the Singapore contract I was also working on when her text came through.

In town. Only free tonight. See you at 8? You pick somewhere.

It was typical of Zoe to send me something so last minute, fully expecting that I'd drop everything to see her. I was tempted to reply that I was busy, but figured that would only result in another call from Mum wondering why I never had time for my sister. Besides, dealing with Zoe would be a distraction from the emptiness at home and take my mind off work for a bit.

Sure, I'll text through the details.

As for choosing a venue? Knowing Zoe, she'd want somewhere that:

Had great lighting so she could be seen.

Was fashionable enough to have a celebrity chef at the helm.

Was fashionable enough to be busy mid-week.

Was fashionable enough that they didn't take bookings.

Was fashionable enough that people were prepared to queue on a Wednesday night.

Had a fashion-savvy front of house who'd

recognise Zoe as being someone fashionable enough to be allowed to glide to the front of the shivering queue, smiling apologetically as she passed them by on her way to her table.

I toyed with the Mexican at the top end of Collins Street. The food was good, the tequila exceptional, and the queues pleasingly long. I had, however, heard that they'd turned away an American movie star who'd attempted to jump the queue, and my sister only liked a queue that she could be whizzed to the front of. For similar reasons, I discounted the great Vietnamese in Flinders Lane that Brad and I loved so much. Also, I didn't want my memories of our favourite places to be sullied by Zoe.

Figuring that she wouldn't be eating, I decided to choose a restaurant that I'd enjoy. My favourite Italian in Bourke Street? Maybe; it was owned by a celebrity chef, but the carbs made it a tad too obvious. Instead I chose a spicy favourite in the Crown Casino complex, where I assumed she'd be staying. Plus they took bookings, which meant I could be comfortable while I was waiting.

By the time she arrived – as expected, thirty minutes late – I was ordering my second cocktail. She looked, as always, gorgeous. Her long blonde hair fell down her back in a tumble of artfully arranged curls worthy of a shampoo commercial, and those cat-like eyes had been accentuated to perfection in her heart-shaped face. As for her dress, it was clinging to her curves perilously, and dipping so low in the front it hinted at her navel. I hated to think how much tape was holding that on … or her boobs in.

She graciously offered me a cheek to kiss before arranging herself in the booth and looking around the room. 'It's a little dark, don't you think?'

She affected that strange almost American, almost European accent that some Australians get when they've been away from home too long. And what happened to 'Hi, Abby, how are you?'

'Yes,' I said. 'I thought you'd be wanting a break from all the bright lights of the runway.'

The decor could best be described as opium den-esque, with dimly lit corners and red-shaded lamps.

'Hmmm, I guess.' She noticed there was no third place set. 'Where's Brad? Don't tell me there's trouble in paradise? I guess it had to happen sometime.'

Her lips curled into the almost sneer, almost pout that passed for a smile on Zoe. The cameras loved it. Most of her red carpet photos showed that pouty sneer.

I felt my spine straighten, and took a sip of my cocktail before replying. 'Not at all. He's in Denmark … or Poland, or Austria … it's not important where.' I waved my hand. 'He's been awarded a fellowship so he's spending the winter there. It's a great opportunity for him.'

'Whatever.' The sneery smile was back. 'I was looking forward to seeing him – I thought he'd like this dress.' She preened a little, running her hands down the slinky, barely there fabric. 'I wish you'd told me he wasn't coming, I would have worn something else. So you're still together?'

'We sure are,' I lied.

'That must make Mum happy – a gardener in the family.'

I fought the urge to defend Brad – it was a waste of time – and changed the subject back to her. 'What about you? Are the reports about you and that guy from that boy band true?'

She lowered her head in what I assumed was supposed to be an embarrassed look and said, 'Yes, okay, we're together. I wish they'd leave us alone. The publicity is so much worse out here than it is in the States.' She raised a finger and beckoned the waiter over.

'Perhaps because he left his wife for you?'

Zoe shrugged one shoulder, her dress in danger of slipping off. 'She's such a plain dowdy thing. She really let herself go when she got dropped from her modelling agency. She's quite fat now.'

'I thought she retired because she was pregnant.'

'Retired, dropped – they're the same thing. You only retire if you're going to get dropped. Besides, if she wanted to hold onto Davy, she should have looked after herself a little better.' She looked closely at me for the first time. 'You should think about that. You're not getting any younger, and Brad won't be around forever. After thirty your face starts to slip, and before you know it any breasts you have – not that you have much – will pull your face down towards your toes. I can give you the name of a good surgeon.' She made it sound like a favour. 'At the very least, I'd definitely consider having those lines in your forehead touched up. Perhaps also the ones around your eyes and mouth. They're only small, but it's about prevention. When you book your appointment, tell them I sent you and you'll get a good deal.'

I was saved from having to thank her by the waiter arriving to take her drink order.

'Would you like anything to eat?' I asked.

She looked horrified. 'No, but you go ahead.'

As I ordered, she amused herself by shifting about in her seat enough to make the waiter think there was a chance of a wardrobe malfunction. Thankfully, the wait staff here were so well used to celebrities that he was almost able to concentrate on what I was saying. I only had to repeat my order once.

'How's Tyler?' I asked once the order had been taken and cocktails provided.

'He's fine, I guess. Mum and Dad are pleased with his results.' I didn't think I'd ever get past the jolt I felt at hearing Zoe refer to Peter as Dad. 'I don't hear from him too often – I guess he's pretty busy with his own life. Does he talk to you?'

'Not really,' I lied. 'As you say, he has a busy life.'

She seemed satisfied with that answer.

My food arrived and Zoe ordered another cocktail.

'You're not really going to eat all that, are you?' She raised an eyebrow at the two small plates in front of me.

'Probably.'

She sneered her smile. 'I wouldn't touch it – the spice would probably make me break out or something. Plus there are carbs in it.'

'I hope so,' I replied.

She made a show of looking at her watch – a slim, diamond-studded creation. 'Do you like it? It was a gift from Davy. Speaking of which, I should be off. He'll be awake by now – he's in London, you know – and I want to Skype him while I'm still in this dress. At least then it won't be wasted.' She downed the remains of her cocktail and stood to go. She bent and almost kissed my cheek, clouding my face in hair and giving me a shot of taped cleavage. 'You can pick up the bill – it was your idea to come here.'

CHAPTER THIRTEEN

Five weeks into the relationship with Clinton, and Sophie's work was suffering. Tiny details that she'd usually be on top of were slipping. I had to check reports that normally I wouldn't give a second glance to. I hadn't said anything to her – I figured that she'd come out of whatever lust-filled haze she was in soon. Bloody Clinton.

On Wednesday, she called in sick, missing a steering committee meeting. When I went through the directory to distribute the documentation on her behalf, I had to completely re-do the status report and chase a number of tasks that had been due for completion but hadn't been updated on the plan.

After the meeting, much of which I'd had to improvise, Clinton took me aside and told me he and Sophie had broken up the previous night. Great.

'What happened?' I asked him. 'I thought it was all going well.'

He shrugged. 'She was getting too serious too quickly for me. I thought we were having fun, but I think she thought it was going in a different direction.'

'From what she told me, that's the impression you gave her, with the calls, the dates, the flowers.'

He'd sent her flowers at work after their first date, and again after, as Sophie blushingly told me, their 'first time'. An ostentatious bunch of red roses had arrived only last Monday to thank her for 'being her'. As I'd read the card she'd held out for me, I was sure I'd tasted a little bit of mouth vomit.

'He calls me all the time,' she'd said, glowing. 'And the texts … they're enough to curl your toes. I wanted to take it slowly, but he's talking futures together already.'

'Already?'

She'd lowered her eyes as a blush spread across her cheeks. 'You know, things like places we'd go together, suburbs we'd like to live in … that sort of thing.'

Now he shrugged again in an 'I can't help being irresistible' way, but I knew there'd be a mess left for me to clean up. Not that Sophie, when she finally made it into the office, seemed keen to talk to me about it.

'Are you okay?' I asked.

Her eyes were red-rimmed from what I assumed were two nights spent crying.

'Do you care?' she said, glaring at me.

What. The. Fuck? I closed the office door. 'Of course I care. What makes you think that I wouldn't?'

She sniffed miserably. 'Because now he's free for you.'

'What. The. Fuck?' This time it came out loud.

'He told me about you two – how you met in Bali, and there was this instant chemistry. He said he'd told you that you couldn't be together until the project was finished, but that seeing him with me was too much for you. I thought you were my friend, and the whole time you've been laughing at me and plotting to steal my boyfriend. It wasn't enough that yours left you, you have to take mine!' Her voice had risen and tears were streaming down her face.

'Oh, Sophie,' I said, 'none of that is true.'

'Of course you'd say that. He said you would.'

'Right.' I scrambled for the words to make her understand. 'The thing is, yes, we did meet in Bali, and we went out twice – once with my friend Andi, and once on our own because Andi had a migraine. He kissed me that night, but I promise you, that's as far as it went – and as far as I wanted to take it. He asked me out again when we first started on this project and I refused – not because we're working together, but because I'm not attracted to him. That's all. Anything else that he's told you is fiction. I didn't want him then, and I don't want him now.'

'Oh,' was all she said through sniffs.

I passed across the tissues. 'Clinton Barclay is pretty enough, but I wouldn't trust him as far as I could throw him.'

'He was so attentive. He completely swept me off

my feet.'

'Guys like that often do.'

'You know, he asked me a lot of questions about you – not so many that I saw anything weird in it, but lots.'

'Like what?'

'General things. Also about Brad.'

'What did you tell him?'

'Just that he'd left the country for a while and I thought you guys had broken up.'

'Okay. Did he want to know anything about the project and the company?'

She nodded. 'Mostly how it related to you. I told him how this project is going to get you your partnership, finally. That you should have had it a few years ago, but it's a boys' club in here and the promotions are always going to guys who went to the right schools and play at the right clubs.'

Hmmm.

'I said too much, didn't I?'

'I don't see how he can use any of that,' I reassured her. 'I think he's just one of those guys who likes to collect information on the off-chance that he'll have a use for it some day.'

I offered her a mirror and compact so she could repair her face.

'My work has been slipping, hasn't it?' she said.

I nodded. There was no point lying to her.

'God, I'm sorry. I was so distracted.'

'Spunk drunk,' I said, grinning.

She returned my smile. 'I sure was.'

'No harm done. File it away in the been there, done that section of your brain and don't let him know he's thrown you. Every girl has to have at least one Clinton Barclay before she finds someone she wants to keep.'

'Did you have one? Is that how you knew to avoid him?'

'Yes, I had one.'

One of each: a Clinton and a keeper. The first ended up in my sister's bed, and the second I wanted to keep, but I let him go.

I hadn't heard from Brad since my birthday, but still checked my cell phone for texts at least a million times a day. I texted him for his birthday, receiving a *thanksx* in return. Every so often, usually late at night – okay, nearly every night – I called his home, just so I could hear his voice on the answer machine. I always hung up before the message tone. My answering machine at home had been getting a lot of hang-ups too, so I told myself that was him doing the same thing.

Now that he'd broken up with Sophie, Clinton's calls had begun to stray into personal territory, with most ending with him asking me out – for a drink, for dinner, for a coffee 'to talk about the project'. I declined each invitation. He seemed to accept my refusals with good grace, but it didn't stop him from asking. It was as if it had become a game to him now. Part of me was tempted to say yes the next time he asked, just to see how he reacted.

The first meeting between him and Sophie was uncomfortable to say the least, but as he acted as if nothing had happened, she rallied quickly. When she overheard him asking me out, and me declining, as usual, she said it made her realise what a lucky escape she'd had.

'I can't believe I fell for his crap,' she said. 'Will you go out with him?' Despite her words, her look was anxious.

'Not a chance.'

Although we had the project back on track within a few days, and Sophie was soon back to her terrier-like self, the incident had ramifications that I hadn't expected. I thought I'd covered Sophie's lapses well: none of her errors had made it into any distributed project documents or to steering committee. In fact, I was convinced that no one other than her and me knew about them. I hadn't counted on Clinton. Somehow he'd found out and gone running to Mark, raising concerns about Sophie's emotional stability and her ability to do the job effectively.

'Clinton is naturally concerned about Sophie,' Mark told me. 'I have to say, this little episode has raised a question for me: is she able to do the job to the standard required? This is a good lesson about why we should be keeping an arm's-length distance between us and clients.' He must have noticed the surprise on my face and corrected himself. 'If you're the type who can't keep her feelings under control. There's nothing wrong with socialising – that's just good client-relationship building. And obviously,' he continued, 'Sophie got the wrong idea. Clinton is prepared to accept that perhaps he might have encouraged her a little, without meaning to of course, but he's asked that you take over the reins of the day-to-day management until Sophie has got her head back in the game.'

'Don't you think that would muddy the waters from a sponsorship viewpoint?'

'I don't know what you mean.'

'I can't effectively sponsor the project if I'm managing it,' I explained.

'It concerns me that you're now raising issues about your ability to multi-task.'

I counted to ten. 'It's not that. It's more that if we go down this track, I'll be effectively reporting to Clinton. That would damage the peer-to-peer relationship we're trying to build. Besides, Sophie is our most experienced project manager. She's far more experienced than me.'

'It's comments like that which concern me, Abigail.'

'How so?'

'If your opinion of Sophie's talents has been mistaken, by extension there's a risk that, in thinking emotionally, your judgement is flawed. I hope that's not the case – I hope you won't let me down. This project is too important to be left to chance.'

'Nothing is being left to chance,' I argued. 'Sophie has every last detail nailed down.'

'Does she? Clinton was telling me that he's been having to question basic structural issues a lot.'

'I can assure you that isn't the case.'

'What reason does he have to lie over something this big?' He didn't wait for my answer. 'Besides, he told me about the history between you two.'

'I'm sorry?' I spluttered. 'History?'

'Yes, how you met in Bali, but that because he knew he'd be working on the project with you, he felt it would be a conflict of interest to engage in a relationship with you.'

'He told you that, did he?'

'Yes, and I'm sure it was difficult for him to confide in me. He has shown great integrity and commitment by putting this project first.' He leant forward over his desk, a concerned look on his face. 'I know it must have been rough to be rejected so soon after your boyfriend had left, but there's no shame in it.'

He paused, but I had nothing I wanted to say that he would be likely to listen to – and that wouldn't turn this into a he-said-she-said situation.

'The two of you need to be able to work more effectively together in order to hit this one out of the park and bring it home. At the moment he's on the right bus and you're still looking for another one to come along.'

Another thing that annoyed me about Mark was the way he mixed sporting and public transport metaphors.

He drew breath before continuing. 'I have to say, Abigail, this lapse of professionalism on your behalf has made me re-think whether you're ready for partner.'

'What exactly are you saying, Mark?' I was still seated, but every muscle in my body had tensed, ready for fight or flight.

'I'm not saying anything, I'm simply suggesting that you should be nicer to him. Clinton said there have been a number of times when he's asked you out for a drink, for the sole purpose of building bridges and discussing the project, but you've declined. I'm suggesting that the next time he asks, you swallow your pride, get over yourself and accept his invitation.'

It was at the tip of my tongue to ask him what else he suggested I do with Clinton, but I restrained myself. 'I thought you said we needed to keep our clients at arm's length.'

'You know that's not what I meant. Oh, one more thing, Abigail … the Singapore due diligence? I've passed that across to Jared to complete. It's becoming obvious that you can't juggle that plus your normal role without the Warner project falling through the cracks. A few months ago I wouldn't have doubted your ability to manage it all, but now I'm not at all confident.'

I needed that deal – I'd been banking on it to help cement my partnership hopes – and I desperately wanted thousands of miles between Clinton and me at the moment. Besides, Jared was my main competition in this year's partner appointments. Not only did he have the required dangly bits, but they'd been dangled at the right school and in the right clubs and on the right golf greens.

'You can't do that!' I said.

'Of course I can. And this is exactly why I have – you're allowing too much emotion to slip into your work, and there's no room for emotion when it comes to these deals. At the end of the day, Jared will be able to maintain his prospective,' I winced, 'but it's becoming patently clear that you cannot.'

'Mark, nothing has slipped.'

'No, it hasn't, and that's no thanks to you. All I can say is it's lucky Clinton's had his eye on the prize. He's stepped up to the plate, grabbed the ball and is running with it. You're still deciding what side you're swinging a bat for. Now that Singapore is no longer on the radar, there are no excuses, so I want you on this project with him one hundred per cent.'

'Remember we've only factored twenty per cent of my time into the project costs, so if I'm billing a hundred per cent against that cost code, the project will blow right out. I'll need to take that back to steering committee as a cost deviation, and re-cast all the unit costs. The margins are tight as they are.'

'I'm not asking you to bill your time against the project, just to be across the project.'

'Do you want me to bill elsewhere?'

'I didn't ask you to do that – that would be contravening financial policy. I'd never suggest that.' It was exactly what he was suggesting. 'All I'm saying is that I won't be expecting any more than the expected hours to be billed to this cost code. You'll have to work the rest out for yourself.'

'But I need to keep up my billable hours to keep my partner hopes alive,' I pointed out. One of the key criteria for partnership was maintaining a ridiculous level of billable hours. The rewards of partnership included not having to.

'Then I guess you'll just have to manage that outside of normal hours. From now on, I want you at all project meetings, on all telephone calls, and across each and every register.'

'Sophie will start to think I don't trust her.'

'Clinton doesn't. And that man has so far proven himself to have very good instincts.'

'Implying that I don't?'

He shrugged. 'Just do it, Abby.'

Somehow I managed to stop myself from

slamming his door on the way out. It was obvious that Mark had been looking for a reason to discount me from the partner discussions this year, and the Clinton and Sophie issue was it.

Rather than settling back at my desk, I packed up my laptop and headed home. After that, after today, I needed to get rid of some anger.

If Brad was here, he'd pour me a glass of wine, listen to me vent as he cooked, pour me another glass, and take me to bed. He always knew better than to suggest solutions when I was in this sort of mood, at least until after my more physical energies had been satisfied.

Once I was lying in his arms, he'd propose a course of action.

'Maybe,' he'd start, 'it's worth thinking about this one from the opposite end. What is it the client really wants? Put to one side, for now, what you're stuck on and consider what they want, then come around it from that angle.'

As I opened my front door, the phone was ringing. I ran for it, but didn't quite get there. Whatever. The walk home hadn't done much to release the fireball in my chest, so I quickly changed into my running gear and took off into the night.

I still ran each morning, but with winter rapidly taking hold, it was now too dark at that time of the morning to run the Tan, so I'd changed my route to stay on well-lit roads. Even though it hadn't worried me in previous winters, this year I felt safer staying out of the park. I didn't remember my confidence being so shaky in previous years. I thought it was because I was so tired. The sort of tired that seeped into the bones and wouldn't let go. Despite my exhaustion, when I did sleep I woke regularly at every little noise, and then lay in the dark wondering where Brad was and wishing he was beside me. Some nights I still reached out, hoping to feel his warmth on the other side of the bed. Winter seemed colder without him here.

Tonight, I was running along St Kilda Road. I slowed a few times, but of course there was no one behind me. When I finally let myself in again, physically spent, the phone was ringing again, but stopped as soon as I reached it.

CHAPTER FOURTEEN

Andi had broken up with Jason again, and was deep in 'this is it, I'm never going back again' heartbreak territory. I hoped rather than believed that this time she meant it.

We'd made a deal that each time he texted her, she was to ring me instead of responding to him. It had been fourteen days and, so far, she'd resisted the temptation. The toughest moment had come on day six when he'd messaged her from the Windsor Hotel, where he'd been having after-work drinks.

She rang me immediately. 'He says he can get a room for us, Abby. She's out of town.'

'Andi,' I warned. 'Never ever … remember?'

'He says he's lonely, and no one makes him feel the way I do. He just feels an obligation to stay with her because her father is having treatment.'

She was definitely wavering.

'Never ever,' I reminded her.

She sighed. 'You're right, I know you're right. He'll never leave her.'

'No, sweetie, he won't.'

Certain songs on the radio still set her off, but she was getting there.

The other night we were drinking champagne to celebrate getting to day ten, when she'd announced her intention to draft a statutory declaration that she'd keep in her handbag.

'I may as well put my lawyerly skills to some use, so the next time I meet someone, I'm going to get him to sign a stat dec to state that he's not married before I even agree to have a drink with him, let alone fall in love.'

'That sounds like a solution.' I reached over to top up her glass.

'Actually,' she mused, 'I might pop in a celibacy clause. That will definitely exclude anyone who's just after something on the side. Did I tell you about the real estate agent from the other day?'

I shook my head.

'I met him at work – we were setting up this complex arrangement of … Actually, you don't need to know that.'

Most of what Andi did was eye-glazingly complicated to me.

'Anyway, he asked me out. I said yes because he was cute, but he seemed so much my type that I decided to do some research first and took myself off to some open homes he was doing in Richmond. I ran into this girl I went to school with – Emily, you'd like her – and we're chatting and doing the catch-up thing when in walks his wife.'

'Lucky escape,' I said.

'I know, right? He still had the hide to text me later that afternoon to check we were still meeting up!'

In other news, Mum had called last week to remind me I'd be required for Peter's campaign launch in Sydney this weekend. I figured the actual invitation was still in the mail.

'Abigail, it won't hurt you to attend this event. Peter is anxious for his entire family to be present to launch this campaign. After all, it's not as if we ask very much of you.'

'Don't you mean that Peter is anxious to make the most of the happy families photo opportunity?'

'Do you always have to be so cynical? Your education was better than that.'

'Are you sure you want me there? Remember what happened last time?'

At the last campaign launch I'd made the mistake of having a few too many chardonnays and had compounded the issue by getting into a conversation with another party-goer about asylum seekers and marriage equality. Unfortunately my opinions didn't match those of Peter's political platform … and the person I was talking to happened to be a journalist. Oops.

'Yes, well, this time keep your opinions to yourself. I'm sure you were led astray by that man you've been seeing. You can leave him at home.'

'That man's name is Brad, as well you know, Mum.'

'Hmmm, well, I think you owe it to Peter to attend. Even Zoe's flying back – she has a shoot for something to do with a movie in Wellington. If she can put herself out with her schedule, I'm sure you can.'

The rumours were that Zoe's 'shoot' was courtesy of her latest romantic interest who happened to be starring in the movie, and who had left his wife and young baby at home in LA. Apparently Zoe's romance with the boy band boy was finished.

At work, Sophie and I were managing the project beyond textbook perfection and had a virtual paper trail for every conversation we had with any member of the Warner team, linking back to one or more of the many registers we were maintaining. Our meetings were relatively quick as we could simply refer back to a phone call that had been confirmed in an email that was referenced to an issue register feeding into a risk register, that had a new numbered task in the project plan matching back to an item in the requirements register, and linked into the development register, test plan and implementation plan, before completing the full circle into a scope inclusion from the original project charter. The meetings were quick, but completing the minutes that came out of them were a nightmare.

The extra effort we were putting in meant that no one on the other side so much as sniffed without us knowing what the impact of that sniff (if it turned into a sneeze) would do. Clinton could try his best, but he had no room for complaint. Everything was as it should be.

It wasn't coming without a cost. These days I rarely left the office before 8.30 pm, and usually worked some more at home, or went for another run, before I was tired enough to sleep. Not that I was sleeping. I passed out most nights through a combination of mental exhaustion and alcohol.

By the time the weekends came along, it was all I could do to drag myself from the apartment – and then it was usually for a long walk or another run. I might have been super organised at work, but my home was a mess of empty wine bottles and frozen-food containers. I straightened my bed each night before I got into it, and ate out of the microwave containers to save on washing up. On more than a few occasions I'd thought about vacuuming, but simply couldn't be bothered.

Even with the extra time in the office, I was struggling to maintain the billable hours I needed to stay on top of targets at work. The Warner project was completely back in green status – not that, as far as I was concerned, it had ever been off-track – so I approached Mark to request I resume an arm's-length sponsor role.

'I don't think so,' he replied. 'Clinton tells me that he and the Warner executive team are *finally* feeling comfortable that you're across everything. Now that you no longer have a helicopter view of the project, but seem to be on the same bus and singing from the same song sheet as Clinton, I'm not going to rock that particular boat.' He pushed his reading glasses further down his nose and peered at me over the top of them. 'I hope this request doesn't mean you're falling behind on your billable hours. Jared is managing to maintain his, as well as staying on top of that Singapore deal you were unable to juggle.'

I went out for a run that night too.

Thankfully, aside from Clinton, the others on Warner's Melbourne team were easy and pleasant to deal with. Not that Clinton wasn't pleasant. He was almost too pleasant. He'd turn up for meetings with a coffee for me, and kept most conversations in the office strictly business. He hadn't asked me out for nearly a month, not since Mark had ordered me to accept his next invitation. I told myself that was a good thing, although the more cynical part of me couldn't help wondering whether his manipulation of Mark was designed to be a power play on me. I imagined Clinton would get a kick from knowing that if he asked me out, I had no choice but to agree. Just because he'd stopped asking, it didn't mean he'd given up. Every so often during a meeting I'd glance up and he'd be watching me, with a strange little smile playing around his mouth.

He'd taken to texting me late at night. On the surface, it all seemed quite innocent – at least at the start:

Hi, have you logged off? I wanted to email through a revision to tomorrow's agenda.

Thanks for updating that register today.

Sorry it's late, but can you send through the revised budget first thing?

Then the texts began to get a little more personal:

Hey Abby, I was just thinking about that sunset cocktail on the beach.

I just heard Van Morrison on the radio and it reminded me of that dinner at Tanah Lot.

Maybe we should take up where we left off … lol.

Even on the nights he didn't text, I'd be on edge and sneaking looks at my phone as I waited for one to come through.

The hang-ups on my landline stopped at about the same time as the late-night texts started. I told myself it was a coincidence. If Brad were here he'd tell me that I was paranoid and off-balance. Then he'd fold me into his warmth and remind me how safe I was.

But he wasn't here.

Todd had emailed a few times since I'd been back from Bali but I'd avoided meeting him. To be honest I hadn't been out much at all in the evenings, not even with

Andi. Mostly I'd used work as the excuse, but the truth was, I wasn't in the mood to socialise. So far Andi wasn't pushing the point, but just lately, at lunch, I'd noticed her giving me the occasional concerned look. She knew I didn't like concern, so the looks hadn't yet moved into concerned words. I couldn't have borne that. I hadn't told Andi anything about what was going on at work or with Clinton. I hadn't even told her that I'd seen him again. She had enough on her plate with getting over Jason, and besides, I was probably over-reacting.

The next time Todd phoned, to invite me out for dinner that evening, he wasn't taking no for an answer. 'Come on, Ab, I haven't seen you in ages – not since your birthday. I miss you – Bert misses you.'

'Is Bert coming out too?'

'No, we'll meet straight after work, but you get the idea.'

I really had missed Todd. 'I have a stack of work to get through …'

He could tell I was wavering. 'The work will still be there tomorrow. Don't make me beg. You know I hate that.'

'Okay, it'll need to be early though – I'm meeting Zoe later. She wants me to go to some after-party thing for the launch she's in town for.'

She'd texted this morning to let me know she was in town for the night, making a big deal about having to be back 'on set' tomorrow.

'Ugh,' Todd said.

He and Zoe had never got on. He thought she was a piece of work, and, despite him being tall, dark and attractive, she thought nothing of him at all. She may have thought differently if he'd been with me.

'My thoughts exactly. I wish you'd phoned half an hour ago – it would have given me a viable excuse not to see her.'

'Maybe I could come with you?'

'Tempting, but no.'

Invitations seemed to be the theme of the day. Sophie also asked if I was free to have a drink with her tonight. As Clinton was in earshot, rather than saying I was meeting Todd, I told her I was catching up with my sister.

'I read she was in town to do that launch in Chapel Street,' Sophie said. 'Isn't she also doing something with some movie in New Zealand?'

'Is your sister a celebrity?' asked Belinda, one of the Warner team.

Sophie answered. 'Abby's sister is Zoe Lockhart, the model.'

'Wow, that's really cool,' said Belinda. 'She's so beautiful. Isn't she going out with that guy from that boy band? And she's your sister?'

'No need to sound so surprised,' I laughed. I was used to that reaction. 'And sorry to disappoint you, but I don't keep up with Zoe's love life.'

That was, unless it crossed paths with mine.

'Oh, I didn't mean it like that.' Belinda attempted to dig herself out of the hole.

'Didn't she do Melbourne Fashion Week too this year?' asked Sophie.

'Yes,' I said, 'she's been in town a bit this year. I caught up with her a few weeks ago.'

Clinton seemed to be concentrating on the printouts of the plan in front of him.

'So you're seeing her tonight?' persisted Belinda.

'Uh huh.'

I looked over at Clinton and he smiled. I looked away.

He stopped by my office on his way out. 'I just wanted to tell you to have a great evening with your sister. Where did you say you were going?'

'I didn't.'

His smile didn't slip.

I'd almost reached Hardware Lane and the restaurant where Todd and I were meeting when a text came through from Clinton. There were no words, just a photo he'd taken of me against the sunset in Tanah Lot. I'd been leaning against the stone wall with my head turned to watch the colours of the sun on the sea. My shorts seemed shorter than I remembered, or was it that my legs seemed longer? Whichever way you looked at it, I was showing a lot of flesh. He'd taken the photo from the side, and zoomed in close so the background was blurred and I appeared to have a dreamy look on my face.

I stopped walking and leaned against a wall, letting the other pedestrians pass me. I deleted the photo and stayed where I was, where I could see the screen of my phone, until my heart slowed. Telling myself I was being an idiot, I shook my head and went to put my phone back in my bag. That's when the next text came through.

I was just sorting through photos of Bali and thought you might like this one. Enjoy your catch-up with your sister. See you tomorrow.

I deleted it too and, taking a calming breath, walked around the corner to meet Todd.

He kissed my cheek and pulled me in for a hug. 'It's been too long.'

'I'm sorry I haven't been in touch,' I said. 'Things have been pretty mad at work.'

'They always are with you.' He grinned ruefully. 'What are you drinking? The usual?'

'Yes, please … and quickly. It's been a shit of a day. And I need to prepare myself for Zoe.' I screwed up my nose.

'In that case, alcohol coming right up!' He signalled for the waiter. 'How long is she in town?'

'Just the night, I think. She made a big deal about having to be somewhere else tomorrow. Whatever.'

As I sat down I couldn't help looking over my

shoulder.

Todd noticed. 'Are you okay? You're acting like you expect to see someone. Are you cold? Do you want to move inside?'

'I'm sorry, I'm not cold … just checking out the passing traffic.'

We spent a few minutes catching up while we waited for our drinks to arrive.

Once they did, Todd raised his glass to me. 'What shall we toast?'

'Do we need to toast? Can't we just clink and get on with it?' I didn't really feel like toasting anything. Why did people always want to toast something? What happened to just drinking?

'How about to absent friends?'

I held his gaze for a second before looking away and taking a sip of my wine.

'You've never asked about him,' he said.

We both knew who he was referring to.

'How's Bert?' I asked.

'He's fine. He misses Brad. I think he misses you too. Why haven't you been over to see him?'

'I couldn't.' It would be too much. 'It wouldn't be fair. What if Bert thought I was there to bring him home?'

'I guess.' Todd pulled his phone out of his pocket and scrolled through until he found what he was looking for. 'Here,' he offered it to me, 'some photos …'

I took it without saying anything. There was Brad, leaning against a wooden shed in what appeared to be a small allotment. He was wearing dirty jeans and had his sleeves rolled up. He was grinning into the camera in that wide-mouthed, crinkle-eyed way. No matter how bad my day had been, that smile would make it all go away. His hair looked as though he'd been running his fingers through it. His face and forearms were tanned, and I could imagine the long, strong muscles in his legs under the jeans. I enlarged the photo on the screen and touched his face as if I could feel him, as if he could feel my touch wherever he was.

In the next photo his foot was propelling a garden fork into the ground; and in the next he had his arm thrown loosely around the shoulders of a smallish blonde woman. He was looking down at her and grinning. I couldn't tell if it was the same grin he saved for me, or just an everyday grin. She looked the type that would need a strong man to take care of her – someone like Brad would be perfect. I decided she was probably Swedish or Scandinavian. She'd have a name that could be in an Abba song, or an IKEA catalogue. Something like Britt or Astrid or Annika.

Todd saw me looking at the photo and grabbed the phone away. 'Sorry, I forgot that one was on there.'

He was looking hard at my face and I was trying to keep my smile from slipping off. I should have told Brad how much I needed him before he went away.

I should have apologised for declining his proposal. I should have asked him to come back, just so he knew that he could come back. Then maybe I'd be counting down the days until he did, instead of being afraid that he'd stay over there forever with his arm around a girl called Heidi who was getting all the smiles he used to give me. I should have said all that to Todd.

'He looks good,' I said. 'Tanned and healthy. He looks like he's having a good time.'

Our entrees arrived, but I wasn't hungry so I picked at mine. Todd watched me push pieces of calamari around the plate, and poured me another glass of wine.

'Do you miss him?' he asked.

'Does it matter?'

'To me it does. He misses you. He always asks how you are. In every call.'

I shrugged and poked some more at the hapless squid. 'It doesn't look like it in that photo.'

'You sent him away.'

'He left.'

'He wanted you to go with him.'

'I couldn't. It was all too much. It was too much to ask.'

'Was it?'

'Yes.'

'Do you miss him?' he asked again.

'I thought we were forever,' I said, 'but I didn't tell him. He always told me, and I didn't tell him. I should've told him.'

'He would've still gone, Ab. He needed more than the words.'

I nodded. I think I knew that. 'Yes, Todd, I miss him.' I finally answered his question. 'All the time.'

'Abby, how long have I known you for?' He didn't wait for my response. 'In all those years I've never seen you like this. You're withdrawn, you're off your food. I've never known you to be off your food. There's something going on with you, and it isn't just Brad.'

'I'm fine.'

'You're not, Ab. You've been bumping me, and Andi said you've been avoiding her too, and acting a little strange when you do see her. She's concerned about you.'

'I don't do concern,' I said. 'Since when do you two gang up on me? You don't even like Andi.'

He smiled. 'Andi's okay, it's just her taste in men that worries me … And you can stop trying to change the subject. Did something happen in Bali? Did you find something out about your father's death?'

I stared at him.

'That's the real reason you were so insistent on going, isn't it? Even though it meant Brad leaving?'

For a moment I considered lying to him, but if he'd been talking to Andi, he'd probably got that much information from her anyway. 'I think so.'

He let out a breath and nodded slowly. 'You

never talked about it. Not even back then. Not ever. Sometimes I thought I'd imagined it happened.'

'Sometimes it feels like it was something I imagined.' I forced a smile, but he wasn't fooled.

'It was only when I saw you that night before you left that it occurred to me what your intentions were.'

'I thought it might have. Andi heard you and joined the dots too.'

I pushed the rest of the calamari away so the waiter could clear our plates.

'Did Brad know?' I asked.

'I don't think so. You two were so wound up in each other, and then all of a sudden you were working longer hours and things were different. You pulled back from him at about the same time you guys booked that trip. He was trying to get closer and he felt you were pushing him away — he just didn't know why, and you didn't have time to talk to him about it. He didn't deserve that, Ab.'

I didn't look at him. 'If I did, it wasn't on purpose. I don't know why things needed to change. I was happy — I thought he was too. Surely that was enough? Why did we need to change anything?'

'It's called evolving, Abs. It's what people do.'

'You're a fine one to talk about evolving — when was the last time you saw the same girl more for more than three dates?'

'We're not talking about me. I haven't found "the

one" yet.' He made quotation marks in the air with his fingers. 'You have, you know you have. Don't you think it was time to take it to the next level?'

'Dreams and happy families mean nothing – it's all an illusion, something people tell you before they leave you and never come back. Or before they go to Denmark or Austria or somewhere and look at plants and dirt.'

My phone text alert sounded. My heart jumped again. I looked down, it was from Zoe.

Sorry, something's come up and I can't do tonight. Maybe next time.

I replied with an *okay*.

Todd was watching me. 'Zoe?'

'Yep. Thankfully someone more interesting has come up.'

'Don't you mean some*thing*?'

'Nope. It's always someone more interesting with Zoe.'

The waiter arrived with our pasta main courses.

'Why do you get so on edge when she's in town?' he asked. 'You were always trying to pick an argument when she was on the scene.'

I shrugged.

'It's as if you always expected her to make a move on Brad,' he said.

'Well, it wouldn't be the first time. I figured it was a matter of time before he gave in – just like the others.

Not that it matters now. He left anyway, and is busy getting his photo taken with Astrid in Denmark or Sweden or wherever.'

The combination of wine and a relatively empty stomach was starting to have an impact on what my mouth was saying.

'Well, that's one less worry you've got now – you've managed to do that yourself.'

I looked hard at him. 'Andi said something similar. You two have been conspiring.'

He didn't deny it. 'You and I both know Brad would never look at anyone else. He only ever had eyes for you. As an excuse, it's not a good one.'

Some of that pasta must have stuck in my throat.

'You know I'm right.'

I managed to nod, and downed the remainder of my wine to clear the blockage.

'What did you find out about your father?' he asked quietly.

I busied myself pouring wine while I considered how much to tell him.

'Have you said anything to Andi?'

'No,' I said. 'And before you ask, I'm not sure why. I know she knows what happened, but she knows a different version of me from that girl. Only you and Brad knew her.'

'You don't think she'd understand?'

I truly didn't know. 'It's not that so much – Andi's

a smart girl. I just don't know that I'm up to revealing it all.'

'Tell me then. I was there … back then.'

He was right: I had to tell someone. I took a gulp of wine and a deep breath.

'You know, the last thing my dad said to me was that he'd be back. "I'll be back before you know it, my magic girl," he said. He used to call me that when he was telling me about all the adventures we'd have when I was old enough to travel. He didn't mean a word of it. He was over there with a woman … a woman he was in love with.'

'Oh, Ab. That's tough.' He reached across to grip my hand.

'I don't think he ever intended coming home. He'd been lying to me.'

'You don't know that.'

'No, not for sure, but it's what I suspect. Why else would Mum never talk about it?'

'Have you ever asked her?'

'I used to ask her about what had happened to him, and she'd say she didn't want to discuss it – it was all too painful for her.'

'Don't you think that maybe you should try again, now that you know?'

'What if she confirms it? What if my father didn't love me enough to stay? I don't want to hear that. Despite everything else that happened back then, I've always thought that to my father I was the most special person in the world. It's the only thing I've known for sure.'

'Is that what this is all about, Ab? Unresolved father shit?'

'So now you're my analyst as well?' I pulled my hand away.

'No, just someone who wants to see his world put back to rights – and that means you and Brad back together.'

I tried to inject some humour. 'Typical fricken Aries – it's all about you.'

'You'd know,' he said.

Brad used to laugh at the self-centred impatience that Todd and I – whose birthdays were only a week apart – had in common. In contrast, we appreciated, and were sometimes frustrated by, Brad's steady Taurean reliability.

We ate in silence for a few minutes. Or rather Todd was eating, and I was pretending to eat.

'You know that whole saying about if you love something set it free?' Todd said.

'Of course I do. Are you suggesting I should wait for him to come back? If he's not too busy with Nina, that is.'

'Who?'

'The girl in the photo. I've decided her name is something Scandinavian, maybe something you'd name a rug after, or a flat-pack set of drawers. Something you have to build with one of those bendy tool things, and there's always extra parts left over. Seriously, why do people buy flat-pack furniture? I only ever did because I had Brad to put it together. If it was left up to me, I'd lose patience at the instruction stage.'

He laughed. 'I used to get Brad to do mine too. I have a bookcase waiting for him when he comes home. You're changing the subject again. I'm suggesting that he's set you free … to do what you need to do. You're the one who has to find her way back to him.'

'But I didn't leave,' I argued.

'You sort of did. He knows exactly what he wants – he always has: you. You're the one who has shit to sort out, and he's given you the space to do that. I know you haven't asked, but walking onto that plane and leaving you behind was the hardest thing he's ever had to do.' He watched me struggle for words. 'You hadn't thought of it that way, had you?'

I shook my head. That damn squid was back in my throat. 'What about Heidi?'

'He trusts you, Ab. Maybe it's about time you trusted him.' He said it gently, a sad smile on his face.

I thought back to that night in Bali with Clinton. I'd very nearly abused that trust, just because I was hurting and wanted to forget the hurt for a few minutes. Todd didn't need to know about that.

'This is now officially way too deep,' I said, 'and

that doesn't go with pasta. Romance and passion goes with pasta, so tell me about your love life so I can pass judgement on that. I want all the juicy details – even the sexy bits you'd usually only tell Brad. *Especially* the sexy bits.'

'Well,' he said, 'seeing as how you've asked …'

CHAPTER FIFTEEN

Todd and I wound up having quite a few drinks and, thanks to Zoe's better offer, our early dinner turned into a very late night. When he announced he was walking me home, I accepted gratefully and without protest.

He said no to coffee and, given the state of my apartment, I was glad – although knowing Todd, he probably wouldn't have noticed. When we parted, he pulled me in close for a massive hug and it was all I could do to not hold on to him. He was the closest thing to Brad I had right now.

He pulled back and looked hard at me. 'You'd tell me if there was something else going on, wouldn't you?'

I nodded, but couldn't meet his eyes.

He kissed the top of my forehead and said, 'Okay, at least promise me that you'll look after yourself, and if whatever it is that you're not telling me about gets too much, you'll call me?'

'I will.'

But it already felt like it was too much.

•

I was feeling even more under the weather than usual the next morning as I gathered my notes for the executive steering committee meeting. Clinton stopped by my office on his way to the meeting room. Great – just what I needed to make the hangover even worse.

'How was your evening with your sister?' he asked.

'What?'

'Yesterday you mentioned you were meeting your sister for drinks after she did some launch?'

I busied myself with organising the piles of printed documents. 'Umm, yes, I met a friend earlier for dinner, and she called and said she'd had a better offer, so I stayed out with my friend instead.'

'A better offer? Really?'

He'd perched himself on the edge of my desk so I had to walk around him to lay out the packs for the meeting on the bench that ran below my office window.

'No, she said something came up, and in Zoe language that means someone better. Whatever.'

He'd stretched his legs out so I had no choice but to brush against them as I walked past.

'Who was the friend you had dinner with? Anyone I'd know?'

I didn't have time for this. 'I wouldn't think so – not that it's any of your business.'

'It wasn't Andi?'

I stopped what I was doing and stared at him. 'Didn't you hear me the first time? It's none of your business, Clinton.'

'Was it a man?'

I shook my head in exasperation.

'Did you get the photo I sent you?'

I ignored him and gathered the piles of documents before leaving my office for the conference room. As Andrew Warner was based in Warner's head office in Perth, these meetings were usually done by video conference. Today he was here in our office, as were two other people I hadn't yet met. As I passed around the meeting packs, Andrew introduced the newcomers.

'Today I've brought along Mike Robards and Katie Chan from Say It Loud Marketing. It's outside the scope of this project, but we're assessing the impact of this project on our brand, and will tailor future marketing accordingly – and that's where Mike and Katie come in. Mike's been in the advertising and marketing industry for nearly thirty years, and wants to get a picture of who we are by looking at our key partners and any strategically important projects. I hope that's okay with you?'

Mike spoke up. 'I promise we won't have much to say. It's getting to know the project that we're interested in.'

He was a charismatic man in his late fifties, good-looking in that way some older men managed. I imagined that would be an asset in his game.

Andrew was speaking again. 'Mike, Katie, let me introduce Mark Jones, the partner managing this deal, and his associate Abigail Brentnall, our project manager extraordinaire.'

'You're way too kind,' I said as the obligatory business-card swap took place.

Mike picked mine up, examined it and looked closely at me. I smiled, but he didn't smile back. I shrugged internally and took control of the meeting, presenting my status report.

We discussed the risk register, and I was about to close the session when Clinton raised an issue regarding a requirement that he felt had been left out of development.

'I don't see anything in the release notes relating to the mandatory filling of field nine,' he said, looking at Mark.

I didn't wait for Mark to respond. 'Thanks for bringing this one up, but if you refer to the requirements register, you'll see it was discussed at our meeting on May 4th and was deemed out of scope. As a result we excluded it from this phase of development and will revisit it during the post-implementation phase. According to my notes, the business felt it wasn't necessary to make the field mandatory. I've noted it as item 5.1 in the post-implementation review so we don't lose sight of it. Did you want to bring it back onto the table now? If so, it will require a change request and formal quoting by the development team.'

Clinton opened his mouth, but Andrew stepped in. 'No, that's fine, thanks, Abby. You're absolutely right. We've already captured and dealt with this item.' He turned to Mike Robards. 'I told you she's good at her job.'

I smiled. 'I can't take all the credit, Andrew. Sophie keeps amazing records.'

Clinton was concentrating very hard on his notes, and when I looked across at Mark it was to see him glaring at me.

Soon after, I called the meeting closed, shook hands with our visitors, and sat back down to complete my notes for Sophie.

Mark saw the others out and returned to the conference room. 'Don't you ever do that again,' he warned.

'Do what?' I looked up from my notes.

'Embarrass Clinton like that.'

'I don't think I did embarrass him. I was just pointing out that we'd already captured and resolved that item.'

'You were point scoring. Any personal issues you have with Clinton need to be left at the door. What you just did was completely unprofessional.'

'That's unfair, Mark. Clinton raised that issue in an attempt to put me in a difficult situation. He waited until the end to bring it up, and if my records weren't as good as they are, I would have been left floundering. I was merely following process.' I closed my notebook.

Mark moved to stand over me. 'Aaah, yes, process. Since when have you and Sophie been taking process to this extent? Registers for this, that and everything in-between?'

'Sophie usually does – it's just that they're not normally as visible as they've had to be this time. We've learnt over the past couple of months to capture everything – it removes arguments and keeps everything crystal clear. Today's issue proved that.'

'Well, I think it's overkill.'

'Because I'm able to keep the steering committee meetings quick and smooth? Because there's been no disputed issues requiring escalation? Or because I was able to score a point against Clinton?'

'You admit that's what you were aiming for?'

'No, that was just an added bonus,' I said, standing too.

In my heels, I was a couple of inches taller than Mark, who had now turned a rather interesting shade of red. He really needed to exercise more. A man of his age shouldn't take chances with his blood pressure.

'I'm telling you now to keep all of those registers of yours to the basics. There's no need to capture emails and phone calls.'

'Mark, if you want me to continue to be as close to this project as I am, if you want this project to be a success, I won't be compromising on the tools we use to manage it.'

He stared at me and I stared back. His eyes dropped first.

'Just leave your personal issues at the door,' he said. 'It doesn't reflect well on your professionalism. And if I were you, I'd be balancing the need for all of those registers you're so keen on versus the billable hours you're dropping behind on.'

He was making it clear that he was looking for excuses not to promote me.

Brad had warned me about this when last year's partner announcements came out. I'd been furious that I'd been overlooked again. When Brad grew tired of listening to me repeat myself, he left the vegetables on the chopping board and came around to the couch where I was sitting. Without saying a word he took my glass from my hand, leaned in and kissed me. When he pulled back and I started to speak again, he gently laid one finger across my lips to shush me, pushed me back onto the couch and slowly unfastened the buttons on my blouse, stopping between each to kiss the skin he'd exposed. By the time my breast was in his mouth, I'd forgotten what I was going to say, and once his hand was between my thighs I was incapable of coherent thought.

Later, he'd said, 'I think the problem isn't that you're a woman, or the club memberships or the hours or the client introductions. The problem is Mark. He doesn't want to lose you as his associate. You're there when he's not. You do double the workload of your colleagues, and you've never let him down. You make him look good. Why would he mess with that?'

'But,' I'd started, snuggling into him on the rug where we'd landed, 'what about –'

He kissed the top of my head and pulled back to look me in the eyes. 'No, babe, there are no "buts". You know deep down, in here,' he ran his finger lightly down to my navel and stroked my belly, 'that I'm right. By the time next year's appointments are due, he'll have found another reason to leave you off the list, and it will have nothing to do with the quality of your work or the hours you put in.'

As he talked, his hand had moved lower, gliding lightly across my belly, the top of my thighs, dipping into the centre of me, before sliding back up to my navel and repeating the journey. Sometimes the pressure was light and teasing, sometimes more insistent, and always his eyes looked into mine, drinking in my soft moans, not allowing me to look away. Even as I went to arch my back and grab at the rug below me, he held my hand and my gaze, finally thrusting into me just when I thought I couldn't bear any more. But I could … of course I could.

'I love you,' he'd said when we were spent. 'I hate to see you working so hard and being taken for granted. But if this is really your dream and you want to keep fighting for it, I'll support you. Just promise me you'll know when to stop.'

My heart, at that moment, had felt like it was too full for me to speak, so I didn't, and when I lifted my head from his chest, his eyes were closed.

Now, in the conference room, I heard Brad's words cut through my anger. He'd known something like this would happen, and he'd known that I knew it too.

'I miss Noodelicious,' Andi complained, 'and I'm cold.'

Even though I'd had pasta last night, we were sitting outside a pasta restaurant at the Spring Street end of Bourke Street. There were no available seats inside, so rather than wait, we'd elected to sit out in the fresh air. I was still too pissed off from the conversation with Mark to feel the cold.

'And you know I shouldn't be eating carbs,' Andi continued, wrapping her coat more tightly around her against the wind that came through in the wake of the trams.

This part of Bourke Street looked like a black and white movie set in Rome or somewhere else in Italy. The sort of movie where Audrey Hepburn would jump on the back of a motor scooter and head into a black and white night. Andi, who was as far removed from Hepburn-esque as it was possible to be, was still Hollywood glamour at its best. She was wearing another figure-hugging tight black skirt, although this one had a ruffle where the kick split should be, her usual high black heels, and a fitted blouse in deep aubergine. It was a look appreciated by the Italian waiters who were now fluttering around us. I felt distinctly tall and dowdy beside her.

'Noodelicious could do with some Italian waiters,' Andi commented. 'Speaking of which, when can we go back there?'

'I thought the change was doing us good.'

'It made life easier when I knew where we were going each time. It's Wednesday so that must mean lunch at Noodelicious with Abby. This takes way too much thought and organising.'

'Sorry about that.'

'But the bread is great,' she said, dipping a piece into olive oil.

'A few carbs won't hurt you.'

'That's easy for you to say. I reckon I'll catch airborne calories. Speaking of thin, how was Zoe last night?'

'A non-event. Someone more interesting came up for her, so she blew me off.'

'Does she really think you fall for her shit?' Andi closed her eyes to savour the olive oil, and used her finger to wipe a little that had dribbled from her lips.

'I don't really care what she thinks. Anyways, I was out with Todd, so just stayed out longer with him.'

'That's why you have shadows under your eyes

today?'

'I guess.' I broke off a piece of bread and dunked it, before popping it back onto my side plate.

'I caught up with Todd the other day too,' she said, not quite looking me in the eyes. What was that about?

'I know – he told me. I didn't think you liked him.'

'He's alright once he stops that judgemental "I know best" thing that he does. You do it too.'

'I don't judge you!'

'You sort of do, but you don't say it out loud. It's the perspective thing. You only see what you see. Take this jug. The side I can see is blue, and the side you can see is red. You'd argue that it couldn't possibly be blue on my side because you can't see it. But I'd admit that there's a possibility it could be red on your side even though I can't see it. Then if I turned it around, you'd say that you knew all along that it was both red and blue and you'd believe you knew that all along. Todd's like that too. It must be an Aries thing.'

'Really? We're talking about the colour of jugs? I guess it's better than talking about Zoe, who I dodged a bullet on, or Jason, who you'd better not have replied to.'

'I did reply to him, after I saw Todd last time, and I told him never to contact me again. I'm done. And I am. He replied to my text and I deleted it without reading it. So there. I've also deleted the photos.'

'Photos? Do I really want to know?'

A wide smile spread across her face. 'No, sweetie,

you don't. It was Todd who suggested I did that – deleted the photos.'

'Of course it would be.'

'He's concerned about you as well. Todd, that is.'

'Please don't, A … Don't say the "c" word.'

She looked hard at me and I concentrated just as hard on the pasta that had been placed in front of me.

'I'm in Sydney this weekend,' I said, changing the subject. 'Peter's campaign thing.'

'Wow, those few years have gone fast. I bet you're looking forward to that … not!'

'Hmmm. I'm looking forward to seeing Tyler though.'

'How hot has that boy got?'

Tyler had stayed with me for a few days earlier in the year and Andi had been impressed – a little too impressed.

'Careful. You're almost old enough to be his mother.'

She giggled and dug into her pasta with relish. 'Oh, I think I've gone to carb heaven. This is so worth the extra gym session I'll have to do this week.'

I felt hands on my shoulders and turned in my seat to see Clinton standing there smiling at me. I shrugged his hands away, but he pulled a chair up and sat beside us.

'What a stroke of luck this is, seeing you here,' he said.

Andi looked between him and me with confusion in her eyes.

'I'm sorry,' he said, getting up to kiss Andi on the cheek. 'It's great to see you again, Andi.'

'I didn't know that you two had caught up,' she said.

He laughed. 'I think Ab wanted to keep things quiet now that we're working together.' He feigned surprise. 'Oh, I thought you might have told Andi about that? Naughty girl.' He tried to place his hand on mine and I pulled it away.

'Check this photo I took of her.' He turned to me. 'Remember that last night down at Tanah Lot?'

He showed Andi the photo he'd texted me last night. She looked at it and then back at me, but didn't say anything. The pasta I'd eaten was mixing with rage and looking for a quick escape route.

'It was the most romantic place I've ever eaten,' he went on. 'All flickering candlelight, crashing waves and those guys on the guitar that I arranged to serenade you ...'

I reached for my bag and threw some money on the table, before turning to Andi. 'It's not what you think.'

'Don't be like that,' said Clinton.

Andi ignored him. 'Does Todd know?'

'There's nothing for him to know,' I said.

'Who's Todd?' asked Clinton.

'What about Brad?' she asked me.

'Brad's too busy getting his photo taken with Bridget to care.'

'Who's Bridget?'

'The Von Trapp family singer who had a rug named after her and was in the photo with Brad that Todd showed me last night.'

'Why didn't you tell me about it?'

Brad and Bridget, or Clinton? The answer was the same. 'I couldn't,' I admitted.

'Is Todd who you were with last night?' asked Clinton.

'Is he why we don't eat at Noodelicious any more?' Andi indicated Clinton.

'Yes.'

'You still haven't told me who Todd is,' said Clinton.

I turned to him. 'And you … you can shut the fuck up and leave me the fuck alone.'

'Talking like that to a client is no way to get a partnership,' he said.

My coat was stuck under the chair. In my haste to get away I pulled it so hard the chair toppled. I ignored it and ran.

Back at my desk, I shut the door on the office noise and stood at my window, breathing hard. Usually I found looking down at the plane trees that lined the top end of Collins Street calming. Today, it wasn't working. I was surprised to notice that my fists were clenched and my jaw was tight. I took three deep breaths and attempted to swallow. Then I was flying out the door and made it into the bathroom just in time, my lunch leaving my body in explosive spasms that felt like they were coming from the very depths of my being.

When it was over, I rested my head on the cool of the tiles until I was sure there was nothing left in my stomach, and until my breathing steadied.

I emerged from the stall to see Paula standing there with a concerned look on her face. I wished people would stop doing that, the concern thing. I smiled weakly at her and rinsed my mouth from the tap. She handed me paper towelling.

'Don't ask,' I said.

'I won't,' she promised.

'Can you do me one favour?'

'Of course.'

'If he calls – Clinton Barclay, that is – you don't know where I am.'

'Is that just for this afternoon?'

'No, it's forever.'

'With pleasure.'

I closed my office door again, with Paula acting as guard – not necessarily to keep anyone out of my office, but rather to keep me in, at least until I calmed down. I didn't blame her – I'd caught a glimpse of my white face in the bathroom mirror.

There were five missed calls from Andi, and a text message: *Call me now!!!!!!!!!!!!!!*

She answered on the first ring. 'This had better be good.'

'It isn't, it's more awful than I can say.'

She was quiet at the other end, and I didn't have the words, so just sat there with the phone to my ear, saying nothing.

Finally she said, 'Ab … are you there?'

'Yes,' I whispered.

'What's going on?'

'I can't tell you, not yet – mainly because I don't know completely myself. But I will tell you as soon as I can get my head around it. Please trust me on this: it isn't like he said. It's a long way from what he said.'

'I thought you said you didn't sleep with him.'

'I didn't. All that happened was what I told you – the rest is in his head. But it's complicated because he's a client here now.'

'Oh.' She got that. 'But I don't understand why you didn't tell me?'

'I don't know why, but I couldn't. I thought I could manage it.'

'Can I help?'

'Not yet.'

'What are you going to do?'

'I don't know,' I admitted. 'I have no idea.'

'You don't have to do this alone, you know. I'm here and so is Todd.'

I couldn't answer her.

'Promise me you'll call if you need me?' she said.

'That's what Todd said. Maybe you two have more in common than you think.'

'Maybe we do,' she conceded. 'Although I think there'd probably be too much competition for the bathroom mirror.'

I appreciated her attempt at humour.

What I needed to do was get Clinton Barclay out of my life. Or, perhaps, remove myself from his.

CHAPTER SIXTEEN

Paula popped her head around my door as I hung up from Andi. 'I don't want to bother you, Abby, but Mike Robards is on the phone again. He's already called a few times and says it's important he talks to you.'

Mike Robards? I searched my brain … Oh, from this morning's meeting. It seemed an age ago.

'Sure,' I said, 'put him through.'

'Hello, Mike, this is Abigail. How can I help you?'

'I'm sorry to interrupt … I'm sure you're very busy.'

I laughed. 'That would be an understatement.'

'It's just … the resemblance …'

'I'm sorry?'

'Abigail, I'm sorry – I need to ask because the resemblance is so strong … Was your father Roger Brentnall?'

I drew in my breath sharply. 'Yes.'

'I thought so. I knew your father well. We were working together until he resigned – just before he went to Bali.'

'Before he resigned? But I thought he was there

on a work conference.'

'No. Where did you get that idea?'

I took another deep breath. 'Mike, is there some place we can meet to talk? You see, no one ever talks about him, and I'd like to … you know, talk about him.'

'I can be downstairs at the coffee shop in ten minutes.'

#

'Abby, your father was a good man. What happened to him was a tragedy,' Mike said, skipping both the pleasantries and the coffee.

'Thank you for saying that. No one really talks about him, yet my memory of him is still so strong.'

'I suppose your mother wanted to move on with her life.'

'Did you know my mother too?'

'I'd met her a few times at company Christmas parties. When your father resigned so suddenly the week before he died, I tried to talk to him, to get him to change his mind. He was a born advertising creative, you know. It was instinctive the way he could get into a client's mind and know exactly how to make the pitch. A natural.' He paused, as if remembering. 'Do you remember that ad for the sugar-free soft drink? The girl in the bikini and all the guys falling apart as she walked by?'

I nodded.

'Then there was that jingle for cough medicine. I

don't think the medicine ever worked, but the campaign sure did.'

I remembered. 'That came from a song he made up for me one time when I was sick.' I sang a few bars … badly.

Mike smiled. 'Did you know that the abracadabra slogan for that children's health initiative about getting kids to eat more vegies came from you?'

'I didn't know that.'

'He always called you his magic girl. He said you were the inspiration behind everything he was aiming for.' He paused again. 'I called your home and spoke to your mother after your father had already left for Bali. I told her that we wanted to talk him out of his decision to resign – it was too sudden.'

'Mum knew that he'd quit?'

He looked at me with confusion. 'Of course she did. She told me she had no way of reaching him, that he'd gone away for a few days. She didn't tell me where … I only knew that after the news broke. She also told me that his decision was final. Why do you ask?'

'It's just that Mum said Dad went to Bali as part of a team-building conference – you know, one of those you advertising boys used to throw money at in the eighties before the crash?'

'Yes, I remember those days with fondness, although the memory of the lunches is a little foggy.' He laughed. 'No, there was definitely no conference.'

I looked away. 'Maybe I misheard all those years ago.'

'Perhaps,' he said. 'Anyway, I just wanted to meet you and let you know how much I respected your father, and that I've often thought of you and your poor sister over the years. I know how much he adored you – he always had a photo of you in his office, or your latest artwork. He'd keep us entertained with stories of your scrapes – you seemed like such a fearless little thing. I remember him telling me about you getting into a fight with the school bullies because they were picking on someone who couldn't stand up for themselves. I'd said that it took a lot of moral courage to do that.' He smiled at the memory. 'He said that he'd never have to worry about you, that you'd always have the strength to stand up for yourself and what you believed was important. Looking at what you've achieved, he'd be proud.'

Would he? I wasn't so sure. I hadn't done much standing up for what I believed in lately. I didn't say that; instead I thanked him. 'You have no idea how much I appreciate knowing that.'

I shook Mike's hand and went back to my office, closing the door softly behind me.

I remembered the day I'd battled the Scotts. When I'd got home that afternoon, Mum had made the noises she usually made when I came home with scuffed knees, dirty face and pulled ponytail. It had happened before. I'd never lived up to her idea of what a daughter should be. She tried to dress me up, tried to get me to play with dolls, but I wasn't interested. I preferred clothes I could run and jump in. I needed to always be moving, seeing what was next, climbing trees (and generally falling out of them), looking for goodness knows what across the suburban roofline. I hated shopping, I hated skirts, and lipsticks were only good for drawing with. I'd once got in serious trouble over that one.

That afternoon, Mum had told me that I had to learn to turn the other cheek, and let people like Lisa McMullen, who were always going to be unfortunate, cope with things themselves. She said something about Darwin, and the survival of the fittest, and how in the scheme of things there always had to be Lisa McMullens. Back then I only knew of Darwin as a place that had a cyclone on Christmas Day before I was born. Dad had told me about it. Dad told me lots about lots of places.

'Nothing good ever came from using violence,' Mum had said.

'Dad says we should never give in to bullies,' I'd argued. 'If everyone just stands by and watches, and no one does anything about it, they think they can get away with anything.'

Mum shook her head in disappointment. 'None of this would happen if your father let me send you to a proper girls' school.'

'Umm derrr, it was girls I was fighting.' Sometimes

I didn't know what planet Mum was living on.

'A proper girls' school has the right type of girls in it,' she pointed out.

'The only difference between the girls at one of those posh schools and the Scott girls is the posh girls can call me a mollface in a different language.'

'Get the ruler,' she ordered.

So I did, and held my hand out for the usual number of smacks.

'It doesn't matter how many times you smack my hand, you can't change my mind on this,' I told her, chin stuck out, palm smarting. 'Besides,' I added as the ruler came down again, 'if everyone turned the other cheek, bullies would be allowed to rule the world.'

That comment earned me an extra smack.

'Don't answer back, Abigail. You'll be laughing on the other side of your face when your father gets home,' she warned.

'Well, that's where you're wrong. I'm not laughing, and it's impossible to laugh on the other side of your face. It's like turning the other cheek – there's no way you can do that.'

She told me to go to my room.

When Dad got home, I heard Mum call him into the kitchen. 'Roger, you need to handle this. You've filled her head with too many ideas. It's not right for a girl.'

'Tess, she's eight years old.'

'Yes, and she's fighting in the playground, and

always running around and climbing trees – that's your influence. If you'd let me send her to that girls' school, this would never have happened. She needs to learn to face reality and act like a young lady.'

So he'd talked to me. Mum had stood in the kitchen door with her face pursed up and her arms folded, interrupting every so often. I'd listened to what they had to say, but, as I said, it had happened before. After Mum considered I'd been lectured enough, and I looked passably contrite, she went back to the stove to finish preparing dinner.

Once she'd gone, Dad ruffled my hair and said that even though he had to present a united front with Mum, and there was no excuse for violence, he was actually quite proud of me for standing up against the Scotts.

'Bullies can only exist when there's no one prepared to take a stand against them. What you did today was a good thing – it was something that Lisa McMullen will remember for the rest of her life, even if you forget it. Promise me this, Abs, no matter what happens, don't you ever let anyone take your principles or your dreams away from you. Trust me, people will try, and they'll pay you well for it, and tell you that it's for your own good. Stand strong and do what you think is right. At the end of the day, your integrity and spirit are the only things you can rely on. Don't ever let anyone compromise them.'

Sitting in my office that afternoon it occurred to

me that all I'd really done was to compromise those things. And for what? Despite what Mike had said, I wasn't so sure that Dad would be proud of the woman I'd allowed myself to become.

Even though it was only 4 pm and I had hours of work left to do, I packed up my laptop and called to Paula. 'I'm out of here. If you need anything, text or call. If Sophie or Mark asks, tell them I'm not feeling great. If Clinton calls, I'm in a meeting.'

'I'm glad. An early afternoon for a change will do you good.'

Once home, I went straight to my wardrobe and the shoebox I kept up on a high shelf. As I lifted the lid, dust flew up my nose and I sneezed. It was a thick layer – I didn't think I'd opened this box since I'd moved into this apartment.

Inside were newspaper clippings. The ones from the time of Dad's accident and the inquest – Brad had ripped them out of his parents' newspapers for me. Mum wouldn't allow them in the house in case I saw them. The later ones, starting from Mum and Peter's wedding, I'd been able to get myself.

I looked at the wedding ones first. I was nearly fourteen, and slouching in the back row. I'd shot up in height a little too quickly, had braces, pimples and, thanks to another ill-advised biking expedition with Brad, a full cast on my left arm and another four stitches in my forehead.

'I suppose it's lucky we can hide the stitches with your fringe,' Mum had said. 'But there's not much I can do about the pimples. I wish you wouldn't eat so many of Mrs Ingram's cupcakes. And you're too tall. If I didn't know better, I'd think you'd done this deliberately to ruin my wedding photos.'

There was still a framed magazine cover on the wall at home showing Zoe prancing down the aisle in a princess dress, daintily throwing rose petals from a basket.

Every time Peter campaigned for office, the story got dragged up again. I wasn't allowed to talk about my father or his death, but the newspapers were. The reporters certainly never mentioned my loss; it was all about the tragedy of the little girl who never knew her father, and how they all lived happily ever after — as shown by the obligatory family picture at the campaign launch party.

I put the campaign articles aside and pulled out the ones from the accident and inquest, unfolding them and flattening them out. Hamish had told me that Dad wasn't in Bali for work, and Mike had just confirmed that. So what was he doing over there? I had no idea what I was looking for — I'd read each of these hundreds of times over the years. Something that I'd missed perhaps? Something that would explain how he'd got to be on a riverbank and in love with a woman who wasn't my mother?

Speaking of which, my conversation with her on the weekend promised to be very interesting.

CHAPTER SEVENTEEN

I took a glass of something bubbly from a waiter, and chased down another bearing a tray of something that looked like they could be spring rolls. God, I hated these political launches, but at least the bar snacks were up to their usual standard.

Casting my eyes around the room, I saw Mum in one corner schmoozing some expensively outfitted stick figures. Peter was laughing a little too loudly on the other side. I couldn't see Zoe anywhere, but Tyler was talking with one of the few party elders that I was not only able to tolerate but actually liked: Jeremy Paulson. Jeremy had briefly been party leader and had come *this* close to winning an election about fifteen years ago. Peter always said he'd thrown it away. I preferred to think that he'd held true to his opinions, and admired him for it.

I grabbed another glass of bubbles, stocked up on some more canapés from a passing waiter, and made my way across to them.

'Baby brother.' I greeted Tyler with a hug, then held him at arm's length to have a good look at him. 'If it's at all possible, you're even taller.' I stretched up to plant a kiss on his cheek. There weren't many people that I needed to reach up to. 'What happened to the stop growing thing? What are you now – twenty?'

He gathered me into a hug. 'It's been too long, Abster.'

I pulled back and looked into his face. 'I know. Hey,' I pinched his biceps, 'have you been working out? The girls don't stand a chance, do they?'

Always on the cute side, Tyler had grown into a really attractive man. He had Peter's height, jaw and dark hair. Unlike Peter, he wore his hair artfully gelled, as if he'd absent-mindedly run his fingers through it. It was the dimple though – just the one, like Peter – that really sealed the deal for him when it came to hooking his catch. I'd say the dimples ran in the family, except I had none.

He beamed his wide smile. 'That's the general idea.'

I turned to Jeremy, who'd been smiling indulgently through this meet and greet, and gave him a warm kiss on the cheek.

'Abigail. Well, aren't you a sight for sore eyes? We were just talking about you, weren't we, Tyler?'

'All good things, I hope,' I said.

'Absolutely. Hang on, where's that waitress gone – I was after some of those satay thingies. Sometimes I think these events are only worth it for the food. My wife doesn't normally allow me to eat this much fat. It's alright for you young skinny things.'

Tyler and I laughed as we lightened the waitress's tray-load.

'Where's your young man tonight?' Jeremy asked me. 'What's his name – Brett? Ben? No, Brad. He's a keeper that boy. He'll go places too, I think.'

I felt a pang somewhere in the middle of my chest, but plastered a smile to my face. 'He's overseas at the moment, looking at some European design ideas. Apparently they've done some innovative work with permaculture, so Brad's taken a fellowship over there for a few months.'

Tyler raised his eyebrows and looked closely at me.

'What were you two gossiping about before?' I asked, eager to change the subject.

Jeremy took a contemplative sip of his wine. 'Oh, yes. Do you remember that painting I bought at the Art Society benefit about five years ago?'

I thought back. 'Yes, and I'm so sorry, Jeremy. Mum got really mad with me when she found out you'd bought the painting I liked rather than the one you were looking at. Unfortunately I'd had a little too much to drink. It's an occupational hazard at these things.'

Jeremy had asked me what I thought of a painting he was thinking of purchasing as an investment. It was by a well-known artist, yet when I looked at it, I'd felt that to have it hanging in my lounge room (or wherever) day after day would surely lead me to depression, or at the very least bring on a strong bout of melancholy. Because I'd been imbibing in the wine on offer – medicinal, you understand; I had a habit of doing that at these gatherings – I'd told Jeremy so. I'd also told him that the painting hanging below it would make me feel as if I was in love, even if I wasn't. The artist was a relative unknown, but Jeremy had bought the piece immediately.

Mum had been horrified when she found out. 'Abigail, no one is interested in your opinions. The artist that Jeremy had been looking at was a good buy. This one is a no name. Next time, try and stay away from the wine; or if you must drink, keep your tongue in your head.'

Jeremy laughed. 'Trust me, Abigail, I've been to enough of these things over the years to know that sometimes the only way to get through them is with a little help from the bottle. Speaking of which …' He hijacked a passing drinks waiter and collected another three glasses. 'In any case, I'm glad you did convince me to change my mind. I just sold that piece for … wait for it … over fifty thousand. She is now the artist to watch, by all accounts. Not bad, hey?' He toasted me.

'Not bad at all. So I've got good taste – who would have known it?' I raised my glass in response.

Tyler laughed and said, 'Remind me to tell Mum, I'm sure she'll be thrilled.'

Jeremy smiled. 'Somehow I doubt that, son.' He

took a mouthful of his drink. 'Well, my pretties, I'd better go and mingle with the party faithful, although I'd rather stay and play in this corner. Abigail, try to stay away from journalists tonight. I happen to agree with your views on the world, but it wouldn't do for anyone else to know that.'

'I'll try,' I promised.

He kissed me on the cheek again, slapped Tyler on the back, and made his way through the crowd. I laughed when I saw him stop the journalist from last time who'd been heading towards me with a bottle of chardonnay and a purposeful look.

I turned to face my brother. 'So, Tylster, where's the miracle child?'

'Zoe? She called earlier today and said she couldn't make it. Something to do with shoot schedules and how important she is. Did you see her when she was in Melbourne?'

'I did a month or so ago. I even agreed to meet her for drinks one night last week after the Chapel Street launch, but she texted me to say she couldn't make it. I managed to recover from the disappointment.' I made a face and used my fingers to make out I had tears running down my cheeks. Tyler raised his eyebrows and laughed. 'She's doing some catwalk shows next month, but I think I'll be interstate, so sadly we'll miss each other again.'

'Awww, Abs, that's too sad,' he sympathised. We

both giggled, and then his voice dropped to a whisper. 'Eleven o clock: mother approaching.'

I screwed up my nose a little in resignation, we both arranged our faces into something more serious, and surreptitiously wiped the evidence of too many canapés from our fingers.

'Abigail …'

I bent down so Mum could greet me with a kiss on the cheek. She raised a finger to brush off a spring roll crumb I must have missed. I saw Tyler grin at the action.

'Mum,' I said. 'You're looking good.'

'Thank you. I bought this outfit especially for tonight. Peter needs to know that some of his family are supporting him.'

'Yeah, I guess it's a shame that Zoe couldn't get away.'

'It wasn't Zoe I was referring to. It's not her fault that the filming schedule was changed at the last minute. She tried to convince the director, but as some senior stylists and photographers had flown in from America especially to shoot this cover, she's had to accept the sacrifice.'

'Such a pity,' I said.

Mum searched my face for signs of sarcasm. Finding none she said, 'What have you done to your hair?'

'I just had it cut and had a few layers put in.'

'It looked so much more feminine when it was a little longer. Oh well.'

I smiled politely and Tyler tried not to.

'And I don't know why you had to wear heels so high. You're already too tall, and you knew there'd be photos.'

I sighed, but she'd turned her attention to Tyler. 'There are people here who want to talk to you. I'd suggest you mingle a bit rather than letting Abigail monopolise you.'

Tyler knew when he was beaten. He raised his glass in my direction. 'Catch you later, Abs.'

Mum turned back to me. 'What's this I hear about you going to Bali?'

'I had a holiday a couple of months ago. I told you I was going away.'

'You didn't tell me where,' she accused. 'I had to find out from Tyler.'

I shrugged. 'I don't see what the issue is.'

'The issue, Abigail, is that Bali is where your father died. Did it not occur to you that I might find it upsetting that you chose to holiday somewhere that obviously has a lot of painful memories for me?'

I shook my head. 'Not really. Anyway, you told me he was in Bali for a work conference, didn't you?'

'That's right. What do you people call it now – an off-site? It was as a reward for achieving their targets.' Mum dabbed at tears that didn't exist. 'Must we go over this again? I thought you would have gotten over all that rubbish by now.'

'It's interesting. I tracked down the company that ran the tours and spoke to the guide who took them out that day, and there was no corporate group booked in at all. Dad was there on his own, with another woman. The guide thought they were a couple.'

Mum opened her mouth to say something, but I held up my hand.

'There's more. I thought he was wrong – after all, my own mother wouldn't be mistaken about something like that. Then, quite coincidentally, I talked to Mike Robards, that guy Dad used to work with? He asked me to give you his regards. He's now CEO at one of the agencies my company is doing some work with. He confirmed there was no off-site. He also told me that Dad had resigned before he went away. I naturally thought you mustn't have known about that, but Mike told me that he'd phoned you to ask you to talk Dad out of it. So, Mum, I have a few questions for you. Why have you lied to me about this for all of these years? Was Dad having an affair? Had he left us?'

'Really, Abigail, why does everything have to be all about you? I don't think this is the time or the place to talk about this.' She turned to go.

'Oh, really? And when is? No one's looking, Mum – they all think this is a touching family reunion. You want a photo op; I want some information – I'll even smile.

I think I deserve to know the truth. He was my father.'

'And that's why I've never told you what really happened – because he was your father and you idolised his memory. But the father you hero-worshipped was not the man I was married to. He was having an affair – with his secretary. She was exactly his type – young, brunette and large-chested. One of those very obvious, forward girls. Your father was a good-looking man – the women all loved him. It's probably why he hardly ever paid any attention to me.' She sniffed, and dabbed again at her eyes. 'See, Abigail, this is why I didn't want to talk about this … it upsets me. Not that you care.'

I looked unimpressed, so she continued. 'He had left us – for her. He was never coming back. He'd told me that before he left. I didn't want you to know. It seemed kinder if you didn't know that he'd lied to you. He never intended to say goodbye; he took the coward's way out.'

I didn't have an answer to that. God, she was good.

She smiled thinly at me. 'Now, let's not talk about this nonsense again. Have you spoken to Peter yet? No? Well, how about we do that? He's about to make his speech to launch the campaign, so now is not the time for you to be difficult, no matter how much you might want to be the centre of attention.'

Sitting on the plane back to Melbourne the following day, my head was still reeling with what Mum had told me. For all these years I'd clung to the knowledge that even though Mum had pretty well ignored me, at least my father had loved me. Now that had been taken away from me too.

But rather than shutting me down, what Mum had told me only made me keener to know the whole story. There was more to it – there had to be. Her story sounded plausible, but something still didn't feel right. It was almost as if she'd told me what she thought would make me stop asking questions. Despite what she'd said, I knew deep in my bones that my father would never have left without saying goodbye. When he went to Bali, he was going on a holiday. I was certain of that. He was intending to come home. I was sure of that too.

If that was the case, it followed that my mother was lying to me, and had been all these years. The question I needed answered was why.

In the eight short years we'd had together, Dad had passed on some key pieces of wisdom:

No matter what the circumstances, the mark of integrity is to stand up and fight for what you believe in, and to accept the consequences of your actions.

Follow your dreams and your heart, and always be upfront and honest about doing so.

And, do what you believe is right – as long as it doesn't hurt someone else.

There was no way he would have ignored his own advice and run off to Bali with his secretary without having the courage and integrity to say goodbye to me, no matter how many imaginary tears my mother pretended to cry. Zoe was obviously not the only actress in the family. Besides, if the woman Dad supposedly left with was as forward as Mum said she was, she wouldn't have shied away from the inquest – but there was no mention of any woman in any of the news clippings.

If I believed that Dad had intended to come back for me, my next step was to prove it. And the only way to do that was to find the woman he'd been on that tour with.

And aside from that, I needed to work out how to get Clinton out of my life.

If Brad were here, he'd remind me to slow down and attack the problem logically. He'd tell me that I'd allowed myself to lose all sense of reason about Clinton, and that was distracting me from solving everything else. I could almost hear him speaking in his calm, practical way.

'The way I see it, Ab, you've got only one problem. It's just that the crap going on at work is clouding your judgement and tricking you into thinking that's where your focus should be. The real issue is the unfinished business with your father. Now, you know that you've been told lies, but you're not sure who told them. It's this one that's stopping you from moving forward – it always has done – so getting to the truth is your real priority. Mark and Clinton and what's going on at work are the distractions, and it's not like you to let that kind of thing drag on as long as this has. Once you've fixed them, you can get to the bottom of whatever it is you need to get to the bottom of with your father. And once you've fixed that, you can fix us.'

Maybe he wouldn't say that last bit.

If we were having this conversation for real, rather than in my head, I'd probably say something like, 'No, that's where you're wrong. Mark and Clinton aren't two problems. Clinton is the problem and Mark is assisting him.'

He'd shake his head, smile patiently at me and say, 'Babe, think about it. Mark's been trying to control you for years with the promise of a partnership that, let's face it, he has no intention of giving you. You've been *this* close for years. He just wants to make you work your arse off for him. You know it, but for whatever reason you haven't been prepared to do anything about it. Maybe because if you had done something about it, you wouldn't have had the excuse to avoid concentrating on what you really need to concentrate on. As for Clinton? Well, he's just a bully. What he's been doing to you is harassment, and Mark should have realised that and put a stop to it. Instead, he's encouraged it and he's using it as this year's excuse not to promote you. Just you wait – at your next performance discussion there'll be something he won't quite say about how the problem with women is that they're too emotional. Then he'll say how you spent too much time this year micro-managing projects you should have been across at a helicopter level. He'll say that you need to learn to balance your roles on major projects with billing hours, and that this experience has proved that you still have a way to go before you're partner material. Then he'll promote Jared who hasn't got any project experience at all.'

I'd yell back that the only reason Clinton had been able to get under my skin was because he, Brad, wasn't here, and he'd taken all my defence mechanisms to Austria or Denmark or Poland or wherever with him.

Brad would pause, look at me in that way he always did when he wanted me to really listen to him, and say, 'You'd be able to see the solution to the Mark and Clinton problem if I hadn't left; and I wouldn't have left if you didn't need to move forward and take a chance on us.' He'd wait for me to digest that, and then he'd add, 'You know I'm right, Abs, you just don't want to admit it.'

And he would be right – not that I'd let him know that straight away. Brad was nearly always right; it was one of his more annoying habits.

The one point where Mum's and Hamish's stories matched was the mystery woman. I had to find her, and the logical starting point for that was Hamish. In the taxi on my way home from the airport, I dug his business card out of my wallet and tapped out a quick email on my phone:

Hi Hamish,

Thanks for your time when I was last up in Bali. I'm wondering whether I can bother you for some more information? Do you happen to still have guest records from back when my father did the tour? I'd like to try and track down the woman that he was with.

I appreciate any help you can give me in this regard,
Abby Brentnall

At home, the phone was ringing as I let myself in. Perhaps because he'd been so much on my mind during the trip home, when I answered it I said, 'Brad?'

There was silence and then the click of a hang-up.

Kicking myself for answering that way, I took my bag to my room, then, cursing my paranoia, double-checked the locks on my windows and the balcony doors.

Hamish didn't return my email for three very long days. His reply arrived as I was checking through the coming week's status pack with Sophie.

Hi Abby,

I hope you are well. Apologies for taking a few days to get back to you, but I've been over in Brisbane visiting my daughter.

As it happens, I do have the records from back then. I don't really want to disclose the details over email, but will be happy to share what I know over the phone. Call me any time.

Regards,
Hamish

As I read his reply, something stirred inside my stomach.

'Abby?' Sophie was asking. 'Are you okay?'

'Yes … yes, everything's fine.'

She looked concerned. 'Are you sure? You've been staring at that screen for minutes and haven't heard a word I've been saying.'

I considered lying, but went instead with a version of the truth. 'Actually, no … something's come through that I need to deal with immediately. Do you mind if we pick this up later?'

'That's fine. We're almost done here anyway. I'll make the changes you've mentioned and we can review that version this afternoon.'

I smiled my thanks, but the smile dropped as she left the office and I dialled the number Hamish had included in his email.

'Hey, this is Extremity, and this is Hamish. How can I help you?'

'Hamish, it's Abby Brentnall. Thanks so much for replying to my email.'

'That's okay. I thought I might be hearing from you again. You're lucky that I don't listen to my wife. When we moved into these offices a number of years ago, she was at me to destroy the old records, but as she says, I have problems throwing anything out. I think it's my Scottish heritage. My mother always said, "We Scots don't like to part with anything", and she kept her accent until the day she died. Anyway, I found the records from that trip.'

'What was her name?' I asked, not even pretending to make small talk.

'Kathleen Tindale. There's nothing else here about her really. She gave her address in Bali as a hotel in Kuta.' He chuckled. 'Well, that place is long gone. I remember some good times around its bar, although that was when I first came to the island. Was I ever that young and carefree? It seems like a lifetime ago.'

I laughed at that.

'I asked around a bit about her – not that I expected to learn anything. I figured that after that experience she would have left the island and never come back. But if she had stayed, someone would have known about it. The island is still pretty small when it comes to expats, especially in the tourist game. Apparently she was pretty distraught and hung around Kuta for a bit, at least until the search was called off. I think she must have left soon after that as no one remembers seeing her for a while. But I was chatting to a guy who used to work in that hotel in Kuta, and he reckons he heard that she was back and over on the other side of the island, maybe around Amlapura or Candidasa. Working in one of the beachside hotels apparently. Well, if it is beachside, that would rule out Amlapura.'

'Oh … why?'

'It's inland. A good base for visiting the volcano, Gunung Agung, and seeing Pura Besakih – our most important temple – but no beachside hotels.'

'So, once a tour guide always a tour guide?' I joked.

'I know, I can't help it. Seriously though, you should get over to that side of the island. It's like Bali was before all the tourists came. Except for Candidasa – you know their beach fell into the ocean in the eighties? They have it back again now, although it's taken a while. Anyway, if I were you I'd concentrate my efforts on the beaches around Candidasa and the coast road. I don't know how good my information is – she mightn't even still be there – but it's a start, right?'

'Do you know anyone I could email or call?' I asked.

'Nah. I wouldn't know where to tell you to start. The larger hotels all have internet, but some of the smaller family-run places and home-stays are off the main road and off the grid. You're probably going to have to search the old-fashioned way.'

'I might just do that. Thanks, Hamish.'

'Well, if you do, let me know if I can be of any help.'

Once we'd said our goodbyes, I stared at the pad I'd been jotting down notes on while Hamish talked. After Mum's revelations at the campaign launch, it seemed imperative that I find out what I could about what had happened to Dad between when he'd arrived in Bali, and when he'd died. It was becoming apparent that the only way to do that was to go back.

Before I could think too hard about it, I'd booked a ticket on a flight the following morning, and told Mark that I had an emergency of a personal nature that I needed to attend to immediately.

'How long are you going to need?' he asked.

'A week should do it,' I said, 'but I'll keep you posted.' Last time I'd checked, I had plenty of holiday leave owing.

'What sort of emergency did you say it was?'

'The personal sort.'

'I don't suppose I have a lot of choice, although I don't like you putting me over a barrel like this. Make sure you do a proper handover to Sophie, and let Clinton know how he can reach you.'

'Of course.' I had my fingers crossed behind my back.

Clinton phoned when he heard that I was going away again, demanding to know where and why. It was the first time I'd spoken with him one on one since the encounter with Andi. I avoided his questions, and Paula avoided those of his secretary. I assured him that all project tasks were currently on track and in safe hands with Sophie. He wanted to debate the point, but I invented another meeting I was late for.

Then I went home to pack.

CHAPTER EIGHTEEN

I'd checked into the same resort in Legian that I'd stayed at back in April; texted Hamish to let him know that I was in town in case he remembered anything else; and engaged the same driver from last time, Wayan, to assist me in my search. We'd left Legian at about eight this morning. It was now well past midday and, despite the air conditioning in the car, I was tiring.

Given that Wayan had spent a large proportion of our time in the car last trip answering Andi's questions about his family, and their family, and their family's family, I'd told him I was looking for a relative that my family had lost touch with many years ago. His face had taken on a concerned look similar to the one I'd seen on way too many faces over the last few months, and he'd vowed to help me find my … aunt. 'Family is everything,' he'd said.

Despite Hamish's advice to the contrary, I'd started my search in Amlapura and some of the surrounding touristy spots. As expected, we'd had no luck; no nibbles even.

Now, as keen as Wayan was to help me in my search, the tour guide in him was just as interested in trying to tempt me away from it.

'We can visit Tenganan, very authentic village,' he said. 'Real Bali people. The men were only allowed to marry girls from inside the village. If they married an outsider, they were no longer allowed to live here.'

'That's a little restrictive, isn't it?' I said.

'No, it's okay. Tenganan women are weavers so don't see the sun as much – they are very pretty.'

'Thanks, Wayan, but I'd prefer to keep focused on finding my aunt. Maybe another day.'

Not far up the road, he tried again. 'Tirta Gangga. The water palace. Very pretty place – the fountain has eleven tiers.'

It sounded impressive. If he were here, Brad would have said something like, 'Really, babe, why settle for nine tiers when you can have eleven?'

I just smiled and asked Wayan to keep driving. 'Maybe next time,' I said.

Back on the road towards Candidasa we stopped at each of the beachside hotels and resorts. Wayan waited while I ducked into reception to ask if they had an Australian woman aged in her fifties or sixties working there named Kathleen.

'No,' they all said.

'What does she look like?' some asked.

'I'm sorry, I don't know. She's a relative who left

Australia when I was very young,' I said. Liar liar, pants on fire.

At the last hotel the receptionist paused and then finally said, 'Australian?'

'Yes.'

'Sorry, no Australian lady like that.'

I figured it was a lost cause – for now. Besides I was hot … and hungry.

'Wayan, where can I get something to eat?' I asked.

'Somewhere near the beach?' he offered.

'As long as they have cold beers, I don't really care right now.'

'There's a nice place here, just outside the resort on the beach. Nice view, cheap Bintangs.'

'It sounds perfect,' I said.

A typical Balinese thatched roof housed a multi-coloured Balinese wooden fishing boat, some tables and a bar. It was the perfect place for a cooling beer and a wander on the beach. I stood for a few minutes on the concrete viewing platform at its side. Below me was a narrow strip of white-ish sand, with palm trees and turquoise sea on each side stretching for as far as I could see.

There were already a number of tourists seated and at various stages of eating, so after a very quick perusal of the menu I decided to play it safe with a serve of chicken satay sticks and a beer.

Whenever I ate satay sticks I was taken back to the

day after Dad had left. Brad and I had spent lunchtime in the library at school, scanning the shelves for anything about Bali or Indonesia. By the time lunch was over, we'd found some books and had been reading about things like gods and offerings, and sticks with pieces of spiced chicken and peanut sauce on top. They were called satays and we thought they sounded very exotic. That afternoon, we took some leftover roast chicken from Mrs Ingram's fridge, chopped it up and threaded it onto the skewer that Mrs Ingram used to check whether cakes were cooked. Then we spread peanut butter on top of it. It didn't taste of anything very special, and certainly wasn't exotic and spicy like the book had described. Brad said that was probably because we needed things that only grew in the jungle to make it taste like it did in the books. That memory of my first experiment with Brad in Mrs Ingram's kitchen never failed to make me smile. These days I knew the secret to a great-tasting spicy satay stick, and had even had a go at making some in the cooking class with Andi back in April. Maybe when Brad came back we could try it together. If Brad came back … best not to think about that.

Surprisingly, the waitress wasn't the usual shy Balinese girl, but rather a weathered, woman of somewhere between forty and sixty. Dressed in a purple singlet and a faded, long olive-coloured cotton skirt, she had bare feet, leather thongs around her wrists and ankles, loose silvery hair untouched by a hairdresser, and a wide, welcoming grin.

'What can I get you?' she asked, with a broad American accent.

I looked up from the menu and smiled back at her. 'I'll have a serve of the chicken satay, please, and a Bintang. You'd better make it a small Bintang, even though I know I'll probably have two.'

She laughed. 'I'll keep the second one cold for you then.'

I settled back in my chair, enjoying the breeze wafting through the pavilion, and listening to the chatter of the other tourists and the soothing sound of the waves as they lapped gently against the shore. The day hadn't been a complete wash-out. I hadn't located Kathleen yet, but this was a gorgeous place to relax in. I'd have some lunch and then head back to Legian, where I could plan my next move from a pool lounge. Depending on the traffic, I should be back in the pool for happy hour.

My waitress was soon back with my beer. 'Are you staying in Candidasa?' she asked.

'No, over at Legian Beach, but I'm exploring this side of the island today. It's beautiful. If I wanted to escape from the real world, this would be where I think I could do it.'

I didn't know why I'd added that last comment – I'd never thought about dropping out before – but the way things were in the office at the moment, it was something I could easily be tempted to do.

'It's lovely here,' she agreed.

'How long have you been here?' I asked.

'It would be nearly thirty years now. My partner and I came out here – oh, it would be sometime in the mid to late eighties. Sometimes it seems like yesterday, but we'd never go back to the hustle and bustle of the real world now.'

'That's nice – to be so sure of where you should be.'

She smiled, and looked around. No one was requiring any assistance, so she settled in for a chat.

'Both of us felt it the minute we landed all those years ago. And then when we found ourselves here … we haven't looked back. There's a lot of others who feel the same way – they landed here for a surf and forgot to go home.'

If she'd been out here for that long, she may have known Kathleen.

'I'm actually here for another reason,' I said. 'I'm looking for a relative that my family's lost touch with … her name is Kathleen Tindale. I don't suppose you've heard of her?'

She thought for a minute or so. 'The name sounds familiar. How did you say you were related?'

I decided to trust her with the truth. 'We're not, not really. My father died in an accident here many years ago, and Kathleen was one of the last people to know him.'

She nodded slowly. 'I see. Well, I don't think I can help you. The name rings a bell, but she's probably long gone by now. Anyway, it's been lovely to chat, but it looks as if your meal is ready. How about I fetch you a fresh beer?'

Some more tourists entered the bar as she returned with my beer, and she was too busy to spend any more time with me. The satays were good. Once I'd given them the respect they deserved, I called for my bill, and left a pile of rupiah on the table. My waitress looked over and waved goodbye.

Back in the car, I leant my head against the window.

On the main highway we passed an area where the rice paddies met the sea, and I saw fishing boats pulled up onto the sand. Three Harley-Davidson motorbikes passed us, the middle rider standing in his seat as they roared past. The other two raised their fists in salute. It was a celebration of the freedom of the road, freedom from rules, and fearlessness. I laughed and Wayan tut-tutted.

At the resort, I changed into my bikini, grabbed a sarong, a notepad and my phone, and headed to the bar overlooking the beach. As I sipped my cocktail and marvelled at the colours of the sunset, I heard Brad's voice again, urging me to slow down and organise my thoughts. It was what he used to say when I had a work problem that seemed too big. 'Break it down, Ab. Work out what you know for sure, and how you know what you know. That will let you see where the question marks are and what you still need to ask.'

Picturing his face in my head, I jotted down answers to the first point – what I knew for sure:

- Mum and Dad had an argument and Dad went to Bali (confirmed by me).
- Dad resigned from his job before he left (confirmed by Mike Robards).
- Dad died in an accident while on a tour (confirmed by the coroner, the newspapers and everything else).
- Dad was with another woman at the time of the accident (confirmed by Hamish Munroe).
- His companion's name was Kathleen Tindale (confirmed by Hamish Munroe).
- Dad left with his secretary who he'd been having an affair with; she was young, brunette and obvious (Mum told me this).
- Dad had no intention of coming back (Mum told me this too).

I imagined talking Brad through my list. He'd nod and say, 'Okay, but you only have your mother's word on those last two points – they haven't been confirmed. She lied about the business trip – Mike Robards told you that – so let's not assume that she's telling the truth about the rest.'

I didn't need Brad's voice in my ear to list everything

I still had questions about:

Was Kathleen Tindale the woman Dad left Australia with?

If she wasn't, maybe the woman he went to Bali with didn't last and he met Kathleen here on the island after he arrived? Could he have fallen in love with her that fast? (Possibly – I did with Brad. I just wasn't brave enough to hang on to him.)

I only had Mum's word that the woman Dad left with was young, brunette and well-endowed.

I tapped out a text to Hamish: *Hi, it's Abby. I don't suppose you can tell me what Kathleen looked like?*

His reply came through quickly: *I can do better than that. I went through the boxes and found some photos. They're faded and a bit blurry, but you're welcome to come up and go through them. There's one of your father you might like to have.*

My hand came to my chest, as if I could hold the breath that felt as though it was trapped there.

I'll see you tomorrow, I texted back.

CHAPTER NINETEEN

Hamish led me into a room behind the reception counter. It was obviously used as an office: packing boxes took up a large portion of one wall, while photos of adventures undertaken wallpapered the remaining walls.

'I remember them well,' he said as he rummaged through a box labelled *1985–1990*. 'Well, I guess you do when something like that happens. They seemed so happy and in love … eyes just for each other. Like you do, I guess.' He realised what he'd said. 'Sorry … I did that last time too, didn't I?'

'That's okay. Do you remember if my dad said anything about their plans?'

'Their plans? No, I don't remember any discussion like that. I was guiding as well as owning the joint back then – although my guiding days are long gone now. You mightn't think so now, being all fit and loose, but one day your knees seize up and all of a sudden you're making noises like an old person. You're tall, like me, and we tall people have further to bend … Aaah, here they are,' he said, emerging from the box with a pile of photos. 'The one of your father is on the top, but there are others in here from that trip – the dates are on the back. You might find him in the background of some of them.'

He indicated a bench and a chair. 'Take your time, and call me if you need me.'

I smiled my thanks and looked at the top photo the second his back was turned. There he was. My dad. Exactly as I remembered him, although, as the colour had faded from the old photo, perhaps a little pinker. Dressed in a pair of white shorts, a sky blue T-shirt and with my smile, he was standing in front of the river that would, just a couple of hours later, take his life.

I put the photo to one side, and began to go through the others, sorting them into date order until I had all that corresponded to that tour.

My cell phone alerted me to a text. Clinton. Again. He'd texted me a number of times since I'd been away and, as all of them had been inappropriate, I'd ignored them. This one was work-related: *Major issue with project. Please phone me ASAP.*

I sighed heavily, put the photos to one side and texted Sophie: *Clinton says major issue with project. What's going on?*

I continued with the photos. I found another few with Dad in the background and added them to my pile. In one of them, he was helping a tanned, curly-haired blonde girl into a life jacket. Although they weren't the centre of the photo, I was sure this was her – Kathleen. It was something about the way he looked at her. The same girl appeared in a few other photos, but there were no more of her with Dad. She wasn't brunette, and she wasn't buxom. Thanks, Mum.

Sophie's reply came through: *I've called Clinton – there's no issue. All under control.*

I tapped out a response: *Thx.*

Hamish ducked his head around the door. 'All going okay in here?'

'Yeah, all good, thanks. Hey,' I picked up a photo of the blonde girl, 'is this Kathleen?'

He studied the faded photo, the crinkles around his eyes taking him back nearly twenty-five years. 'Yes,' he finally said. 'She was gorgeous – that long-legged variety of surfer girl that the Californians do so well.'

'She was American?'

'Sure. Didn't I mention that?'

I shook my head. 'No, you didn't. Do you mind if I take these as well?'

'Be my guest.'

I looked closer at the photo. Could it be? Yes, it was my waitress from yesterday. I was sure of it.

Before I could change my mind, I sent off a quick email to work advising them that I'd be away for another couple of days.

As I was re-booking my flights a text came through

from Mark: *Abby, project is at risk. Clinton keen to know when you're back to fix. Whatever this personal issue is had better be important. If you're unable to cope with it, call him and let him know where you are and he can take over what needs to be done.*

I replied: *Mark, all deliverables are on target, no dates have slipped or are at risk of slipping. Will be back in office next Wednesday and will deal with Clinton then. Sophie has it all under control.*

For fuck's sake, I was on partner track. I shouldn't even have been micro-managing this project to the extent that I was. For the first time in my career I was feeling like I didn't really care much whether this client stayed or left. For that matter, the elusive partnership no longer seemed to matter either. Attaining partner wouldn't make Brad love me enough to stay, so why had I been so hell-bent on sacrificing our relationship for the sake of my job?

It was as if the sheer rage I'd felt towards Clinton that day in Bourke Street had cleared my mind of everything that was no longer important. I felt the urge to fight for something again, and it wasn't my job. I hadn't really wanted to go into battle for years and I kind of liked the feeling. I was tired of compromising my sense of what was right in favour of what was just plain unreasonable and bordering on harassment and bullying.

In fact, it was no longer bordering on harassment

– things had gone way past that. Despite what had been happening with Clinton and work, despite the crusade I was now on to find some truth behind my father's death, what I was feeling tasted like, looked like and smelt suspiciously like … freedom. Just like the bikers I'd seen on the highway yesterday.

Early the next morning I checked out of the resort, and greeted Wayan, who was driving me over to Candidasa. I'd booked into an ocean-front villa at a resort adjacent to the bar I'd visited yesterday.

After spending what was left of the day between the pool and the white-sand beach, I dressed simply in a lilac spaghetti-strap cotton dress, flip-flops and my leather ankle bracelets, and walked across to the bar.

The waitress from yesterday wasn't around. Instead I ordered the happy hour two-for-one beer special from a smiling Balinese girl, negotiating for my second to be poured after the first had been drunk. Then I settled back to watch the sunset. That was the thing about Bali – there was always a bar, a beach and a sunset, or so it seemed.

I wondered if that had been the attraction for my father all those years ago, or if it was just the siren call of young flesh with no strings attached that caused him to run away from Mum and me, and, of course, Zoe. I doubted that I'd ever know the answer to that, but if I could just speak to someone who'd known him as he was before he died, I might go a little way to understanding. Surely Kathleen, wherever she was, would remember a young, good-looking, carefree Australian man on the run from a wife he no longer had anything in common with and one and three-quarter children he would never see again?

When the waitress came back I ordered the nasi campur, a mixed rice dish. I'd taken to ordering it a lot, and even though it consisted of rice, a curry or satay stick, egg in some form, vegetables, peanuts, fried shrimp and whatever else, no two restaurants prepared it the same way. Eaten with a variety of sambals, it was never boring.

'Is the lady from yesterday working tonight?' I asked the waitress.

'Kate? No, not tonight. She has a holiday. Mr T,' she indicated a tall, baseball-capped man behind the bar, 'lets her stay home.'

'Is he the owner?'

'Yes.'

'Okay, thank you.'

'You're welcome,' she said in her singsong English.

Kate/ Kathleen … I took the picture of Kathleen and my father out of my wallet. I was convinced this Kate and Dad's Kathleen were the same person. She mightn't be here tonight, but I was staying in the villa for the next couple of days. At this rate I'd be able to work my way through the menu, which would be no great hardship if all the food was as good as the nasi campur I was eating.

I finished my meal, and my second beer, and moved to the bar to pay my bill. The bartender looked up from behind the counter and I received the biggest shock of my life.

When people said things like that, I was always heavily sceptical. How could they know it was the biggest shock of their life? Relative to what? More of a shock than watching a huge spider crawl across your car windscreen and realising it's on the inside of the glass? More than finding out that your boyfriend's slept with your model sister? More even than receiving an accidental and unexpected proposal from the man you've loved your whole life?

Often the biggest shock in people's lives was really just a small surprise. Something like, "I was thinking about you and then the phone rang – it was the biggest shock", or "Why'd you grab me from behind like that? You gave me the biggest shock". Or even the shock of seeing a photo of the man you love, and should never have let go to the other side of the world, with his arm around someone called Agnetha or Annafrid.

This shock was bigger than all of those things.

The man in the cap who was staring back at me was the spitting image of a younger Grandpa Brentnall. No, I'd go further. The man who was staring back at me was the spitting image of my father. Or rather how my father would have looked if he hadn't been … well, dead. Given that he was dead, I could only assume that my eyes were playing tricks on me … weren't they?

The man who couldn't possibly be my father didn't appear as shocked to see me as I was to see him, although his face was pale and his hands shook as he processed my bill.

'I hope you enjoyed your meal,' he said.

'It was lovely,' I managed. 'It's the best nasi campur I've had this trip.'

'I'm glad. I'll let the chef know.'

He counted out my change and turned away. It was all perfectly normal. A normal conversation. Nothing more to see here. I could walk out of here, go back to my room and begin to breathe again.

'Wait,' I called.

He didn't turn to face me.

'Is Kate your partner?' I asked.

'Yes,' he said.

'She's not working tonight.'

'No. We were expecting a quiet night.'

'I was in here yesterday.'

'I know.' He still hadn't turned around.

'I was looking for someone,' I persisted. 'Someone I thought she might know.'

'She told me.' He finally turned back to me. In the twilight he looked even more like the photo of Grandpa Brentnall at nearly sixty. He looked even more like I thought my father would look if he hadn't been killed in an accident when I was nine. I didn't want to consider the possibility that was now edging its way around my brain and towards my mouth.

'Do you think she might know that person? Is that why she isn't here tonight?' I asked.

'Yes.'

I waited. He took his cap off and rubbed his hand through the short, spiky grey hairs on his weathered head. It looked as if he'd taken the easy way out and attacked what was left of his hair with a number one clipper.

'Kate knew it was you. She said she thought you looked like a picture of my mother at your age,' he finally said.

'How do you know what my age is?'

'You were thirty-four in April, weren't you, Abby? It is Abby, isn't it?'

'Yes, my name is Abby, and yes, I just turned thirty-four.'

I was starting to shake uncontrollably and the terrible thought that had edged its way around my brain had put down roots and wouldn't let go.

'You know, don't you,' he said. His eyes didn't leave mine. They were my eyes.

'I think so.'

'I need to hear you say it.'

'You're my father, aren't you? You didn't really die

in the accident?'

'Yes, Abby, I'm your father, and no, I didn't really die.'

The blackness came at me then. It started at the back of my head and took the light away. I collapsed into the closest seat. The shaking didn't stop. I put my head between my knees and tried to breathe, taking in air in great gulps until the dark behind my eyes began to drift away. I still didn't want to sit up, and I absolutely didn't want to open my eyes, but I knew I couldn't keep them screwed shut forever.

The man who said he was my father brought me a glass of water. 'Drink this,' he said.

I did as I was told.

'Now this.'

This time the glass contained a clear spirit. I drained it in one gulp, relishing the burn as it hit the back of my throat, proving that I was really awake, this wasn't a weird dream, it was really happening – but still not able to look at him.

Neither of us said anything for a little while.

Then he spoke. 'So what do we do now?'

I had no idea what the normal protocol was for when you met your dead father in a bar in Bali.

'You talk,' I managed.

'Kate knew it was you,' he said. 'We've collected photos from the Australian newspapers over the years, although you haven't been in them for a while.'

'No, Peter and I have different political allegiances.'

'I can imagine that,' he said, his mouth curving just a little at the ends. 'I knew that if you were the Abby you were at nine, you'd be back here.'

'Is that why Kate isn't in tonight?'

'Yes … hang on, let me sort this couple out for a drink.'

He busied himself getting beers for the couple who had just walked in, and had a word with the waitress, before walking back to me with another couple of Bintangs.

As I watched him, the numbness I'd felt began to be replaced by something else. My memory of my father was of a tall, lanky man. The type of man who kept active – running, walking, swimming, surfing when he could. He'd taught me to ride a bike, he'd taught me how to not run like a girl, he'd read me stories that had made-up endings. He used to read the book and then say, 'Abracadabra, this ending just doesn't work for me. Let's make our own adventure.' So we did.

Mum caught him once and he got in trouble. 'Roger, how is she supposed to learn to read properly when you can't follow the book?' After that, we never let Mum catch us again. I preferred the made-up endings – they were always more fun. Our heroines never simpered; they could look after themselves, and were capable of doing anything they wanted to.

Mum thought that was setting me up for

disillusionment, as our made-up stories had nothing to do with the real world. 'Boys don't like girls who don't need them, Abigail,' she'd told me.

When Dad died and Zoe was born, there was no more time for stories.

Now, as I watched him come towards me, it all came back – the stories, the adventures, and the promises. How could he do that? I got that he and Mum weren't working, but how could he leave me like that? And Zoe? Although knowing her as I did, I didn't blame him too much for that one. But why didn't he come back for me?

'Why were you looking for Kate?' he asked. 'Were you looking for me?' He plonked down the Bintangs and sat at the table beside me.

'No. You died, remember.' I spat the words out, still unable to look at him.

'So I did.'

I had a sick feeling in my mouth, so took a swallow of beer. It didn't remove the taste. I could feel him watching me, but kept my gaze on the table.

'I wanted to know what happened to you, how you died,' I finally said.

'You didn't know?'

There was something in his tone that made me raise my eyes to his. They were filled with tears. I looked away from him again, in order to keep my anger where it should be.

'No. Mum never talked about it. She told everyone that you were here on a work conference. There always seemed to be something she wasn't telling me, though. I think I'd always wondered, but then I booked a trip to Bali and just knew that now was the right time.

'I did some research, spoke to a few people, and found out that you'd done the tour with a woman, not with the company as Mum had always said. Mum told me she'd said that to protect me. She said that you'd left us and didn't intend to come back. I couldn't believe that, so I came back to find out. Then I spoke to a few more people and found out the woman's name was Kathleen and the last anyone knew was that she was over near Candidasa. Someone else said they thought she was working in a bar. I figured that there couldn't be that many middle-aged white women around Candidasa working in a bar, so I thought I'd come for a look. It threw me a little because I thought I was looking for a booby, brunette Australian woman.'

'Why would you think that?'

'Because Mum said you'd run off with your secretary.'

'Your mother said what?'

I shrugged. 'She only told me last month when she knew that I'd been here on a holiday. I told her that I wanted to find out what made you come here on your own and leave us behind.' I laughed a little ruefully. 'I don't know what I was expecting, but it certainly wasn't this. You weren't supposed to be alive. I thought that I'd talk to Kate and she might be able to tell me about you. Mum wouldn't even talk about you after ... well, after you died. I just wanted to know ... I don't know what I wanted to know ... maybe just that what Mum had said was a lie. I couldn't believe that you'd go and never come back without saying goodbye, not to me. But that's exactly what you did. She was right – you left me.'

I met his eyes, and he looked away first.

'Your mother and I didn't part on very good terms,' he said softly.

'You see, I didn't know that either. Not then. Besides, none of that was my problem. You weren't just walking away from her – you were leaving me behind.' I could hear my voice getting louder and struggled to control it. 'That wasn't fair.'

'I think it was hard for her, Abby. She was pregnant, and I needed space to ... to sort things through. She was always very concerned about how things looked. When I ... well, when I didn't come back, I guess she didn't need to let anyone know anything different.'

I wanted to ask him why he'd done it, why he'd left me when he could have just left her, but all of a sudden, it was all too much for me.

I stood up. 'Umm, I don't even know what I should be calling you ...'

'Roger?'

'You didn't change your name?'

'I'm known as Roger Tindale. I took Kate's name.'

'Okay, Roger … I have a lot more I need to say to you, and many more questions to ask, but I … it's too much. Right now, it's just too much. I have no idea what to … I have no idea.' I could feel my eyes filling and that absolutely was not allowed. Not now. I turned my head and blinked a few times until I was sure that all traces of moisture had gone. 'If I leave here tonight, will you still be here tomorrow?' I paused for a second. 'I mean, you're not likely to run off and not die again? Are you?'

We looked at each other without speaking for a bit.

Then he said, 'No, Ab … I'm not going anywhere. I … I guess you're handling this better than I deserve. I had a little warning at least – I knew I was supposed to be dead, and I knew you were likely to come back here – but you had nothing to warn you about me.'

'You think I'm handling it well?' I shook my head. 'Don't be deceived by appearances. I'm far from okay with this. I'm so far from being okay. I've just learnt how to fake it over the years of being a corporate warrior.'

'You? No! Please tell me it isn't so! Not my fearless, adventurous Abracadabra!'

I realised it was his attempt at a joke, but just now it was more than I could bear.

'It's not like you were around to talk me out of it,' I said.

'I know. If it means anything, there's not a day that's gone by in the last twenty-five years that I haven't thought of you.'

My eyes filled again. This time I couldn't hide it. Roger grabbed at my hand.

I shook my head. 'Not yet.'

He dropped my hand and nodded. 'It's okay – I get that this is weird.' He paused. 'How long are you here for?'

'I fly home Monday night.'

'That gives me a few days.'

'What for?'

'To try to explain … and to get to know you. I want to get to know you. I want to know the woman you've grown into. I want to explain. What happens after that … what you do with the information after that – well, I guess that's up to you.'

I rubbed at my eyes, keeping my palms over them as he talked.

'Lunch tomorrow with Kate and me?' he asked.

I nodded. It was all that I was capable of.

Somehow I made it back inside my hotel room. My legs were shaking; in fact, all of me was shaking. Even the room was shaking.

They said that in an earthquake you should find a door jamb to sit under, but everything was still rumbling down there on the floor. I leant against the door in a little heap until the room stopped moving. Even then my hands were still trembling, so I sat on them until I couldn't feel them any more.

Finally I staggered to my feet. My feet and hands had gone to sleep so I hobbled across to where I'd left my phone. Then I rang Brad, or rather I rang his answering machine. In the past I hadn't left a message. Tonight I did.

'Hi, Brad. Umm, I know I shouldn't be ringing you, but, umm, something so weird is happening, and I know I can't tell you on this message, but I wish I could. You're the only person who'd understand, the only person I could talk to about what's going on –'

End of message.

I rang back.

'I had everything under control, as it should be, and now nothing is as it should be. You've gone, and everything's fallen apart. I've made a stupid mistake, my job's unbearable, and now … I wish I could tell you what's happened now, but I can't – there's no way you'd believe me even if I could tell you. And I miss you more than I can say –'

End of message.

I dialled again. 'I know I've never told you before, and I should have, but …' I took a deep breath before saying, 'I need you. I really need you.'

This time when the message cut off, I didn't ring back. I already wished I could erase the messages.

I needed someone to invent something to do that – an application that allowed you to erase messages that you'd accidentally left on someone else's voicemail. It would certainly solve the dialling-under-the-influence problem that existed in society today. You could take it one step further and erase texts too, for those occasions when you'd got your drunk text on or had been playing away from home. Not that I'd done either of those things recently, but the principle was the same as the issue I was facing now with Brad's voicemail.

I thought about calling Andi or Todd, but the hugeness of what I'd have to tell them was too much. How could I explain it to someone else? How could I even begin to talk about what had just happened? Who would believe it? I wasn't even sure that I believed it.

So I curled up into a ball and lay there dry-eyed in the dark.

CHAPTER TWENTY

The next morning when Kate came to pick me up, I was waiting in the lobby. She seemed to be more worried about meeting me than I was about meeting her. After all, she'd known that my father was alive for all these years. I, on the other hand, had thought he was dead for that long.

She greeted me with some hesitation. 'I don't know what should happen in these circumstances.'

'You mean how do you greet the daughter of your very much alive partner who's supposed to be dead?' I sounded as bitter as I felt.

She shrugged and smiled. 'Yes, something like that. It must be tough, Abby.'

I swallowed and nodded. 'It is.'

'How about you and I get going?' she suggested. 'We can talk more at the house.'

I nodded again, accepted the helmet she offered me, and climbed onto the motorbike behind her.

We took the main road out of Candidasa and drove for a few more kilometres before turning down a dirt track beside a small village. At the end of the dirt track was a beach with palm trees and white sand and gentle waves lapping the shore. The type of beach that any man who'd previously died would never want to leave in his Balinese after-life.

Kate parked the bike in front of a stilted timber house. The bottom floor was loosely walled by bamboo screens, while the top floor appeared to be a sleeping platform. I imagined the cooling breezes would waft through those open windows in the evening. A shower was hanging from a tree out the back, and a dog displaying the characteristics of a number of different breeds wandered out to inspect me. Kate lightly rumpled his head and led me to the main part of the house … and my father.

Roger moved towards me and held his hand out to shake mine. I ignored it and kissed him lightly on the cheek. How else were you supposed to greet your dead father? His smile was grateful.

Inside the house, the space had been loosely divided into a basic kitchen and food preparation area with a few seats scattered around the bench, and a lounge area. In the kitchen, raw spices and vegetables were arranged around a chopping board. There were no appliances in sight; just a bamboo grater and the largest stone spice grinder I'd ever seen. Brad had a smaller version on his kitchen counter. Every so often he'd fill it with garlic or chilli or something and tell me to pound away. He had a way of knowing when I needed to take out my frustrations on some innocent spices.

Roger arranged cold drinks for the three of us, and Kate started chopping shallots and chillis.

She indicated one of the seats near the bench. 'Why don't you sit down? We can get to know each other while I chop. Roger was out early this morning catching fish for our lunch,' she explained. 'We'll pop it on the barbecue and serve it with this salad and some steamed rice.'

'It's smelling wonderful. Can I help with anything?'

'Sure.' She passed me the grater, a bowl and a roughly chopped coconut. 'This needs to be grated, and I have enough dicing to go around.'

Roger smiled at us and headed outside to prepare the fire for the fish. Kate and I chatted lightly while we chopped and grated.

'So does this salad have a name?' I asked, keen to talk about anything other than what we all needed to talk about.

'Yes – sayur urab. Essentially it's a mixed vegetable salad. I'll throw in some beans and that coconut you're grating, mix through some garlic, chilli, shallot and shrimp paste. Smell this.' She passed over something truly foul-smelling.

'We're eating this? It smells bad.'

'The beauty of shrimp paste is that you never really know whether it's off.' She grinned. 'Trust me,

Abby, it adds something truly Balinese to the mix – the dish won't be the same without it. Then we'll mix up some lime juice and coconut oil as a dressing.'

She watched me as I clumsily grated the coconut. 'You're not a cook?'

'It shows? No, I'm more of an eat-out girl. I've tried to enjoy cooking, but Brad was always so much better at it than me.'

'Brad? Is he your boyfriend, partner? I assume you're not married – I noticed there's no ring.'

'No, I'm not married. And Brad – well, there's no Brad now either. There was, for years … there's not now.' I shrugged.

Why was I telling this woman I didn't know anything about my life? The alternative was talking about my dead father, so this somehow seemed more appropriate.

'What happened?' she asked.

'He went to Denmark – or Poland or Austria or somewhere – to look at watering systems or gardens … or something. He likes dirt and plants.' I paused from grating. 'Perhaps if I'd taken more notice he wouldn't have gone.'

'Would you have wanted him to stay?'

I thought for a minute, then shook my head. 'No, it was too good an opportunity for him. He wanted me to go with him, but we'd booked to come here and … I know this sounds silly, but I felt that I really needed to find out about … you know … find out about my father. Not that I expected this.' I continued grating as I talked. The bowl was filling up. 'He sort of asked me to marry him, but there's no way I could commit to anyone. Not then, not now … not without knowing what happened, and not without knowing if I was likely to do the same thing my father did – run off or something. Even without knowing about what my father did, I've always thought that someday I would just snap and leave. And that wouldn't be fair to him. And even if I didn't snap and run off, I didn't want to love him so much that I couldn't do that – if I wanted to, you know.'

I didn't think I was making any sense, but she was nodding as if I was. 'Did you tell him that?'

'No. I just said "no". If I ever was going to get married, I wanted the proposal to be special, and it wasn't. So I got a little irrational and said a few things that I probably shouldn't have said. Is this enough coconut?'

She accepted my change of subject. 'It's definitely enough coconut. Lucky they grow on trees around here.'

She laughed and I joined her.

Roger had grilled the fish to perfection, brushing it with lime, garlic and chilli, and dolloping a spicy shallot and ginger-based sambal on top. Served with the salad, the perfectly grated coconut (if I did say so myself), steamed rice and more beers, lunch was delicious.

By unspoken agreement, conversation was limited to general chit-chat. It wasn't until Kate cleared the plates away that Roger raised the subject we'd been avoiding.

'I guess you want to know why I did what I did?'

Part of me didn't want to hear the answer, but I knew that I needed to. I nodded. That awful shaking was starting again. I placed my beer back on the table and sat on my hands.

'When I left Sydney, I had every intention of coming back. Your mother and I … I know it sounds like a cliché, but I needed space.'

Kate returned with a bowl filled with rambutans and mangosteens. Good – things that needed peeling; something to do with my hands.

'Don't you think you should tell Abby the real reason that you left?' she asked.

Roger looked at her for a couple of seconds before replying. 'I'm not sure that's my story to tell.'

'Rog, she's come all this way – she needs to know the whole story. It's up to Abby what she does with that.'

'Has your mother said anything about it?' he asked me.

'She didn't even tell me that you'd left us until I confronted her after I was here in April. Then she said that you'd had an affair with your secretary and she hadn't wanted to tell me because I'd idolised your memory all my life.'

He smiled at that. 'Did you really? Idolise me?'

'Of course I did. It's what happens when the father you adore dies when you're a kid.'

'Rog …' Kate was keen to bring us back on track. 'Tell her what really happened.'

'Yes, Roger, tell me what really happened.' I took a mangosteen from the bowl and clumsily began peeling it.

'I didn't have an affair, Ab. It was your mother who had the affair.'

I stared at him in disbelief. Mum's world was always about doing the right thing, living in the right suburb, Dad having the right sort of job, me going to the right school and the right university and behaving like a girl should behave. There was no way she would have had an affair. To even suggest it was ludicrous.

'I don't believe that. Mum would never have cheated – she was always too straitlaced.'

Roger and Kate exchanged looks.

It was Kate who said it. 'Abby, before he left, your mother told Roger that the baby she was carrying wasn't his.'

Zoe … not Dad's? I stopped eating mid-bite. 'No …' I shook my head. 'No. Dad, say it isn't true.'

Dad? Where did that come from?

'I'm sorry, Abby. It's true. Your mum and I … well, things hadn't been good for a long time. We probably should never have got married. It was just that …'

'Just that she fell pregnant with me and you had no choice?' I completed the sentence.

He paused.

'It's okay – I figured that part out myself,' I said.

'Well, yes. We got married because we had to – that's what you did back then.' He shrugged. 'But we had you, and that was great.' He smiled at me. 'Your mother though … she was never satisfied. She felt that she'd given up so much – she'd been studying law, you know.'

I didn't know. 'She never spoke about her ambitions. I always assumed that she wanted to get married and have a family.'

'I think that came after. She wanted someone a little more respectable than I was. Sure, I was doing well at work, but I was in advertising and that wasn't what she wanted. I was away too often, I had a lot of client functions – I couldn't give her the attention she wanted. And I didn't have the same ambitions that she did. I wanted to see more of the world – I wanted that for you, for us. She wanted the income, the good private school and a respectable career. There was nothing wrong with that, with what she wanted – it was just different to what I wanted. We had different priorities.'

'Well, she certainly got all that with Peter,' I said.

Kate and Roger exchanged looks. I decided to let that go uncommented on … for now.

'Yes, we saw the wedding in the Australian papers – we've been able to keep up with events from here,' said Kate.

'Did you two ever get married?' I asked.

'No.' Kate looked with fondness at Roger. 'Your father is already married … to your mother.'

I raised my eyebrows at that. 'Seriously?'

'I know,' she said. 'It sounds a little strange, but we're fine as we are.'

He reached over and rubbed her shoulder with affection.

'Hang on … who is Zoe's father?' I asked.

'I'm not sure that's my story to tell,' he said. 'In any case, your mother was disappointed with me. Things hadn't worked out the way that she wanted.'

'I certainly hadn't worked out the way she wanted,' I said, and turned to Kate. 'Mum was always disappointed that I didn't grow into my name. Abigail was supposed to be a princess – you know, like the Abigail in the soap opera she loved, all curves and hair and pouts and boobs. You probably didn't see it in America.'

Roger chimed in. 'And Abby as a little girl was fearless, a real tomboy. Her best friend was the boy down the road, a kid named Brad Ingram. The pair of them were inseparable. Did you ever hear from him after you guys moved?'

I shot a look at Kate. She smiled; she was quick on the uptake.

'Am I missing something?' he asked.

'Later.' I took another swallow of beer.

'Your mother wasn't happy, and bit by bit she withdrew from me. We didn't really … well, we didn't have much of a relationship after that.'

'Is this getting into too-much-information territory?' I asked. No kid wanted to know about their parents' sex life.

'Perhaps. Then all of a sudden she was interested. At the time I thought she might have been trying to start again, make a go of our relationship, but it was just the once and afterwards she withdrew again. It was as if she'd retreated into herself. We barely spoke. She announced she was pregnant soon after that, and was completely absorbed in the baby. Neither you nor I existed for her; it was all about the pregnancy.'

I nodded. 'I often heard her say that Zoe was a miracle of love. I just assumed it was because she was born immediately after we found out you'd died. I thought it was your memory that made her so special.'

He smiled ruefully at that. 'It wasn't love for me she was talking about. Zoe's father was the love of her love. He always had been. It was only when I found out that she was further along in the pregnancy than she'd told me she was, that I put two and two together and realised the baby couldn't be mine. So I confronted her, she admitted it, and I left for Bali. It was only going to be for a week or so, just to decide what to do. I was coming back for when the baby was born – I owed your mother that much. After that I had no plans. Not then.'

'But you quit your job? Why did you do that if you were intending on coming back?'

'I wasn't acting rationally. Your mother had never liked what I did for a living, and part of me thought that if I wasn't in advertising, but something that she thought was more respectable, she wouldn't have needed to find someone else. I know, it doesn't make any sense at all. Then, on my first day in Kuta, I met Kate and everything changed.' He smiled at her. 'We fell in love immediately. It was like a bolt from the blue, and I just knew it was the real thing. I decided to go back to Sydney, separate formally from your mother, and Kate and I could be together. I was going to make arrangements about having you with me.

'Then the accident happened. I got washed down the river and separated from everyone else. Things were a lot more remote back then. I wandered a while, and a local family found me, took me in and patched me up. I'd been whacked on the head pretty badly and had no idea who I was. I stayed there until everything came back. It was months before I made it back to where Kate had been staying at the time of the accident, and more months before I found her again. She'd stayed on the island. I was apparently dead to the rest of the world – you should have seen her face when I turned up on her doorstep. That's when I realised I didn't need to go back, not if I didn't want to. I could have another life out here. I didn't think any further than that.'

'But what about me?' I asked. Tears were rolling down my face and I made no effort to wipe them away. The tears felt old, as if they'd been sitting in the back of my eyes for more than twenty years. Perhaps they had.

He leaned forward and took my hands. 'You were my only regret, Abby. My abracadabra. My magical girl.' His eyes were also full of tears. 'I've missed you every day of my life.'

'And I've missed you too. But I … I can't pretend to understand … and I can't pretend to forgive you. I can't. It broke my heart and … all the adventures we were going to have … How could you do that?' I pulled my hands away.

'I didn't think about it, not at the time. And when I did think about it … well, it was all too late. I couldn't come back from it. By then … well, I'd read about your mother. If I came back then it would have ruined everything for her, and would have thrown your life into even more disarray. I was better off staying away. There was the life insurance she'd already claimed … and there was Peter.'

I looked between Roger and Kate for clarity. 'I get what you're saying, but the dates don't add up. Mum and Peter didn't get married for a few years after you … well, after you went away.'

He seemed surprised. 'But I read about the inquest.'

'How Peter represented your mother at that,' added Kate. 'To come back then would have ruined everything for her again.'

'I figured that was what you meant, but …' A light went on in my head. 'Oh my God. Are you saying that Mum and Peter knew each other before then?'

Roger nodded.

'There's more, isn't there?'

He glanced across at Kate and nodded again.

The light bulb glowed brighter. 'Is Peter Zoe's father?'

CHAPTER TWENTY-ONE

'Is he?' I asked again. 'Is Peter Zoe's father?'

Roger looked at the table and nodded. 'Tessa knew Peter at university.'

'Theresa,' I corrected. 'She prefers Theresa these days.'

He sighed. 'Of course she would. Theresa knew Peter at university. They had a brief thing – it didn't mean anything to him, but Tess … your mother … fell in love with him.'

'So how come you two …?' A dreadful thought occurred to me. 'Please don't tell me –'

'No, Abby, you're definitely my daughter.'

'Thank God for that!'

Roger and Kate both laughed.

'Your mother and I met at the university bar one night,' he said. 'I'd noticed her for a while, but she'd never paid me any attention at all until that night. Of course, looking back, I think I was a rebound from Peter, but at the time I was thrilled. One thing led to another, and when she found out that she was pregnant

– well, it seemed the right thing to do. Your mother had to give up university, though – in those days, there really wasn't any question about it, and, as I said, it seemed the right thing to do …'

'Did you ever love each other?' I asked.

'Looking back, I don't think so. I think we were content for a time. Things were alright. And after you were born, we had a few good years. I fell in love when you were born.'

I smiled at that.

'Then Tess ran into Peter one day in the city. You were with her. They got talking. She was married, he was married, and he had political ambitions so there was no question of it going any further. There was no question of anyone getting divorced. They continued to meet – lunch, coffee, phone chats. I don't think your mother had ever really got over him, so when it happened, she didn't have far to fall. As for Peter? I have no idea – I never really met him. We all moved in different circles at uni. He and his law cronies associated with very different people to us hippy arts students. When the inevitable happened, your mother told Peter about the pregnancy. I think she expected he'd leave his wife and everything would all fall nicely into place. You would stay with me, and Tess, Peter and the new baby would start a life together.'

'Wow, a nice, neat little package.'

'Exactly. That was until Peter told her it had all

been a mistake and he couldn't leave his wife. She'd been recently diagnosed with breast cancer and to leave her in the middle of treatment would have destroyed his career. He offered to pay for an abortion – apparently he knew a doctor who would do it – but when your mother declined, he broke the relationship off immediately. So she decided to try and pass the baby off as mine. Which, of course, was why she came back to me briefly.'

'So that's why she started crying?' I asked.

He looked confused. 'What do you mean?'

'I remember that she started crying a lot, then you died, then Zoe was born. In that order. When I got older, it was the order that made me wonder what else had been happening. I remember asking Grandma Brentnall once – I must have been about thirteen, I guess. It was before Mum and Peter got married. Grandma told me I was confused, that it was after you died that Mum couldn't cope. But it wasn't, was it?'

'No, I don't think so. Peter broke her heart, but she knew she had no choice other than trying to make things work with me.'

I nodded. There didn't seem to be much I could say to that.

Kate replaced our beers, and I smiled my thanks. At the rate that I was consuming them, I'd be going back with a little belly.

'You still have the scar,' Roger said, peering at my face. My finger touched the little raised line automatically. 'What happened again? I recall Brad was involved.' He turned to Kate. 'Brad and Abby were always getting up to something. They were as thick as thieves those two.'

'It was brake-free day and there was a lot of blood,' I said.

Kate raised her eyebrows in question.

'Brake-free day,' I explained, 'or BFD as we called it, meant that we weren't allowed to use the brakes on our bikes for a whole day. We had to use our feet, or steer away. Anyways, I didn't steer away in time and ended up in Mrs Ingram's clothes line, and then in hospital for stitches in my chin.' I pointed to the scar, now barely visible. 'This one,' I held my hair back from my forehead, 'I did a week before Mum got married. I broke my arm too. Mum thought I did it on purpose to ruin the photos.'

'When I asked about Brad before, you avoided my question,' Roger said. 'What was that about?'

I grimaced. 'It's a long, boring story and I'm afraid I don't come out of it smelling of roses.'

'Tell me anyway,' he encouraged.

So I told them both the whole sorry tale, all of it. I talked about leaving Brad as a kid, missing him, finding him again, loving him, and saying no to him. I talked about how he'd left me, and I even talked about my almost-mistake with Clinton.

'I think I had to do this,' I said. 'But I wish it hadn't

meant losing him.'

I sat back in my chair and surveyed the horizon. Brad was out there somewhere.

Roger had stayed quiet during the telling. Now he asked, 'Is it forever? The separation?'

I shrugged. 'I have no idea. I hope not.'

He nodded slowly. Then he opened his mouth as if to say more, glanced at Kate, and shut it again. Kate was right: it was too soon for him to be offering me any sort of advice, well-meaning or otherwise.

I felt her eyes on me. 'Abby, why don't you go for a swim while Roger and I clean this up? The beach is too beautiful to miss.'

Her smile was gentle, but her gaze was concerned. She was giving me a chance to begin to process what she must know was almost impossible to process.

I returned her smile. 'Thanks. I think I will.'

The swim was a good idea. I needed to feel the water around me, cooling me, calming me, shaping me, supporting me. Too much had happened over the last couple of days. I'd come looking for information about my dead father. Instead, I'd found that everything I thought I knew about my life was a lie. Nothing was real.

The only thing that seemed real was right here, in this little house on stilts beside the palm-tree-fringed beach, just outside Candidasa. Even that didn't seem quite real – it felt as though I was in the pages of a travel brochure, or an article about the best places in the world to leave the real world behind.

I rolled onto my back and floated in the calming warmth and stared at the cloudless blue sky, allowing the gentle swell to lift and soothe me.

Brad. He was real too, but he was in Denmark, or Austria or Sweden or somewhere. And I'd let him go there. Without me. To have his photo taken with Annika.

In the past I'd always been able to do something about whatever was bothering me. Take the appropriate action to fix it, or control the outcome. For anything else I'd swallow a glass of harden-the-flip-up and move on already. Neither of these alternatives fitted this situation. I couldn't fix it, and I couldn't ignore it.

I had no idea what to do with what I'd just found out. Dad was alive – I still faltered on the word 'Dad'; Mum was the one who'd cheated; Zoe was only my half-sister; and Mum and Peter had a bigamous marriage. It was no wonder that Mum had virtually ignored me once Zoe was born – I represented everything that had taken her away from the man she loved. It was no wonder there'd been no argument when I'd refused to take Peter's surname. I was the only one in the house who wasn't entitled to it. It also explained the lack of dimples.

Maybe the only way of managing this situation

was to not manage it at all. Just let it unfold and see what happened.

I flipped back onto my tummy and dove below the surface.

I spent the next few days with Roger and Kate.

I worked a couple of shifts at the pub – Roger introduced me as his niece from Australia – swam a lot, and we talked some more. I got to know them both, and found that I genuinely liked them. In my mind, Roger wasn't my father – not yet. I couldn't think of him like that. In my mind he was an old surfer I'd randomly met who I'd come to enjoy spending time with. With time and repeat visits we might get there. I hadn't forgiven him – I didn't think that I ever would – but I was closer to understanding why he did what he did.

I watched him when I thought he wouldn't notice. I watched him at work, watched the way he interacted with the staff, and saw their respect for him. When the surf was up, I watched him pick up his board, pat whatever dog was around, and bound into the water as if he was still the young man I'd known when I was a kid. I watched the way he concentrated over bar figures and stock orders, the way he furrowed his brow – the same way that I did – when he was thinking. I watched him when he smiled, that wide grin that lit up his whole face. It was my grin, and he grinned it a lot. It made me question when I'd stopped smiling as much. Was it when Brad left? Or sometime before that, when the pressures of chasing my ambitions started to take away my enjoyment of the every day?

Mostly I watched him when he was with Kate. The love and respect between them was palpable. It was in the way they looked at each other, an understanding smile, a quiet glance, a soft touch on the arm. There was no wonder in it; it just was. It was how Brad and I were, before I ruined it.

On my last night in Candidasa, Kate and Roger hosted a small dinner for me and invited the bar staff I'd met and worked with. Amazing dishes came out from the kitchen, there was a good supply of Bintang flowing, and much laughing and dancing as the sun went down. I'd come to love this little stretch of beach and these beautiful people.

When the others had left, Roger and I sat at the table and argued over Australian football codes.

'I can't see why you abandoned rugby league to support aerial ping-pong,' he said, using the slang term for Aussie Rules football. 'If ever there was a reason for me to come back, it was to make sure your sports education was being properly administered.'

We now talked about his absence as a fact of life rather than something awkward that shouldn't be mentioned.

'Think yourself lucky I'm not a rah-rah girl,' I said, referring to rugby union. 'After all, with Peter around, that's all I was exposed to growing up. I horrified him once by actively supporting the All Blacks. I think he could tolerate my politics as long as I supported his football team. The idea of me barracking for New Zealand was almost too much for him.'

Roger laughed at that. 'So, Abby, what are you going to do about Brad?'

'I'm starting to wish I'd never told you,' I joked.

'Be that as it may, someone needs to talk some sense into you. What scares you the most?'

'Who says I'm scared?'

'I do. You used to run headlong into anything that you thought needed to be conquered, tackled or hunted down, yet with this one you've run away. Why is that?'

'Maybe I've changed over the years. Maybe I grew up and had to take responsibility for things, and now I fight only the fights I know I can win.'

'Maybe you've been listening to bullshit.'

We commenced a stare-off. I won. He shrugged.

'I always win a stare-off,' I said. 'I should have warned you.'

'Don't think that's going to change the subject. What are you running from?'

I played with the label on the Bintang bottle.

'Abby,' he warned.

'Okay, I'm scared that if I need him too much he'll leave me just like Mum did, and you did, and like I left him before. I know it sounds ridiculous, but I'm scared that I love him more than he loves me.'

'Your mother didn't leave you.'

'She did, you know. As soon as she fell pregnant with Zoe, I ceased to exist. Actually, it was earlier than that. When she met Peter – that's when I felt she could no longer really be bothered with me. After that it was just a case of ticking the boxes – making sure I was fed, clothed, educated, occupied. Mum told me that you didn't love me enough to stay, and as for Brad … well, Mum took me away from him when we moved.'

'Man,' he said, rubbing his head, 'between us, we've done a good job of screwing your head, girl. What's this "loving more" shit? You love. He loves. That's the only equation that matters. Whoever sent you to accounting school needs to be shot.'

'Umm, that would be Mum and Peter.'

'I rest my argument. But that illustrates my point – you can't apply an equation to emotions. Trust me on that one. Kate and I … I couldn't give a shit who loves who more. We love each other – that's all there is. I could die tomorrow, she could die tomorrow, and there would be sadness, but no regrets. You need to live like that too. Marry or don't marry, I don't care – these days it really doesn't make a difference. It certainly hasn't made any difference to us. But if you love each other, there's no harm in compromise, and there's no such thing as doing the right thing – unless it's the right thing for your relationship. But for God's sake, Abby, surely it's worth the risk?'

'Since when do you get to lecture me?' It was only half a joke. My brain was telling me he'd lost any right to tell me what to do, but there was a larger part of me that liked it because he was my father.

He held my eyes. 'Since the day you waltzed into my bar.'

I shrugged. 'Fair enough.'

'Good. Go home, sort out whatever it is that needs sorting out with your mother, and then go find Brad. Next time I see you, I'll be asking about him, and the answer had better be a little more positive.'

'You've got a deal.'

'And, Abby? If the job isn't making you happy, there's no shame in jumping off the treadmill and trying something different. Remember how I always told you to be true to yourself?'

I looked at him sideways.

He laughed. 'I know – that's a fine thing coming from a man who's pretended to be dead for twenty five years. I'm not proud of what happened, and I know there could be consequences associated with it. That's up to you, and I'm prepared to accept that. But what Kate and I do, how we are? We're living our dream. I want the same for you – although perhaps without the dramatics.'

I believed him.

'Do you want to know what I'm going to say to

Mum?' I asked.

'Not particularly. That's your call.'

'I won't say anything about you, you know.'

'Ab, I trust you enough not to even ask you that question.'

On the flight home I jotted down some notes. As far as I could tell, I had three priorities:

- My job was no longer making me happy. I knew this for sure. I was never going to be made partner while I worked for Mark. There would always be an excuse. Part of me wondered whether I'd put up with the situation for as long as I had because I knew somewhere deep inside that this wasn't really my dream. Taking care of the job situation would also take care of the Clinton distraction.

- I needed to have a difficult discussion with Mum. Although I wasn't intending to tell her about Roger, there were things that needed to be said. I'd get that over with next weekend.

- Brad and I were meant to be together. I wanted for us what Roger and Kate had. That meant fighting for him, and I was now ready to do that.

CHAPTER TWENTY-TWO

'The contract needs to be amended to include a volume clause,' I said. 'Their volume only needs to decrease by less than two per cent for our profit to be completely eroded. The annual increases for CPI won't be sufficient to keep pace – our margins really are that tight.'

We were talking about a new project that Mark was considering submitting a bid for and I was attempting to summon some enthusiasm for.

Mark leant back in his seat and tapped his pen against the arm of his chair. 'That's all very well, Abby, but if we insist on a volume clause, the risk is that they'll go out to tender when the contract comes up.'

'True, but if we're losing money on them, do we really want them as a customer? In any case, our competitors will also insist on a volume clause, and will be looking to make money from the deal from the start – as should we. Anything else is poor business practice.'

'How would you put it to them?'

'Exactly like that. We're in a falling market where the natural rate of attrition is currently five per cent.

I understand that they have strategies on the table to alleviate that, but they haven't yet been implemented, nor is there any guarantee that they will be implemented. Unless something is done to stem the flow, the volumes we process will be declining by that attrition rate, or more, right from the start. We'll be losing money on the deal by this time next year.'

He leant forward, rested his elbows on the desk and clasped his palms together, propping his chin on his knuckles. 'I understand that, but given that your judgement has been less effective than usual of late, I don't think I'll be taking your advice.'

I raised my eyebrows. 'Seriously?'

'You've been away a lot this year.'

'Mark, I haven't taken leave for years. Surely not taking leave has more potential to impact my judgement than taking it?'

'Yes, that would normally be the case, but Clinton has raised some concerns about you disappearing in the middle of the project. It's not a good look for a project manager.'

'You have to be joking. I didn't disappear and it wasn't the middle of a project. A proper handover took place, and all milestones were green. In any case, I shouldn't be managing this project – I'm an associate, for God's sake, not a junior project manager. Sophie is more than capable of handling this deal. All tasks are up to date, all development completed and all training scheduled. Clinton Barclay has no grounds for concern.'

'Abby, you need to look at it from his viewpoint – you wouldn't even tell anyone where you'd gone.'

'No, Mark, because it was no one's business but mine. It certainly wasn't anything to do with Clinton. When I said I had personal matters to take care of, I meant it.'

'Clinton wants you to work closely with him in relation to the training. In view of that, I need you to be in Perth tomorrow for a planning meeting with the Warner executives.'

'The big guys?'

'Yes, plus Clinton and his Perth team. I don't think I need to tell you that a lot is riding on this project, and not just from the company viewpoint. There's a lot riding on this for you personally.'

Whoa. I nodded slowly. 'What you're telling me is that if I don't toe the line on this, I can kiss goodbye to my partnership again this year?'

'I didn't say that.'

'Actually, Mark, I think that's exactly what you're saying.'

'I don't see what your problem is with him. He's a good-looking, successful man and, last I heard, you were single. He seems to like you, and being nice to him would help us out.'

I let out a laugh and shook my head before standing. Straightening my skirt, I leant over the table towards him. 'Being nice to him? I'm going to pretend you didn't say that and I didn't hear it. Any and all contact from Clinton Barclay to me, or about me, outside of this office is not only inappropriate but completely unwelcome. I've told him that and I've told you that. I will be in Perth tomorrow, but I won't be taking one for the team, regardless of what other business his company can bring us.'

'That's not what I was saying. I don't appreciate your inference.'

'That's exactly what you were saying. And this might just be a coincidence, but nor do I appreciate yours.' I walked to his office door and shook my head again. 'I know that you need to be ambitious and ruthless to make it in this world, but I didn't know that you had to sell your soul as well. I'm hanging on to what's left of mine, thank you very much. Oh, and I'll drop my advice about the volume clause into a memo. Just in case the issue about my failure to warn comes up at next year's partner discussions.'

Back at my desk, I called for Paula.

'Can you please get me on a flight to Perth tonight? I won't be staying at the usual hotel – could you book me in somewhere else? Please also call Clinton Barclay's office and find out the details of tomorrow's meeting before booking my return flights. Oh, and I won't be flying Qantas – get me on another airline. I won't risk being on the same flight as him.'

She nodded.

'If his secretary asks for my flight details,' I added, 'say that you'll email them through, but feel free to be incompetent. Tell her that you assume I'll be staying at the usual hotel and let them think I'll be staying an extra night. Then book me on the red-eye home.'

Paula looked at me for explanation. I normally hated the red-eye, so called because after a night spent sitting up in economy that's exactly what you had – red eyes.

I shook my head. 'Don't ask.'

'Is that all?'

'Yes, thanks. Paula, I appreciate this.'

She smiled. 'He called while you were away – Clinton – wanting to know where he could contact you.'

'I thought he might have. What did you tell him?'

'Exactly what we agreed – that you had some personal issues that needed to be attended to and you hadn't told me your destination, but that you had cell-phone coverage so could be reached in the event of an emergency.' She paused before adding, 'Your sister called too.'

'Really?'

'Yes, it was weird – she phoned just a few minutes after he did. It was such a coincidence. Anyway, I told her exactly the same story.'

'Hmmm.'

When it came to either Zoe or Clinton, I didn't believe in coincidences.

'You're back.' Clinton came up behind me at the coffee bar. Warner Enterprises had laid on a lovely morning tea. I'd selected a fruit Danish pastry and coffee, and was on my way into the meeting room.

'So it would seem.'

As expected, his secretary had asked Paula about my travel plans. By the time I arrived in Perth I had a number of messages waiting for me from Clinton:

Hi Abby, I thought you might have been on this flight. I'll see you at the hotel I guess.

Hi Abby, I just checked with the front desk here at the Duxton, it seems you're not booked in. Give me a call and let me know your movements.

Hi Abby, not sure if you'll be here in time for a meal, but I think it's imperative that we catch up before tomorrow as a quick status check.

I sent through a brief reply to the last one: *Thanks for the offer, Clinton. I've already ordered room service and need an early night. Will see you at the office in the morning.*

His response was just as quick: *Where are you staying?*

I didn't reply.

'So, how was your holiday?' he asked now, helping himself to the espresso machine.

'As you know, it wasn't a holiday.'

'Where did you go?'

'I don't think that matters, do you?'

'I was trying to get hold of you. We had issues with the project.'

'There were no issues with the project, Clinton. Sophie had everything under control. If you had concerns, you could have raised them with her.'

'Perhaps. Don't you think that you've played this game for long enough?'

What the fuck?

'I'm sorry, Clinton, I have no idea what you're talking about.'

'You know exactly what game I'm referring to.'

'Was there anything specific that you wanted to talk about in relation to the project before the meeting starts? No? I didn't think so.'

As I moved past him, he grabbed my arm. 'Be careful, Abby. Mark listens to me. You don't want to see that partnership of yours slipping away. Besides, we got along well once before.'

I shook off his hand. 'That might be true, but you're assuming that what you're threatening me with is important, and I wouldn't be making any assumptions about that if I were you.'

His eyes narrowed. 'Oh, by the way, I've met your sister … lovely girl. Strangely, she didn't know anything about any family emergency.'

He looked smug. I hoped my surprise didn't show, although as I'd said, there was no such thing as a coincidence when it came to either Zoe or Clinton.

'Who said anything about a family emergency? I had to go away for personal reasons. And my personal reasons are none of your business, nor Zoe's.'

At that point we were joined by some members of Clinton's project team, so we all made our way into the meeting room.

Clinton opened the session by thanking everyone for attending, and stating that the purpose was to agree the proposed training and transition schedule. At that cue I handed around the memo Sophie had prepared.

'In this pack you'll find the roll-out schedules for each of the sites. You'll notice that in Sydney and Melbourne we'll run six two-hour sessions, including two after normal hours, to ensure that all operators have the opportunity to attend. In each of the other states we'll only run four sessions. This should be sufficient to ensure full attendance by appropriate personnel at those sites. The sessions will be facilitated by my senior project manager, Sophie Martella. She'll be supported in Sydney and Brisbane by the manager of our Sydney operations team. Support in Melbourne, Adelaide and Perth will be provided by the manager of our Melbourne operations team.

'I'm aware that Clinton,' I turned to smile sweetly at him, 'requested that I personally attend each session. As flattering as his faith in me is, that would add a substantial cost to the project. After talking to Andrew this morning,' I acknowledged Clinton's boss, 'we've agreed that there's no real justification for that spend, not when we have such competent trainers available within our existing scope and budget. As you know, any change to the cost will require a variance to be approved by the project steering committee, and I'm sure none of us are keen to inherit any more paperwork, or explain any budget creep.'

I paused for the inevitable laughter. Game, set and match to me. Clinton had been pushing for us to travel to each of the sites together. There was no way I was allowing that to happen.

'Does anyone have any issues with anything I've gone through so far?' I asked, pausing for a response. 'No? Great. Let's work through the expected outcomes of each session. Can you please turn to page five of your pack? You'll see that I've also included a copy of the requirements register and the development register. Each item agreed on the requirements register has a reference that is replicated in the development plan and also flows across to a training session. See that? Terrific.'

The rest of the meeting progressed as expected. We finished right on schedule and, despite Clinton's best and most charming attempts to the contrary, all of my proposals were accepted.

As I stood in the reception area chatting to Andrew and a couple of the other directors, Clinton approached. I was struck again by just how good-looking he was, yet he did nothing for me, if indeed he ever really had done. Way too pretty.

'Andrew, I'm taking Abby out for dinner tonight. Would you like to join us?' Clinton watched my face as he waited for the answer. Bastard.

'Sorry, I'm due home for dinner,' Andrew said, 'but make sure you go out for a few drinks first, on me. Abby, thanks for everything you've done. I have to say, I was surprised that Mark put you so closely onto the project. I thought you were way too senior for that, but Mark insisted. We've appreciated the attention though, and Sophie has done an exemplary job to date. You must be very proud of her.'

'Oh, I am. I'll let her and Mark know how satisfied you are with her. Mark had the impression that there was some problem with her performance? Had that come from you?'

'Absolutely not. In fact, I'll drop Mark a line this afternoon just to confirm how satisfied we are.'

'Thanks. I'm sure Mark would appreciate the feedback.'

'Great. I'll do that now while it's fresh in my mind. Now you two go off and have a nice meal out. When are you flying home, Abby?'

'I'm on the red-eye later tonight, so it'll be a quick dinner, but I'm sure Clinton will take me somewhere nice.'

Clinton's eyes narrowed.

'Speaking of which,' I said to him, 'do you mind if I just go back and freshen up? You're at the Duxton, right? I'll meet you there at seven thirty.' I held my hand out to Andrew. 'It was a pleasure to see you again. We'll talk next Tuesday as usual in the steering committee?'

Nice one, Abby. I was still congratulating myself when Clinton grabbed my arm and directed me to the lift.

Once inside he said, 'Nice move back there.'

'Thanks. I thought so. Sophie will be pleased to know there are no problems with her project management skills after all, and I'm sure Mark will be reassured to know everything is on track, despite your concerned calls of the last couple of weeks.'

He moved closer to me, backing me into the corner. The heel of my shoe snagged the edge of the carpet and he took the opportunity to push himself against me.

'Alone at last,' he breathed into my ear.

I screwed my eyes shut and turned my head from his mouth. He pulled my head back and forced my lips open with his, filling my mouth with his tongue and slamming me against the wall. I could feel his erection against me and was aware of just how alone we were. His mouth was hard and insistent and I was having difficulty breathing. I pushed ineffectually at his chest, but he just laughed and pinned my arms above my head. How could I ever have thought this man even vaguely attractive?

I cursed the tightness of my skirt, knowing that my wriggling to free myself was only exciting him more. Finally I managed to release my snagged heel and slammed it down into the top of his shoe. That had to hurt.

He let go of my arms, jolted back and slapped me across the face. 'Bitch!'

He grabbed at my arm again, but the lift doors opened and I rushed out into the lobby. The evening peak had died down and the space was deserted.

'Don't you ever touch me again,' I said through gritted teeth.

'I take it dinner is out of the question?'

I shook my head in disbelief and turned to walk off.

'By the way, Zoe says hi. She's a beautiful girl, so … responsive. Strangely, it didn't seem to worry her that you and I were together. If anything it seemed to turn her on. She likes me to compare her performance to yours.'

I tried not to rise to his bait, but somehow my feet wouldn't take the steps required to cross the beautiful marble floor and leave the building.

'She likes me to tell her how you like it,' he continued.

I was tempted to knock that pretty smile off that pretty face. 'You'd need to use that active imagination of yours then. How did you meet my sister?'

'Easy, I introduced myself to her after the launch of that shop in Chapel Street. I went along because I thought you were going to be there, but you didn't show. Anyway, I told her that I knew you, and she very quickly put two and two together and figured there was something between us. Okay, I might have let slip that you were a little taken with me. We met for a drink after the show and, well, you know how it is … your sister can be very persuasive when she wants someone.'

So he was the someone more interesting that Zoe had thrown me over for. She would've got a kick out of that.

'There's nothing between us,' I said. 'How many times do I need to tell you that?'

'You don't mean that.'

'What is it, Clinton? Am I the only woman to have said no to you?'

His smile didn't falter. 'So, this personal emergency that Zoe knew nothing about?'

'What about it?'

'I'd hate for Mark to somehow find out that you lied to him – he's already questioning your judgement. Whatever story you've convinced Andrew to spin, it won't take much from me to make Mark really start to doubt you. And from there it's a very quick farewell to that partnership you want. Then there are those rumours about cutbacks that will occur if this project isn't a success. So, what do you say – are we having that dinner? You have a flight to catch, so maybe you'd prefer to skip dinner and go straight to my room for dessert. We can "talk" some more about the best way for you to keep your job.' He used his fingers to illustrate the quotation marks. Wanker. 'Maybe you'd like the opportunity to compare your sister's performance?'

There was a time only a few months ago when I would have searched for a diplomatic solution to this mess. A way of keeping my job and ambitions alive, and Clinton at arm's length – a win/win situation. The thing was, diplomacy and win/win solutions weren't applicable when it came to dealing with bullies, and Clinton Barclay was a bully. Just like Debbie, Sharleen and Kylee Scott. His methods may have been different, but his motivation was the same – power, or the illusion of power, over someone else. He only wanted me because I'd refused him, so he thought he'd force me. But I was a very different Abby from the skinny kid who'd fearlessly launched herself at Sharleen Scott all those years ago. A different Abby from the one who'd freewheeled into Mrs Ingram's washing line, or dragged a car bonnet to the top of a grassy hill before jumping into it and pushing off the edge.

Or was I? Maybe that Abby had just been hidden under a few layers of highly polished veneer. That Abby would never put up with shit like this from a master slimebag. That Abby would never have let Brad go to Denmark, or Poland or Austria, or wherever, alone to have his photo taken with Brigitta. That Abby would have been up for the adventure, and she would have fought for her man. That Abby would never have tolerated Clinton Barclay, and she'd have made damn sure he wasn't able to bully her again. Deep down, I was still that skinny pigtailed girl. I was still my father's daughter.

'You know, you're right.' I allowed a smile to curl across my lips. 'Maybe skipping dinner is a great idea.'

I pulled my skirt up just a little, to give me room to move. Clinton saw the movement and moved closer, smiling all the while. I let him get near enough so I could rest my hands loosely on his shoulders. His smile grew wider.

I leant forward and whispered in his ear, 'Go fuck yourself.' Then I lifted my knee and jammed it hard into his balls.

CHAPTER TWENTY-THREE

'What's this about, Abby?' Mark hadn't opened the letter I'd given him.

'It's my resignation.'

'I don't understand,' he said, handing the letter back. 'You're on partner track.'

'A road to nowhere, so it would seem. And one I've decided to turn off.'

'I still don't understand why.'

'Really? You allowed Clinton Barclay to influence your opinion of me and your opinion of my judgement. I expressed my concerns about working closely with him from the start, but you ignored them. As a result, I've spent the last few months being virtually stalked by him. He's attempted to blackmail me into sleeping with him by threatening to tell you that I'm not cooperating. While I was away on leave he phoned family, friends and my colleagues here attempting to find out where I was. I've allowed all that to happen over the last few months because of the implied threat of losing the partnership that's been promised and promised, but never delivered.

Every time I've expressed an opinion, you've thrown it back in my face with the implication of impaired performance. Two nights ago I found myself pinned to the back of a lift with someone very unpleasant telling me that if I didn't sleep with him, he'd be reporting my insubordination to you, and that your relationship with him was such that you'd believe him. That's no longer a situation that I'm prepared to put up with.'

He looked shocked. 'What did you do?'

'What did I do? I rendered him incapable of using those parts on anyone else that night.'

'You assaulted a client?'

'A client who was sexually harassing me and who had assaulted me. Don't worry, I doubt he'll be pressing charges. The only charges you need to worry about are the sexual harassment ones that, according to my solicitor, I would be well within my rights to press. Apparently I have a right to feel protected by my firm, not exposed.'

'You wouldn't dare. This profession will close its ranks against you – you'd never get another job again. As for any hopes of being a partner, well, they'd be gone.'

'You're assuming that (a) I want another job in the profession, (b) that I still want to be a partner, and (c) that I haven't made detailed notes of every single one of our conversations concerning your Mr Barclay.' I held up a manila folder filled with paper.

His mouth dropped open. 'Clinton told me that the two of you had a relationship in the past and you were jealous because he preferred someone else.'

'And you believed him? Of course you did, because he's a man, a good-looking man, and because he told you over a beer, I assume.'

His face gave me my answer.

'Not that it's any of your business, but I met him by accident in Bali. We had a brief interlude after which I told him that I didn't want to see him again. That was why he insisted I be primary project manager. If you recall, on …' I opened the manila folder, 'May 21st, I first asked you to take me off the project as I didn't feel comfortable working with Clinton. That request was repeated in June, and again in the first week of July. I think you know what I'm saying?'

The colour in Mark's face was changing. I noted it and continued regardless. 'I'm good at my job, and my integrity has never been called into question before, so I have to conclude that the only judgement that should be questioned is yours, not mine.'

'What do you want?' he asked.

'I want what's owed to me. I want a glowing reference, as is my due. I also want a guarantee from you of confidentiality regarding this conversation and my dealings with Clinton.'

'You're implying that you don't trust my integrity.'

'Am I? I'm not being sufficiently clear then.'

His face got redder.

'I've already phoned Andrew Warner and explained that I've resigned. I didn't tell him why. He's disappointed of course, but understanding – and he's offered me a role in their firm. I told him that I wouldn't feel right accepting it until this project is complete. He respects that.'

'Why would you do that? That would mean working with Clinton.'

'Sadly, no. It appears our Mr Barclay is in a spot of bother – something about using company money to entertain potential clients and suppliers at a certain gentlemen's club. A random audit showed up some anomalies. You wouldn't know anything about that, would you?'

The red now had tinges of purple.

'I didn't think so. So I'm guessing that some mutual confidentiality is in order? I took the liberty of having this agreement made up. I trust you'll sign it?'

Sometimes it was worth having a lawyer as a best friend. Speaking of which, I still owed Andi a full explanation.

Mark signed it without comment.

'Thank you. I'll now clean out my office. I've explained to my staff that I have some personal matters that need to be sorted out, and as such have reluctantly tendered my resignation and you've reluctantly accepted it. I've assured Paula that she still has a job here for as long as she wants it. I'll know if anything else is said.'

He nodded his agreement.

'Oh,' I added, 'you'll be needing this.' I handed him my resignation letter. 'I trust that you'll ensure payroll get the details right, particularly in relation to my contractual entitlements regarding pro-rata bonuses and long-service leave. I've taken the liberty of making my own calculations.'

Mark took it and read it before speaking. 'You've had a busy couple of days.'

'I have. I had a pretty good reason. That episode in the lift was the last straw.'

'Are you going to take action?' he asked.

I paused, then shook my head. 'No. I have to take responsibility for some of what happened. And, after all, I did knee him in the balls.'

He shook his head, in exasperation or amusement I couldn't tell. 'Abby, I hope you understand how truly sorry I am that this has happened. I didn't realise it had gone as far as it had and was causing you that much pain.' I raised my eyebrows, but he ignored the movement. 'You're the best associate I've ever had.'

I shrugged. 'Perhaps you should have remembered that when you were listening to the poison Clinton was feeding you.'

'Perhaps I should have. I wish you good luck.'

He held his hand out. I accepted it.

•

Andi balanced her tray as she teetered through the lunchtime crowd to our table. We were back at Noodelicious – there no longer seemed any reason to stay away.

'Why do we always come here?' she asked as she took what was left of her miso soup from the tray and popped it on the table beside her teriyaki chicken. She then removed the water bottle that had caused the mess when it fell over. 'That's right – we haven't been here for ages, because you were avoiding someone.'

I grimaced.

'You'd think I'd remember to lie it down flat, wouldn't you?' she added, not expecting a response.

She bent over to put the tray on a spare chair and a number of male eyes appreciated the view. It was all so familiar and normal that my eyes welled up. I blinked quickly before she noticed.

'So,' she said, 'I have some News.'

'This sounds like man type of news.'

'No, Ab, this is bigger – this is capital "N" News. It's just that with the way things are between you and Brad, I feel a bit bad telling you, but I'm honestly so happy that I can't not tell you, and anyway, I live in hope that you two will make up. And when I told him that I was going to tell you, he said, "Andi, take it slowly, you know Abby's feeling fragile", and I'm like, "As if I would just blurt it out. I'm more sensitive than that". And, after all, you are my best friend – he just thinks that because he's known you longer, he has the biggest say in how I tell you – but honestly, I've never felt like this before, A, it's all so amazing. The sex is incredible. He does this thing –'

I put my fingers in my ears. 'Too much information … Am I missing something? Who is this man and who's he married to?'

'Oh, Abs, you've seriously been AWOL. He is completely, beautifully single – well, he was, now he's not because he's completely, beautifully with me.' She smiled widely and waved her chopsticks around. 'I seriously can't think why I dismissed him all of these years, and then suddenly, bam! And we're together. How did that happen? Actually, how did that happen? One minute we were arguing and the next …' She didn't seem to expect an answer. 'We bumped into each other the other week. I was telling him about that sleazebag – what's his name again?'

'Clinton?' I guessed.

'Yes, him. We're out having a drink and then he's there, like he was that day at lunch, almost as if he knew I was going to be there.'

'He probably did know you were going to be there,' I suggested wryly.

'Really? Do you think he was following me? That's a little melodramatic, isn't it? Anyway, he was asking where you were and making out like you'd want him to know and stuff. He tried the same thing on Todd as he did with me that day. I was worried that Todd would believe him – he can be really convincing, you know.'

I knew.

'It really creeped me out, so Todd told him to piss off. Honestly, Abs, what were you thinking with him?'

'I thought he was harmless – we both did.'

She shook her head and sighed dramatically. 'Of course, I had to tell Todd the whole story – well, as much as I knew, which I guess really isn't that much. And then Todd was like, "What was she thinking?" And I'm, "I know! I have no idea what she's thinking". I mean, Brad's gone for just two minutes, and we think this guy is stalking you, and you seem to have gone all helpless and weird when you're always fearless and together. And Todd is like, "I don't know how we're going to get her out of this one before Brad comes home", and "What happens if it's serious?" And I'm saying that there's no way you would be serious with him because he's such a sleazebag, and anyway, you and Brad were on a break so it was technically okay for you to be with someone else, even though you did nothing more than kiss him. He didn't agree with me and said that Brad would be devastated. I told him that Brad was the one who left, so what right did he have to expect you to live like a nun. And how you'd told me that Brad was over there with his arm around some girl a rug was named after. He told me that was fine talk coming from me, and then ...' She looked at me expectantly.

I was shaking my head in confusion. 'Andi, I still have no idea who or what you're talking about.'

'Todd Reynolds, Brad's best mate. We hooked up, and now we're … well, we're together, and it's all because of that sleazebag. We originally got talking when we tried to work out how we could stage an intervention. I told him that we didn't need an intervention, that there was something more creepy going on below the surface because there was no way you'd replace Brad with someone like him. And he agreed and said he wished you'd had the sense to go with Brad and then none of this would have happened. And I said that there was so much more to it than just simply deciding to go with him, and that I thought there was something going on with you that you weren't telling us about. And there was, wasn't there?' She didn't give me time to respond. 'And then Todd remembered how you were when you met him that night that Zoe didn't turn up, and said it was the first time that you'd let him walk you home, so that had to mean you were feeling concerned. I told him that you weren't running the Tan any more in the mornings, and that's when Todd really believed me and said that he was trouble, Clinton, that is, and that he thought you'd got yourself into something weird you couldn't get out of, and we had to help.'

Oh, I'd missed the chaos of Andi.

'Yeah, sweetie, I had got myself into something weird. I'm sorry I haven't seen you – there's been so much going on. And you're right, Clinton is a sleazebag.'

'Of course he is. He could only be more my type if he was married.'

I laughed at that. 'I can't believe that you and Todd are together. Brad and I often thought you'd make the perfect couple, but every time we put you in the same place at the same time, you were in the middle of something with someone who belonged to someone else, and Todd was being Todd.'

'And the two of us would argue – yes, I know. It wouldn't have worked then. I thought he was a tool, but now I like his tool!'

I spluttered chicken broth, and the chopsticks full of noodles I'd been bringing to my mouth fell in a splash back into the bowl.

'I'm not sure that I want to know,' I said, pretending to be outraged and shocked.

It was fantastic news – really it was; of course it was. I just couldn't believe that Andi had been off falling in love with Todd while my world was imploding. I'd had this idea that everything else would stop while I sorted my shit out, and then start turning again when I was done. Apparently, it didn't work that way.

'Sure you do,' she said, 'and I'll tell you every last erotic detail as soon as you tell me where you've been and what's been happening. You know your spoilt brat of a sister rang me looking for you the other week? I had to tell her that I had no idea where you were. So where were you?'

'Bali.'

'Again?'

'I found out what made my father leave when he did. I found the woman he fell in love with over there, and I found out that my mother has been lying to me all these years. Then I went to Perth and Clinton fucking Barclay tried to blackmail me into having sex with him, so I resigned. So now I have no job, no Brad, and by this time tomorrow, after I confront my mother, I will probably have no family.'

She stopped, speechless for once, a chopstick full of teriyaki chicken dangling over her bowl. So I told her. Everything. Well, nearly everything. I didn't tell her about Clinton in the lift, and I didn't tell her the part about Dad being alive. The only person I would ever trust with that information would be Brad, and he wasn't here. He was still in Poland or Denmark or Austria or somewhere. With his arm around Astrid. I wanted to ask Andi if she knew when he'd be back, but I couldn't.

At the end of the telling, she ate the (now cold) piece of teriyaki chicken still at the end of her chopsticks, and managed, 'Wow.' Then she said, 'I thought I had the news today – great, amazingly unbelievable sex with someone you'd be surprised about – and you've managed to trump me. How did that happen?'

I shrugged, and pushed my half-eaten soup away. 'You had fantastic news.'

I was dismayed to hear a crack in my voice, just a waver, so tiny that anyone who didn't know me wouldn't have noticed, but I couldn't say any more because the crack was widening. My eyes welled again, but this time I couldn't hide it and the reaction from the last week, and the last couple of days, and ever since Brad left, escaped in the form of salt water down my cheeks, in wide rivers that took with them my mascara and makeup and dropped into my soup bowl in great big plops.

In all our years of friendship, Andi had never seen me cry, and now looked as if she had no idea what to do. It was usually the other way around, me comforting her. I mopped ineffectually at the flow, but nothing seemed able to stop it. It was as if years and years of tears were making a bid for freedom into my Thai noodle soup with thick rice noodles, chicken, extra chilli and no bean sprouts. I couldn't stop them.

Andi grabbed at my hands and held on. 'Oh, babe, I don't know what to say.'

'There's nothing you can say,' I blubbed. 'I've been so stupid, so incredibly stupid. And I miss Brad so much, but you are absolutely forbidden to say anything to Todd, especially about me missing Brad, even though he knows. And you can't tell him I cried – he's never seen me cry. No one needs to know how much of a mess I am.'

'Cross my heart.' She made a cross against her cleavage, and all the men who'd thought there could have been some girl-on-girl action, based on my tears and her clasped hands, hoped again.

I smiled a watery smile and absently stirred tears into my soup with my chopsticks.

'What happens now?' she asked.

'I'm not sure. I'm going to Sydney tomorrow, and I'll have it out once and for all with my mother. Then, somehow, I have to try and work out how I can possibly explain everything to Brad and fight for him – because I do want to fight for him. I have no idea why I let him go. None of this would have happened if I'd gone with him. Then I need to find another job. That's all.'

'You're right, A – none of it would have happened if you'd gone with him, but it would have happened at some point. You needed to find the real story about your parents, you needed to trust yourself enough to fight for Brad, and you needed to stop being scared that Zoe was going to breeze in and take it all away. Even if you went with Brad, that was all still waiting. Now you've got the chance to do something you *really* want to do instead of what you've always been told you *should* do.'

'I don't know what that is though.'

'Think of the fun you'll have working it out.' She shrugged, causing her wide-necked blouse to dip off one shoulder, exposing more cleavage and a perfect collarbone. I didn't know how she did it. 'And, sweetie? It's okay if you can't do it all.'

'About Todd,' I asked. 'Is he "the one"?'

'You know, Abs, I'm absolutely positive that he is.'

'How did you know?'

'He said no to sleeping with me that first night.'

'Wow … how long did he make you wait?'

'Too long – until the third date. I mean, how did he hold out against this?'

One of the things I loved most about Andi was her healthy confidence.

'Since then, though …' She proceeded to tell me all about it.

'Are you going to be okay?' she asked after she'd finished her X-rated story.

I wasn't sure I'd be able to look at Todd in quite the same way again. There were a number of very graphic pictures in my head, and apparently on Andi's phone.

'Do I really look that miserable?'

'Yes,' she said, looking at me with that dreaded concern again.

'How about now?' I plastered a smile on my face.

'Nope, still miserable.'

'Wanna hear something funny?'

'Sure.'

'You know the other week when I was supposed to meet Zoe and someone better came up?'

She nodded.

'The someone better was Clinton. They hooked up.'

This time she was the one who spluttered.

CHAPTER TWENTY-FOUR

'He's a very nice young man,' Mum said. 'Very good-looking.'

I smiled politely. Zoe wouldn't go out with someone unless he fitted the good-looking requirement. The other criteria were that he should be: (a) famous, or (b) rich, or (c) both of the above, or (d) my boyfriend, or (e) someone else's husband, preferably both rich and famous.

Mum was still speaking. 'You know him – Clinton Barclay? Zoe said that you two went out for a while and you got quite silly about it, to the extent that both of you lost your jobs. You never have handled rejection well, Abigail.'

Whatever.

'As a result, she and Clinton have made themselves scarce today. She's concerned that you'd make a fuss like you did that other time.'

Oh, would that be the time she shagged my boyfriend before Brad? Or the one before that? The one who'd asked me to marry him? Sure I'd said no –

he didn't really want to get married, and he knew I'd say no; he just wanted to be able to say that he'd asked. Zoe caused the break-up of that relationship and then swanned off to Milan. Yes, that time I did make a fuss. Besides, right now I was in no mood to get into any discussion with Mum about Zoe. I was here for other reasons. It did, however, surprise me that Zoe had missed the opportunity to parade Clinton in front of me. I suspected that Clinton had spun some story about his comfort levels. It would have been something like, 'Zoe, it would hurt me to see your sister so devastated', or, 'It would make me feel uncomfortable if there was a fuss, and Abby is so jealous that there would be a fuss'. In actual fact, he was probably more concerned that I would act uninterested, or, Zoe's worst nightmare, give them my blessing. I had to give Clinton credit though: he'd hit on the best way to keep Zoe interested in him – make out that I was.

'You know, Abigail, you've always been jealous of your sister, and it's so unseemly. It's really no wonder that you've never managed to settle down with anyone.'

I took a deep breath. We were moving further into 'whatever' territory. 'Where are Peter and Tyler?'

'At the rugby. It wouldn't have hurt you to give us a little bit of notice rather than just arriving. Of course you're always welcome, but …'

'Don't worry, Mum, I'm not staying. I just had a couple of things that I wanted to ask you about Dad.'

She was bustling about the kitchen, making a show of preparing a teapot. 'I thought we'd been through all of this. I don't understand why you want to drag it all up again. It was a very painful time for me. I think you should have some more sensitivity.'

'Do you, Mum? He was my father and I loved him. I can't understand why you lied to me, and I want to know why you did.'

She turned to rummage through the perfectly organised pantry, looking for the tea that was sitting on the third shelf in the china canister she'd been putting the tea in for as long as I could remember. 'I don't think I know what you're talking about.'

'Mum, stop making the bloody tea and listen to me!'

'Abigail, there is no need for that language in this house.'

'Oh, that's right, I forgot. We need to play happy families in this house. In this house, it's okay to lie to your daughter and tell her that her father ran off with his secretary when the truth is that your mother was pregnant with another man's child.'

Mum dropped the cup she'd been holding and it smashed on the tiled floor. The colour disappeared from her face and she stared at me as if she'd never seen me before.

'Where did you hear that rubbish?' she whispered.

'From a very good source.'

'Was it that Robards man?'

I shook my head. 'I know some of the story, and I think I've figured out the rest. Now all I need to know is why.'

There was silence, and the china remained where it had fallen.

'Shall I start, Mum?'

She buried her head in the cupboard under the sink looking for the dustpan and brush.

'I know that you fell in love with Peter at uni, and I know that he didn't want you,' I said.

She flinched at that, but I was in no mood to be kind.

'I was an accident from a rebound shag that tied you into a marriage you didn't want to be in. I know that you began an affair with Peter, and I also know that it stopped when you found out you were pregnant with his child. I figure that you started back up with him soon after the inquest, and kept things quiet until his wife died, but that's all guesswork.'

She tutted as she bent to sweep up the china. 'This was one of my favourite patterns. Now I won't have a complete set.'

'It explains a lot,' I continued, ignoring her efforts to avoid the subject. 'About how once Zoe came along, I ceased to exist; about how I was shunted off to that school and enrolled in anything that meant I didn't need to be at home. I was a constant reminder of the one time that you stuffed up and the life you threw away. Zoe and Tyler were your real family.'

'You never made an effort to like Peter,' she said.

'He wasn't my father. My father died because you disappointed him. Nothing he ever did would live up to Peter and the life you thought you'd given up with him. Dad and I never stood a chance.'

'That's ridiculous,' she said, taking a fresh bin bag from the roll in the drawer and making a production of shaking it out and placing it in the bin.

'It's not such a perfect fairy tale now, is it, Mum? The press wouldn't like that side of the story so much, would they?'

'You wouldn't dare.'

I'd finally hit a nerve. 'Wouldn't I? As far as I'm concerned, you've lied to me most of my life. You attempted to damage the image I had of my father; you certainly tried to make me hate him. That was unfair in so many ways.'

'I didn't have a choice,' she said, finally looking at me.

'Actually, Mum, you did. I know I was always a disappointment to you, and I know I always reminded you of Dad, but that was no reason to do what you did.'

'You were always too much like your father – always so idealistic, so reckless, so uncaring of consequences. You never thought enough about appearances, and you certainly never mixed with the right people. Do you have any idea how that could have hurt Peter's career over the years? The least you could have done was support his campaigns – like Zoe did.'

'Even though I don't believe in either his politics or hypocrisy? Or are they the same thing? I forget.'

She shook her head at me. 'You have no idea how unhappy I was with your father.'

'You never even gave him a chance. You spent the first however many years of my life pining for Peter and resenting Dad and me because Peter threw you over. Then you resented the things Dad and I did together. Nothing Dad did would ever have made you happy.'

'You don't understand – I was supposed to marry a lawyer, not an advertising man.' She said the word 'advertising' with disdain. 'I fell in love with Peter during the first week of university. I knew I wasn't the usual type of girl that he went out with, but eventually he noticed me. We spent hours planning our future – I really believed that despite the differences between us, there would be a future for us. He was my soul mate, the man I was destined to be with. And then he got Loretta Sheridan pregnant and her father made them marry. Peter didn't want to, but Loretta's father was a judge in the Supreme Court and Peter couldn't afford to upset him.'

'In other words, Peter was cheating on you back then as well.'

She glared at me.

'How did you end up with my father?' I asked.

'I was lonely, and I was upset with Peter. I thought if he knew that I'd been with someone else, he'd be jealous. But then I fell pregnant so the laugh was on me. Your father immediately offered to do the decent thing, and there was no question that I wouldn't accept him. I also had to give up my studies. I think I hated him more for that than I did for getting me into trouble. At least at uni I had the chance to still see Peter.'

She paused for a second, as if she was remembering. 'Then, one day in the city, I saw Peter again. We started to meet for coffee while you were at school. I realised that I'd never fallen out of love with him. He wasn't happy with Loretta, but was trapped because of her father's influence. He said he'd never forgotten me. When I found out that I was pregnant, I told him. I thought he'd be pleased, that it would be an answer to our problems. You could stay with your father, and Peter and I could have a life together. But he panicked and told me that he couldn't leave his marriage yet, not when she'd been so recently diagnosed, but that one day he would be able to come and get us. Until then I should have an abortion or pass the child off as your father's. I felt like my heart was broken, but I trusted that we'd be together one day.'

For a minute I almost felt sympathy for her. She had placed her faith in Peter all those years ago, and was clinging firmly to it, despite all the signs that said she shouldn't.

'You're a very ungrateful daughter,' she said. 'We've given you a good education, and put you in the path of the right people. And you repay us by associating with people like that boy who lived up the road. Do you think I need a reminder of those times? That's what happens every time you bring that man to this house – it reminds me of how unhappy those years were.'

'It's all about you, Mum, isn't it. Did you even think about me at all? After Dad died, Brad was the only person I had, and after we left I never heard from him again. I wrote to him, but he never replied.' I looked hard at her. 'Did you have anything to do with that?'

'I suppose there's no point in denying it now – it was years ago. He wrote to you, but I didn't give you the letters. Eventually he got the message and gave up.' Her tone was matter of fact.

'He said he wrote to me – I didn't believe him.'

She shrugged and finally emptied the dustpan of china into the bin. 'That was my favourite teacup.'

'What about the letters I asked you to post for me?'

'Apart from that first one you posted yourself, which I suppose was how he got your address, I didn't post them. Don't look at me like that, Abigail. It was for your own good.'

I stared at her. My head was beating, and at that

moment I didn't think I'd ever disliked anyone more. That flash of sympathy I'd felt was gone.

I pushed my stool out from the bench. 'You know what? I'm done. Say hi to Tyler for me … Actually, no, don't bother – I'll email him. As for you … we're done.'

'You don't understand,' she said. 'You've never understood. When you're really in love, you'll understand. You'll understand that you'll do absolutely anything to save it. I did what I needed to do for the good of this family.'

'Don't you mean, for the good of Peter and his career? Are you still that scared that he'll leave you if something happens? After all, he did it before, when you found out you were pregnant.'

'That was different. He had a family that he needed to protect. You don't understand.'

'You keep saying that – are you trying to convince yourself? And what about his indiscretions over the years? How do you justify those?'

'How do you know about that?'

'I don't. I just assumed that if he cheated on his wife with you, it's likely that he cheated on you with others. I guess infidelity isn't a good look when you run on the platform that Peter does, though.'

'That's none of your business.'

'If I wasn't so angry, I could almost manage to feel sorry for you.'

'I don't need your pity. And don't you go trying

to cause trouble for Zoe either. Clinton said that you'd made up some rubbish about him being abusive.' She shook her head slowly. 'I've never understood why you've always felt the need to ruin things for Zoe.'

I smiled without humour. 'Zoe and Clinton are well matched – I wish them much happiness. But if I were you, I wouldn't tell them I said that.' I pushed the stool back under the kitchen bench. 'I've said what I needed to say.'

I picked up my bag and let myself out of the house. I didn't look back.

Starting today, I wouldn't be doing that any more. It felt as if I'd spent most of my life looking back – to a time when Dad was around, and Brad and I were able to pretend that our bikes were really horses, and problems could be solved with cupcakes. It was time to leave the past where it belonged and move forward.

CHAPTER TWENTY-FIVE

I'd booked myself into a hotel in the city, in case Mum wasn't home when I called by. I hadn't intended to leave until I'd said what needed to be said. I dumped my bags in my room and took a walk down George Street to the harbour. Being a sunny Saturday afternoon, the streets were filled with shoppers. I weaved my way along the narrow pavement, dodging bags, prams and strollers.

It was here by the harbour that the differences between Sydney and Melbourne were most apparent to me. It was as if the cities were two beautiful women: one wearing a blue sequinned evening gown; and the other in a classic black dress. One so obviously showy and sparkly; the other more refined and subtle. One, you just couldn't help but notice her beauty; the other quietly elegant and refined. Both gorgeous, but very different.

I'd always liked this part of town, where the Bridge met the Quay and the Opera House. Here, everything seemed perfect – as if all of life was like that. The cloudless blue of the sky emphasised the white sails of the Opera House, and the harbour itself glistened like a million diamonds. God, I was that screwed up I was moving into cliché territory; and, like concern, I didn't do clichés – another 'c' word.

My phone beeped with a message from Tyler: *Hi A, heard you're in town. Mum seriously pissed – what went on there? Are you still around? Can we catch up for a drink?*

My baby brother had always been the one ray of sunshine in my family. Even though Tyler was closer in age to Zoe – five years' difference between them, compared to the fourteen between Tyler and me – when they were kids, Zoe rarely acknowledged his existence. Tyler was representative of the fact that attention had to be shared. But I'd always had a lot of time for Tyler, and as a result we were close. Mum and Peter were hell-bent on turning him into a replica of Peter, but I suspected Tyler had his own ideas about that.

Sure. Not flying out until tomorrow, I texted back. *Hotel bar at 6? I'm staying at the usual.*

I was nursing a glass of wine when Tyler strolled into the bar. Actually it was more of a saunter – that loose-limbed, confident walk that some great-looking guys have. And Tyler was a very good-looking man. I felt a little dull beside him.

'I should have thought to wear heels,' I said, stretching up to greet him. 'If anything, you're even taller and hotter than you were a few weeks ago.'

He grinned. 'Is that possible?'

Tyler may have had Peter's confidence, but thankfully he had none of his arrogance.

I smiled back. 'It's good to see you.'

'You too. What are you drinking? I'll buy my impoverished, unemployed big sister a drink.'

'So you heard about that then?'

'Yep. You drinking white?'

'Please.'

He was soon back with drinks and a couple of bags of potato crisps. 'So tell me about this fuckwit that Zoe's brought home.'

'Wow, I bet you don't use that language in the family home! What happened to "How are you, Abby?" or "You're looking good, Abby"? Instead you jump straight into Clinton and Zoe territory.'

'Sure, I'll play.' He grinned. 'How are you, Abby?'

'Fine, thanks.'

'Well, I know that's a lie.'

I giggled and took a sip of my wine.

Tyler grinned at a group of girls walking past. The blondest of them turned back and waggled her fingers at him. He raised both hands in a gesture of defeat and mouthed, 'Sorry, I'm with someone.'

She mouthed back, 'Too bad.'

He watched until her pert little bum had disappeared from the bar.

'Really?' I said.

'What's wrong? So you're a cougar.'

'Hello, I'm only thirty-four – I'm far from being a cougar. As if I'd be with someone your age.'

He shrugged. 'Yeah, but you gotta admit it, I look pretty good. Most women would love to show me off.' He gave me a cheeky smile.

'Don't go out in the wind – those tickets you have on yourself will blow off.'

'You've always been good for my ego, Ab.'

'Isn't that what big sisters are for?'

'Yeah, true. Maybe you should tell Zoe. Hey, is it my imagination or does that girl get worse every time she comes back? And Mum and Dad let her get away with whatever she wants. Speaking of which, tell me there's no way you ever had anything to do with this latest guy of hers.'

'Clinton? Well, that's not a simple question to answer.'

He groaned. 'No, Ab! Please tell me you didn't go there? Sure he's good-looking, if you like the pretty type, but he's a serious player, and you've never been into players.'

I sighed. 'I know, but it's one of those things that happened just the once – when I was in Bali earlier in the year. He was there too. He was persistent, and I was feeling pretty shitty after Brad went to Denmark, or wherever he is. So, you know how it goes – one thing led to another and we almost hooked up. I backed out at the last minute. I thought it was just a one-night thing and I'd never need to see him again, but he turned up on the other side of a meeting table.'

'Awkward.'

'It certainly was. It could have all stopped there, but Clinton doesn't like to be told no and made it his mission to try and convince me to say yes.'

'Is that why you lost your job?'

'Yep, I resigned. Clinton had somehow convinced my boss that my judgement was off. He also managed to convey the impression that it would be within his power to bring extra business our way if only I would, shall we say, be a little nicer to him.'

'You're fucking joking! Your boss told you to take one for the team?' Tyler sounded furious.

'Not in so many words, but it was pretty clear what he meant. Anyway, haven't we just spoken about your language? Mum and Peter would have a fit if they heard you.'

'Yeah, shocking, isn't it? Mum and Peter would have a fit if they knew half of what I get up to.'

'Cheeky bugger.' I laughed. 'And here's me thinking you're a chip off the old block.'

'Aaaah, maybe I am.'

'What do you mean by that?'

'Come on, we both know that Dad isn't as pure as either he or Mum make him out to be.'

I stared at him.

'Abs, really, I'm not *that* stupid. Anyway, what did

you do to Clinton?'

'He bailed me up in a lift, so I kneed him in the balls and told him to go fuck himself.'

Tyler roared with laughter. 'Go, Abs! Poor bastard – he's obviously never come up against you in a fight!'

'Then, somehow, his boss found out that he'd been frequenting a certain gentlemen's club on company money.'

Tyler grinned. 'Really? Who would have thought.'

'Yeah, strange. And before you ask, I had nothing to do with that part – although I think Mark is convinced I was behind it all. I'll let him think that.'

'What caught him out?'

'A random audit of corporate card expenses brought up the club. A further investigation showed some other anomalies and things like improper use of taxis and hotels. They've been investigating him for a few months. Anyways, I handed in my resignation. I couldn't work with someone who was prepared to pimp me out to the highest bidder. Unfortunately Mark was one of the clients Clinton had been "entertaining".'

'Even more awkward.'

'Indeed. But it gets better …'

'It couldn't possibly.'

'Trust me, it does. Sadly, Clinton was dismissed.'

'Sad indeed.'

'And the best bit? I've been offered a job by his old boss, with more money. I'm taking a few months off first.'

Tyler rolled back onto the bench seat, laughing. 'Fuck, that's good! Does Clinton know they've offered you a job?'

'Nope, and I don't intend to tell him – at least, not until Zoe gets sick of him.'

'And am I right in thinking that as long as Zoe thinks you're keen on Clinton, the longer she'll hang on to him?'

I smiled. 'How long have you known about that?'

'About Zoe stealing your boyfriends? For as long as I can remember. She never managed it with Brad – that's when I knew he was a keeper. I could never work out why she wanted anything and everything that you had.'

'I have no idea either, but she's always been like it.'

'How did she and Clinton meet?'

'He tracked her down when she was in Melbourne doing the fashion shows, engineered an introduction using my name, and I can guess the rest.'

He shook his head. 'She's a piece of work that sister of ours.'

'I do worry that he'll attempt to control Zoe, and after the behaviour I saw in the lift, it concerns me that he might be abusive. I sort of tried to tell Mum, but she said that Zoe had said I'd say something like that to try and ruin things for her, as usual.'

'I wouldn't worry about it, Abs – you've done what you think is right. It's up to her if she listens to you.'

I replenished our drinks and settled back into my seat. 'So, how's uni?'

Tyler was a couple of years into a law degree.

'Yeah, it's good. Dad wants me to join the practice when I'm done. I think he still has plans for me to follow in his footsteps into politics.'

Peter had kept up partnership naming rights on his old law practice even after his move into Federal politics.

'What do you want?' I asked.

'Not that. Maybe go to the Caribbean and work on a dive boat or something.'

'I'd like to be there when you tell them that.'

Tyler changed the subject. 'Why do you let Mum believe the stuff that Zoe tells her?'

'Unfortunately, appearances are more important to Mum than old-fashioned qualities like honesty.'

'Yeah … she's been covering for Dad all these years.'

'I still can't believe you know about that.'

He shrugged. 'You get to read the signs after a while … and they love each other in their own way. While we're on the subject, I didn't read the signs for you and Brad breaking up. I thought you two were together for life. You were my idea of what it should be like when you meet your soul mate.'

'That sounds corny. I don't know that there's such a thing as a soul mate.'

'Of course you do, Abs, don't fool yourself. What happened with you two?'

'Who says we've broken up? He's overseas on a fellowship.'

'The look on your face when you were explaining it at the campaign launch. You hid it well, but I saw some pain behind the smile.'

'Pain behind the smile? Have you been listening to boy bands again?'

'Ab …' he warned.

'You're not going to give up, are you?'

He shook his head.

'I was stupid and let him go.'

'What happened? Did he do something ridiculous like propose?'

'What the fuck?'

'Come on, A, you and I both know all about your commitment phobias. You're scared that anyone you love will be taken from you – I think it's left over from your dad dying and from when Mum pretty well withdrew … I've figured that much out over the years.'

My surprise must have shown on my face.

'I've made law a little bearable with some psych units. You're a classic case.'

'Gee, thanks a lot.'

'I'm being serious now. Come to terms with the father stuff, let go of the mother shit, trust that Zoe won't take everything you love, and you'll be fine.

Too easy.' He laughed at himself. 'And in that single sentence we have the reason why I'll never go into a therapy practice.'

I laughed with him. 'Yeah, too easy. Listen, can we change the subject?'

'Nope. I'm on a roll. So, fess up – did Brad pop the big question?'

'Yes, sort of. But I don't think it was a real proposal. It was like he just blurted it out in the middle of an argument. I don't even know if he meant it, or it was just something he thought he should do. He knows how I feel about marriage.'

'Now you're just being an idiot. Fine, it didn't work out with your parents, but you two wouldn't be like that. He loves you, and even though you used to pretend to be all cool about it, you love him too. Did you ever tell him? Dudes like to be told.'

'No, not enough. I didn't want to be like Mum and be the one who loved more.'

'I know I'm only twenty and still shagging around, but even I know that sounds like a crock of shit.'

'Don't hold back.' My eyes were welling again.

He saw and covered my hand with his. 'Go and hunt him down and bring him back where he belongs. Dudes like that, and you like a challenge. That makes it a win/win solution.'

'Dudes like that? What about if you love him set him free and blah blah blah he might come back or he might go and screw someone called Astrid or Heidi or something?'

'Like what you did with Clinton?'

'That's unfair.'

'But true.'

'I didn't screw him,' I argued.

'When Brad left, that was him setting you free to sort your shit out. You're just too thick to have worked that out. See, this is why you need me, big sis.'

'That's what Todd said. When did you get to be so smart?'

'As I said, a few units of psych – much more use than fucking torts. Anyway, who's Astrid and Heidi?'

'A blonde girl he had his photo taken with. I figured she'd have a Scandinavian name because she looks like an Abba song.'

'In other words, you've jumped to conclusions so you don't feel so bad about nearly shagging Clinton.'

'Stick with your torts, law boy.'

Lying in bed that night, I thought about what Tyler had said – about how Brad had set me free. Todd had said something similar. Now I needed to find Brad and somehow convince him that I was worth being given another opportunity.

With spring coming and the possibility of work picking up, he must be due home soon. He'd be keen to put into practice the things he'd learnt in Denmark, or Austria or Poland or wherever, like he did with the rooftop bars after his last European trip.

Hunt him down and bring him home was how Tyler had put it, and that was exactly what I was going to do. Although I hated to admit it, he was right about Brad, and about how it was up to me to make the first move. Who'd have thought that I'd be taking life advice from my twenty-year-old brother?

CHAPTER TWENTY-SIX

I met Andi and Todd for dinner. They looked right together, as if they'd both come home to each other from wherever they'd been. They still bickered, but there were smiles beneath the words. I saw how Todd glanced at her when she wasn't looking, and how she did the same to him. It seemed as though they needed to check that the other was still there and it wasn't all a wonderful dream. Brad and I used to be like that too.

Todd was a little uncomfortable with me when we first greeted each other at the restaurant, but I could understand that. I hadn't spoken to him since the Clinton episode, and even though I knew Andi would have put him straight, it did matter to me what he thought about me.

Andi asked how things had gone with Mum, so I told her about Clinton and Zoe. 'Apparently he said that he'd feel uncomfortable if I was upset.'

'I bet he was more concerned that you'd give them your blessing,' said Andi.

'My thoughts exactly.'

Todd's face closed over. 'Do we need to talk about him?'

Andi playfully smacked his hand and said, 'Oh, lighten up. He put the hard word on Abby but she didn't go there.'

'Oh, right,' he said. 'But I thought –'

'Never mind what you thought,' she said.

He turned to me. 'He put the hard word on you?'

I attempted to avoid the question. 'It doesn't matter now.'

'Abby … what did he do?'

'I was in Perth for work. He jammed me against the back of a lift, forced himself on me, then slapped me when I drove my heel – in self-defence – into the top of his foot to get him to move.'

Todd and Andi stared at me with their mouths open.

'And then,' I continued, 'he told me that if I didn't have sex with him he'd find a way for me to lose my job. So I kneed him in the balls and got the hell out of there.'

'Jesus, Abby, you could have been in a lot of trouble with him,' Todd finally managed.

'I've sort of figured that one out for myself.'

'Why didn't you tell me, A?' Andi was concerned again.

'I was embarrassed. I always thought I could look after myself – you know, be the one in control. Then I was in a situation where I'd never felt less in control. I knew logically that nothing could have happened, not in the lift or in the lobby, but to be honest, I was scared.'

'Did you get him good?' asked Todd.

I nodded. 'He wouldn't have been much good to anyone else for a couple of days.'

'Do you think he's abusive?' Andi said.

'I wouldn't be surprised. He's used to being obeyed, and hated the fact that I said no to him as often as I did. My only regret is that I allowed him to get away with the harassment at work for as long as I did – that's another reason I didn't tell you.'

'Don't feel bad, sweetie,' Andi said, 'you've been vulnerable this winter.' She glanced at Todd. 'The business with Brad threw you off balance, and then there was all the family stuff. I'm not surprised that you didn't deal with him in the way you normally would have.'

'Thanks,' I said. 'Somehow, though, that doesn't make me feel any better.'

Todd refilled our glasses.

'Do you want to know the best bit?' I asked, and told them about how Clinton got fired and I got offered a promotion at his old company. 'And now he's gone back to Los Angeles with Zoe. Apparently she's really hooked on him and thinks she can get him an audition. Of course, it helps that she thinks I'm interested in him. When you think about it, it's all neatly tied up for the best really.'

Except for the part where Brad still wasn't here.

They laughed.

'Oh, Abby, I haven't seen that fighting spirit of yours for years,' said Todd. 'Remember when you single-handedly took on the Scott gang?'

'You've known me for too long,' I said.

'I've known both you and Brad for too long,' he said quietly.

That was my opportunity to ask about Brad. I opened my mouth, but the words didn't come out. Drat, what was this new tear-welling thing? I must be going soft in my old age. I'd cried more in the last few days than I had in the last twenty years.

Andi noticed and jumped in to change the subject. 'Well, it sounds to me as if the two of them are welcome to each other.'

Todd shook his head. It felt awfully like he was disappointed in me, and I didn't blame him. I was disappointed in myself.

Andi spied someone across the room and excused herself for a few minutes. Todd took the chance to ask me how I was really coping.

I shrugged, not wanting to give too much away. 'It's been a long winter.'

'It's nearly spring,' he said, watching me closely.

I played with my coaster, then blurted it out before I could stop myself. 'I miss him so much, Todd. I …' I was trying hard not to let the emotion out, but biting the inside of my cheek and trying to talk at the same time didn't work. 'I miss him every day. I don't think I'll ever stop missing him. I had to do what I did – I know that now – but I should have trusted him with that.'

I hung my head and a fat tear plopped onto the table. I wiped it away, but he saw it and held his finger out to catch the next one.

'I need to find him,' I said. 'Wherever he is, I need to find him and tell him everything and bring him back. There's so much I have to tell him – things I should have told him before and new stuff. I mean, seriously, look at me, Todd – I don't cry and now it seems I can't stop. It's happening all the time. Sometimes I don't think I'll stop crying until he's home.'

Todd laid his hand over mine. 'It's about time you let go of that legendary control and joined the rest of us.'

'You make me sound like a control freak.'

'Well, Ab, you've got to admit it – you do tend to get your own way fairly often, and you know how to engineer the outcomes you want.'

'Not this time. Not since he left. Nothing has gone as I expected since he left. And now I feel very far from being in control.'

He looked steadily at me. 'Perhaps that's not such a bad thing. You used to fight for what's important, and you haven't done that for a long time.'

I thought about that for a second. 'I didn't fight for Brad.'

'Why do you think that is?'

I lowered my head again. 'Because it would mean admitting how much I need him, and people I need have a habit of either not being there or preferring Zoe.' I'd never said that out loud before.

After a short silence he said, 'Oh, Ab, it's okay, it's going to be okay.'

I looked up. 'How do you know that?' I was sure my mascara had smudged.

'Because it has to be. You two are all I know – and you know everything has to be about me.' He grinned. 'You have no choice but to make it work, Ab, and if that means swallowing your pride and admitting that you need him, you have to do that.'

'Where is he, Todd? I need to find him. Even if he's with Nina or Brigitta.'

'How about I text you the details tomorrow.'

'I'll be packed,' I said.

Despite having way too much to drink last night, and being out way past sensible o'clock, I stayed up into the early hours packing a suitcase and then going through old photos of Brad and me.

After not enough hours of restless sleep, I gave up and went for a run. By the time I got back to Flinders Lane, I was exhausted. I jogged around the corner to my apartment and stood for a moment with my hands on my knees, panting. I'd really pushed myself this morning.

I lifted my head and noticed the dog sitting on my steps. It was Bert. He saw me and bounded across, jumping around me in waggy, doggy ecstasy.

My heart, already pounding, felt like it had stopped. And then I saw Brad, leaning against the door. He straightened and I stared at him through the leftover sweat.

'You're home,' he said. 'I was wondering if you ever would be.'

'Where did you come from?' I panted. Oh, he was a sight for sore eyes.

'Oh, Abs, aren't you a sight for sore eyes?'

Didn't I just say that, or was I just thinking it?

'You're not supposed to be here,' I said. 'You're supposed to be in Denmark or Austria or Poland or somewhere, and I'm supposed to get my shit together and hunt you down and bring you home. Tyler said that's what dudes like.'

'What do dudes like?'

'They like to be hunted down, thrown over their woman's shoulder and brought home.'

He was smiling. 'I'd like to see you do that. Were you going to come and find me?'

'I saw Todd last night. He was going to text me the details and I was booking a flight this morning.'

His smile got wider. 'But I'm here.'

'You're not supposed to be.'

'I thought I'd save you an airfare, seeing as how you're now unemployed.'

'Todd told you?'

'He told me. I listened to my messages – did you mean it when you said you needed me?'

I nodded.

'You've never said that before.'

'I've never meant it before.'

He smiled and moved closer.

'No, don't touch me – I'm gross and sweaty, and you're not supposed to be here, and if you touch me I'll cry, and I've been crying too much lately.'

'You never cry.'

'I do now. I can't seem to stop.'

'Why don't we go inside? You can have a shower and then we can talk.'

I nodded, but I still couldn't take my eyes off him. I was afraid that if I went inside and stood under the shower, he wouldn't be there when I came out. I was scared he wasn't real.

'I'm scared you're not real,' I said.

He moved even closer and hauled me to him. He smelt real and he felt real. I was beginning to think he could be real.

'I'm sweaty,' I said into his chest.

'I don't care – you're beautiful,' he said into my hair.

And then he kissed me and the tears came. I didn't

want him to see me cry, so I blinked a bit and pulled away, biting at the inside of my mouth.

'I'm sorry. I'm crying a lot these days and I don't know why,' I sputtered. 'It's just lately.'

'So you've said.' He took the keys from my pocket and led me upstairs. The first thing he noticed was the mess. 'Jesus, Abby, this place is a pig sty. What's been going on?'

Then he saw the suitcase in the hall. 'Where are you going?'

'To find you.'

He pulled me to him and kissed me deeply again.

'Go have a shower and we'll talk when you're finished,' he said.

'Will you still be here?'

'I'll still be here.'

I grabbed some clean clothes and went into the bathroom, before running back into the hall. 'I can't believe that you're really here.'

'I promise I'll still be here when you're no longer smelly. Now, go have a shower.'

So I did. And when I emerged he was still there, sitting on a kitchen stool eating toast. Bert was curled up in his usual spot on the mat near the balcony door. He lifted his head and wagged at me some more, his tail beating against the floor. It all looked so familiar and normal that the tears threatened to spill out again.

'I couldn't find anything else to eat,' he said. 'Your

fridge should be donated to science.'

'Did I have bread in the freezer?'

He pushed across a plate and a cup of coffee for me. 'Yep, I had to chip it out of the ice. What have you been eating?'

I shrugged. 'Not much.'

'So it would seem.'

We sat at the kitchen bench and munched and sipped, and looked stupidly at each other. He'd collected the wine bottles and moved them to a central location near the bin, and done the same with the microwave boxes and other rubbish. He'd also located stray glasses and plates and stacked them in the dishwasher. Maybe I'd vacuum this afternoon. I'd have time now that I didn't have to catch a plane.

I asked him how he knew I was at home.

'Todd told me. I flew in yesterday afternoon and knew he was seeing you last night. I made him swear not to say anything to you about me being back. I needed to know how you feel.'

'What did he tell you?'

'Enough to bring me here this morning.'

'I've missed you,' I said. 'I miss you.'

The tears were falling again. He leant into me and kissed them one by one from my eyes.

'I've missed you too.'

'I can't cope when you're not here. Everything's gone wrong since you left.'

He smiled that wonderful, wide, crinkly-eyed smile, and traced my face with his finger, chasing a few leftover tears as they made their way down my cheek. Then, finally, he kissed my mouth.

'I wasn't going to do this, Abby,' he murmured between kisses. 'I was going to make you come to me, and beg and grovel.'

'I'd deserve it. And as long as you don't stop what you're doing now, I promise that I'll find something to grovel about later.'

I moaned as he kissed his way down the length of my throat and along my collarbone.

'What about the begging part?' he asked as his hand found its way to my breast.

'Oh, I think I'm about to start begging,' I said.

Afterwards, we lay facing each other. I reached out a hand and traced his lips. He caught it and brought it to his mouth, sucking gently on my fingers. When he let go, I trailed my fingers down his chest and around his nipples, before sliding my hand further down his body. He caught his breath, so I allowed my lips and tongue to follow the same path.

This time our lovemaking was slower and sweeter. When the orgasm hit, it was less a release than a joy.

CHAPTER TWENTY-SEVEN

Sometime later, wrapped in his arms, I asked him how his trip was. We seemed to have skipped that question earlier.

He kissed the top of my head and began to describe some of the places he'd seen and the ideas that he'd brought home.

'I love the sound of those vertical gardens,' I said.

'The Europeans are so much more advanced than us in design and permaculture. It's because they don't have the land that we do, so they tend to look after it more and make the most of the resources that are available. And if that means going up, well, that's what they do. I have some amazing sketches for corporate office spaces and precincts.' His hand idly stroked my arm as he talked. 'You should see this herb garden I've designed for a new restaurant fit-out in Abbotsford. It sits up in the rafters under a skylight that opens up. It's operated by a system of pulley ropes. Not only will it look amazing, but it will be completely functional.'

He sounded excited, and by the way he described

his ideas, I knew they'd be a success. I told him so. He looked a little surprised and I realised that was another thing I hadn't done often enough – taken an interest in his work, or listened to his ideas. It had always been about me being busy, me being stressed, me having to work late, me wanting to attain partnership, and him being there to support me. When had I ever been there to support him?

Eventually he asked me about work. 'Todd said you left your job. What happened?'

'I resigned.'

'Why, Ab? You were so desperate to be a partner.'

'By that comment, do you mean I was so desperate to be a partner that I chose not to go with you?' I moved away slightly in his hold.

He pulled me back. 'No, it was just a comment.'

'Sorry,' I said meekly.

'Don't do meek, sweetheart, it doesn't suit you. So what happened – why did you resign?'

'Because Mark asked me to do something that I didn't agree with.'

'Did it involve that guy Todd told me about?'

'Yes.'

'Always so honest.' His arms fell away from me.

'It was nothing,' I said.

'The way Todd told it, it sounded like more than nothing. It sounded like a whole lot more than nothing.'

I shrugged. 'What do you want me to say? It was

one stupid night of nothing, a kiss that blew up into a few months of pure shit.'

He didn't say anything.

'We had broken up,' I justified.

'I'm aware of that.'

'You'd gone to Denmark or Poland or …'

'… Austria or somewhere,' he finished.

'Yes.'

'It was Denmark.' He wasn't smiling any more.

'Brad, I'm sorry.'

He nodded but didn't say anything.

'Anyway, Todd showed me a photo of you with some blonde Swedish girl.'

'As you say, we had broken up.'

'Who was she?'

'Her name's Max and she's English. She was travelling with a Kiwi mate of mine, Richie. You saw that photo because I asked Todd to show it to you. I needed to know if you were missing me as much as I was missing you.'

'Oh.' I felt inexplicably happier. It was short-lived.

'Instead I find that you're into something with some guy you met in Bali.'

I attempted to defend myself. 'It wasn't like that.'

'What was it like?'

'Do we have to talk about this now?'

I moved away from him and found a T-shirt to cover my nakedness. He pulled on his shorts and sat on the other side of the bed.

'I think we do,' he said.

'Nothing happened. Well, not what you think anyway.'

He waited.

'Okay, fine. I met him in Bali, and on the last night I was there I had a little too much to drink and we kissed. I went back to his room and … well, I changed my mind.'

'Is that it?'

I shook my head, and sat cross-legged on the bed. I had one pillow propping me up against the bedhead and another in my lap. 'It should have been, but it wasn't. I'd seen him before, at Noodelicious – you know the place where Andi and I have lunch?' He nodded. 'Well, I'd seen him there. I thought he was interested in Andi – you know how everyone is interested in Andi. Then he was in Bali.' I took a breath. 'It wasn't until I'd gone back to work and he was in the project meeting for Warner Enterprises, and somehow managing to convince Mark that I needed to personally be involved in the project management, that I put two and two together. He knew who I was and where I worked because of the tender documents.' I shrugged.

Brad looked at me. 'I'm not liking the sound of this.'

'At the end he was essentially threatening me that if I didn't sleep with him, he'd make up all this shit about me and tell Mark. As it was he'd got in quite thick with Mark. He'd told him that we'd hooked up, he'd had to reject me, and now my judgement was flawed – woman scorned and all that.'

As I talked, I didn't look at him. I couldn't. It still felt like I'd betrayed him.

'I felt like I couldn't do anything about it because I had actually kissed him. Who would believe that I hadn't encouraged him? Besides which, he had Mark wrapped around his little finger. Then when I went back to Bali, he was phoning around trying to find out where I was, to the extent that Mark texted me and ordered me to ring him and disclose my whereabouts. And constantly there was the inference that if I didn't do it, my partnership was gone. Anyways, things came to a head last week – he forced himself on me in a lift, I jammed my heel in his foot, he slapped me, I kneed him in the balls, and then I resigned.'

I didn't know what the look on his face was. Disgust, disappointment?

'Shit, Abby, I had no idea. I should have been here.' He rubbed his face with his hands. 'You couldn't talk to anyone else? What about Andi, or Todd? Todd was supposed to keep an eye on you. Look at you – you're so thin … What the hell has been happening here?'

'Don't blame Todd. I could have told him, but I didn't know there was a real problem until I was in the middle of it, and then I was embarrassed that I'd let it happen. How did I let it happen? I have more sense and control than that. Then I was afraid that Todd would be disappointed in me, and I couldn't have borne that … not with everything else that had been happening.'

'What do you mean, everything else that had been happening?'

'A heap of things blew up regarding my father, and then, when I went back to Bali, I got the biggest shock of my life and found out that my mother had been lying to me for all these years. That's where I was when I left those messages on your phone. You'd gone, so when Clinton came in with his stalking and whatever, I had no idea what to concentrate on.'

He held his hands up. 'Whoa. Working backwards, what had your mum lied about, and what's this "back to Bali" thing, and what the fuck does any of it have to do with your father? He's been dead for years.'

'Mum never told me the real reason why Dad went to Bali,' I said, hugging the pillow to my chest.

He looked at me for a second and I saw the realisation cross his face. 'Christ, I'm an idiot. You know, I'd forgotten that your father died out there. Is that why you kept saying you needed to go?'

I nodded.

He shook his head. 'I'm sorry, Abs. I didn't understand.'

I shrugged one shoulder. 'It's okay. I don't think I did either – at least not until I got out there – then it was like something that I'd been needing to do for years. I was so used to no one ever talking about him that I didn't either. It was almost like he'd never existed. Mum wouldn't let me talk about him, so as I got older I figured that he must have had an affair. She was so bitter about him that the only explanation was that he'd left her.'

'Yeah, that's what my parents always assumed.'

'Well, that wasn't the case. It was her who had the affair. With Peter. Peter is Zoe's father.'

Now he was staring at me with his mouth open in disbelief. 'What the fuck?'

In the kitchen my cell phone was ringing. I ignored it. Eventually it stopped and I heard the tone of a voice message being left.

'That's why he left, because Mum had cheated on him. Peter had turned his back on her so Mum was trying to pass Zoe off as being Dad's.'

Then my landline started ringing. It eventually stopped and the answer machine clicked in.

'Abby? Are you there? If you are, please pick up … It's Kate … Roger's had a heart attack and he's asking for you. Please ring me … please come.'

I scrambled off the bed and started hauling clothes out of my closet.

Brad grabbed me and held me by the shoulders. 'Abby, settle down … what are you doing?'

'Where's my suitcase? I need to repack it.'

I squirmed out of his arms, but he caught me.

'Where are you going?'

'Bali – Roger's had a heart attack.'

He forced my head up to look at him. 'Abby, who the fuck is Kate, who the fuck is Roger, and why is he asking for you?'

'Kate is Roger's partner and Roger is my father.'

He looked at me in confusion.

'He's my father,' I whispered this time.

'Abs, your father died a long time ago,' he reminded me gently.

'I know … but here's the thing, he didn't actually die. And now I need to see him again before he dies for real.'

CHAPTER TWENTY-EIGHT

'I can't go into this now,' I said. 'I need to call Kate and I need to get myself booked on this afternoon's flight.'

Brad was still staring at me, disbelieving.

'Brad, snap out of it. Can you please grab my wallet and passport out of my handbag and get me a seat on that plane, while I ring Kate? Then I promise I'll tell you everything.'

He seemed relieved to have something to do.

I called Kate.

'Oh, thank God you're there, Abby.'

'How about you slow down and tell me what's happened.'

'It's a heart attack – they said it's a major one, but I don't know what the difference is. Surely a heart attack is a heart attack?'

I was sure there was a very big difference. 'It's okay, Kate. He'll be okay. He's fit and healthy.' I was trying to convince myself as much as her. 'Where is he?'

'He's been taken to the hospital near Kuta. They say they need to operate.' Her voice broke.

'Okay, he's in the best place possible then. I'll get onto this afternoon's flight and be with you as soon as I can. Hold on.'

I emptied the bag I'd packed for the European summer and replaced it with lighter Bali-weight clothes. In the meantime, Brad had booked my tickets, and been out for sandwiches and coffees. We sat on the lounge and drew breath.

'It seems you owe me a story, Abs.'

'I do.'

I began talking, and he listened without interrupting. I told him about how I'd found Kate, about how I'd met Roger, and about the confrontation with Mum.

'So, that's how it is,' I finished.

'I can't believe I didn't realise why you were so hell-bent on getting to Bali.'

'You mean instead of coming with you?' He nodded. 'Yes. It's something that had been weighing on my brain for a while, but I didn't know it until I did something about it. I figured I needed to go and see if I could find anyone who had known him back then. I didn't think the whole thing was as simple as it sounded, as I'd been told. I didn't expect to find anything – I certainly didn't expect to find what I found – but I needed to do it in order to move on. I needed to do it to let go of some things. I just didn't know it then.'

'You never said. If you had, I would have come

with you.'

'And forgone your trip? No, I didn't want that on my conscience. As it turns out, it was something that I needed to do on my own.'

'Haven't you realised what this means, Abby?'

'Yes, it means that my father hated his life with us so much that he faked his own death.'

'No. It means that he was so unhappy that when the opportunity came up to start again, he took it. Sure it was cruel, and it was wrong in so many ways. But more than that, it means your mother was never really free to marry Peter.'

'Yeah, that was one of the first things I thought of.'

'Are you going to tell her?' Brad asked.

'No, I can't do it to her. And I can't do it to Peter either, regardless of how I feel about him. I especially can't do it to Tyler. Can you imagine what publicity like that would do to him? You know he wants to mess about on boats, not go to law school?'

Brad nodded. 'I think you're right – it's not information that can do anyone any good at this point. Is it something you can keep to yourself?'

'I think so. You and I are the only people who know the story, and I see no reason why that has to change. As far as I'm concerned, my father died when I was a little girl. I cried for him then, I grieved for him then. The man I met in Bali is an old expat who came over for a surf a couple of decades ago and never went home. I was just getting to know him better. I hope he recovers and I can grow to love him – him and Kate.'

'What about Kate? Tell me about her.'

'She's lovely. She's gentle and wise and she loves him, and he loves her. It's an unconventional set-up, but it works, and he's stayed with her all these years. You know, they never married because Roger felt that he was still married to my mother. He took Kate's surname and managed to get all the right papers. He calls himself Roger Tindale and introduced me to everyone as his niece.'

'So he's not the same man who left?'

'No. The man I met is happy. The father who left wasn't, and I don't think he ever would have been. It was a selfish thing that he did, but Roger isn't a selfish man. I'm glad I met him … I'm glad I know him. He's not my dad, not yet, but there are things still to say. That's why I'm going back now.' I laughed. 'I like the idea of him living his dream. He's been happy, and I'm pretty sure he would never have been if he'd stayed with Mum. She would have broken his spirit, and he would never have been able to give her what she wanted. He was never going to live up to Peter Lockhart. It's probably easy to say now, but Mum had been in love with Peter all those years so, in the weirdest of ways, I guess it's all worked out for the best.'

'Yeah, it's funny how things work out. I think that's

always been the issue between you and your mum – she sees your father in you. You have that same tendency to look for adventure.'

'You mean the same inclination to recklessness?'

'Yeah, but they're also a couple of the things I love most about you. You've always had this fearless independence that I think you tried to bury under the respectable career. I still remember seeing you on the ground battling the whole of the Scott gang. You were remarkable.'

I grinned, a little ruefully. It seemed like a lifetime ago. I guessed it was. 'Todd reminded me of that the other night too.'

'I remember overhearing Mum talking to Dad one night after your father died – how long is it going to take before I can say that without thinking it's weird? Anyway, it was just before your mother married Peter. Mum said she was worried that your mother was trying to turn you into the type of girl she wanted you to be. She told Dad that she was afraid that all of that wonderful spirit you have would be tamed. What did she call it? Like you were a triangle that they were trying to fit into a circle.'

'It felt a bit like that at times. Do you think it has been tamed? My spirit?'

'I think you let them for a while.'

'You should have seen me knee Clinton Barclay in the balls.'

He laughed. 'I think I would've liked to have seen

that.' He shook his head. 'You shouldn't have had to deal with that. It shouldn't have been allowed to get that far. Heaven help him or Mark if I ever see either of them.'

'Perhaps, but I allowed myself to be in that position in the first place.'

He stared at me. I looked away first.

'What happens next?' he said. 'With us?'

'I don't know. I have to do this, I have to go back. And I have to stay until I know what to do next. I don't know how long that will be.'

He nodded slightly, but there was sadness in his eyes. 'The next move is yours to make.'

'I can't make a decision on that yet.'

He studied me closely. 'I think I know that. Do you want me to come with you?'

I shook my head. 'No. I have to finish this on my own. So much has happened … I don't know where to start making things right again – with you, with what I do. I don't know what I want any more. To be honest, I'm not sure that I ever did. I think part of the whole partnership thing has been me looking for a way to make Mum proud of me, or at least bring me a little positive attention.' I took a shaky breath. 'But I now know that's never going to happen, and I have to accept that, and the reasons why.'

'I love you,' he said.

I smiled at him. 'I hoped you did, but I don't deserve it. I've taken you for granted too.'

'Do you love me?'

'You know I do.'

'You hardly ever told me.'

'I know, and it's another thing I'm sorry about. I didn't want to be the one who loved the most … I didn't want to be my mother. That sounds stupid, doesn't it?'

'It does a bit.'

'How did you do it, Brad? Trust in us the way you always have?'

He shrugged. 'I don't know, Ab. I've loved you most of my life, and that day in the garden centre when I saw you again … well, I just knew. It sounds corny, but it felt like you were my destiny. The rest was easy after that.'

'I'm sorry I didn't trust you. I'm just used to leaving, or being left … you know?'

He nodded. 'I know.'

'You always saw through me.'

It felt like I was pulling away from him again. I think he felt it too.

'Do you want me to wait?' There was no expression on his face.

'I don't know how long I'll be.'

He stood and moved to the balcony door, looking down into Flinders Lane. Bert stood beside him and nuzzled his nose into Brad's hand.

'At least you haven't managed to kill the plants,' he said.

'They've had to fend for themselves this winter.' I think he knew that I wasn't only referring to the plants.

'Do you want me to wait?' he asked again, still looking outside.

'If you can.'

He deserved more than this. I walked over to him and stood beside him, also looking at the mess on the balcony. I struggled for the words.

'Yes, Brad, I'd love for you to wait for me. I want nothing more in this world than for you to wait for me. But after everything that's happened, I don't feel I can ask you to. And, in truth, I don't want to ask you to – I want to beg you to … wait, that is. But I know you've already waited years for me, so it isn't fair … not to you.'

He looked at me in silence for a few moments.

'I wouldn't blame you if you can't wait.' I shrugged. 'I'd regret losing you for the rest of my life, but I can't not do this.'

'It doesn't seem as though you've left me with a choice.'

'I'm sorry, Brad. I'm so sorry, but …' I had no idea what to say. 'I'm sorry.'

'So am I, Abby. I've loved you my whole life, and I'm ready to commit to a lifetime with you.' He shook his head sadly. 'But I can't keep waiting around for you to decide what you want. I thought I'd given you the space you needed while I went away … you have no idea how hard it was for me to leave. I won't do this again –

come looking for you. What happens now is all on you.'

We stood in my hallway with my packed bag looking accusingly at me. He took a step towards me and I took one towards him and we were in each other's arms, kissing as if it was the last kiss we'd ever share. Hard, hungry and desperate kisses, as if we were drowning. Perhaps I was drowning.

He wrenched himself away, whistled for Bert, and left, shutting the door softly behind him. I put my hand to my lips to try and keep the imprint of his there.

It was like it was all those years ago. Then it had been me driving away, watching him trudge up the road, his hands shoved awkwardly into the pockets of his jeans. He hadn't looked back then either. That day, from the rear window of the Commodore, I'd watched him until I couldn't see him any more. I knew it would be the last time I saw him, but I didn't want him to look back and see my tears. I didn't want the possibility that the last time he saw me, I was crying.

This time, I raced to the balcony and watched him shove his hands into the pockets of his jeans, walk to his ute, climb in and drive away. He didn't look back, but just like last time, I felt that somehow he knew I was watching him.

I watched until I couldn't see the car any more. Then I watched some more, just in case. Then I let the tears fall. Again. This was becoming an inconvenient habit.

CHAPTER TWENTY-NINE

Being mid-week, late and outside the tourist season, the queues at Denpasar for visas and passport control moved quickly. I didn't have checked luggage, just a small cabin-sized wheelie bag, so within forty minutes of landing I was in a taxi and weaving through the narrow streets around the airport, dodging the usual motorbikes and stray dogs.

The air conditioning wasn't working so I opened the window, but the heat and darkness had already wrapped itself around me. The taxi driver was communicating in the universal language of taxi drivers everywhere: one short beep for 'Excuse me, I'm coming through', one longer beep for 'Watch where you're going, idiot', and multiple blares for 'For fuck's sake, this is a one-lane road and two of us don't fit, so where the hell do you think you're going?' Tonight it all blended into one long noise.

I could still see the look on Brad's face as he forced himself away from me earlier today. I raised my fingers to my lips as if I could still feel his lips there, as if I could still taste him. I closed my eyes and saw him smiling at me, saw the way he looked into my eyes as we made love. I kept my eyes shut so I could keep him there.

By the time we pulled up at the hospital, it was almost midnight local time and I'd been up for over twenty hours. I was tired in that way that attacks the bones, yet I knew that I wouldn't be able to sleep just yet, even if there was the opportunity. I paid the driver, retrieved my bag and walked through the hospital doors.

After I'd explained who I was, a nurse led me down some corridors and into the intensive care unit, where Roger lay hooked up to a series of tubes.

'Your uncle, he is a very lucky man for you to come all the way from Australia to see him,' she said.

I nodded and smiled, but my eyes were drawn to Kate who sat beside his bed. At the sound of my wheelie bag, she got to her feet and gathered me into a hug, sobbing. I held her tightly until her tears subsided.

'I'm so glad you're here,' she said. 'It happened so suddenly.'

'What have they said?'

'It's now a wait and see. The first twenty-four hours are crucial.'

'He's too young,' I said.

I didn't say that Grandpa Brentnall was in his early sixties when he died. We both knew that.

'I know, sweetie. The doctors are running tests, but I guess it's a good sign that he's always looked after himself. He's fit and strong – that has to be in his favour, doesn't it?'

She separated from me and sat back down beside Roger. I took a chair on the other side of the bed. He looked old and frail, far removed from the lanky, vital man I'd met just a few weeks ago. He looked even more like I remembered Grandpa Brentnall looking. I picked up one of his hands and held it.

'Ab?' His eyes flicked open.

I moved closer. 'I'm here.'

He smiled faintly. 'How's that bloke of yours?'

'I told him how I feel, Dad. I decided to hunt him down and bring him back, 'cause Tyler said that's what dudes like, but he found me first, this morning … or was it yesterday morning?'

'Will it be okay?'

'I don't know. I hope so. Don't you tire yourself.'

'Don't over-think it, Ab. That's when the trouble starts.'

'I won't.'

'And don't go getting any of those tears on me either. After already dying in a jungle, do you think I'm going to go in a place like this?'

'I guess not,' I said, wiping my eyes. He had a point.

'I liked it when you called me Dad.' He closed his eyes.

Kate and I settled down to do some serious waiting and seeing.

'Thanks for coming, Abby,' she said again. 'It means a lot … and I wouldn't have blamed you if you didn't.'

I smiled weakly. 'I had to come. He's my father, and despite everything, I can't lose him again now.'

So we waited. I must have dozed a little, but I didn't think Kate slept at all. I watched her holding my father's hand and almost willing his heart to recover. They'd been together for so many years and their love for each other was obvious. Roger was right: in a true partnership, where there was love and respect on both sides, there was no room for the equations and other power games that people played.

I thought again about Mum's marriage to Peter. For all intents and purposes, they had what the papers called a fairy tale romance, and what the political spin-doctors held up as the perfect marriage. I remembered how she used to react when any of their friends divorced. Often the trigger would be the husband's infidelity, but I guessed the root cause would have been something very different. Who really knew what went on inside a marriage?

Her and Peter's closest friends, Tony and Frances, had split up while I was at uni, so I must have been around twenty. The story was a common one. He'd been playing away from home for years, and neither had any respect left for the other. She'd turned a blind eye to his infidelities over the years, just like Mum always did with Peter, and they'd stayed together for the sake of the kids. Once they were free of school fees, Frances found someone who treated her with respect and finally left. Mum blamed Frances for the split, talking about how she'd betrayed Tony with another man, as if Tony's actions over the years hadn't mattered. Mum had said something like, 'She should have made more of an effort. It's a woman's role to keep the family together.'

The sad thing was, Frances had been Mum's friend initially, yet after the divorce Mum refused to take her calls. Mum and Peter still saw Tony and his trophy wife. Word was, Tony was now considering trading her in for a younger model.

I'd said something about how it was better for children, especially girls, to see respect and love in a relationship, rather than a situation where the woman had to put her own needs aside.

Mum's answer was simple. 'Don't be so naive, Abigail. When you're married, your responsibility is to keep your husband happy and your children healthy. Your happiness doesn't come into it, nor should it. You have to work at marriage, it's not supposed to be fun. Look at Peter and I – we've weathered the years.'

True, but at what cost? Who was happier at the end of the day – the couple who'd been together for thirty years but hadn't spoken for the last twenty-five; or the couple who'd been together for thirty years while she turned a blind eye to his philandering (or vice versa) and made sure he had a clean, freshly ironed shirt each day and a hot meal; or the couple who separated and went on to have new, mutually respectful relationships with others and each other? At the end of the day, did you want to be able to say that you'd weathered the years, like Mum and Peter, or really lived those years, like Roger and Kate?

I looked across at Kate and the unashamed love in her eyes for my father. They'd fallen in love more than twenty-five years ago. Since then, nothing else but building a life together had mattered. It had been enough for both of them. Yet if you held their partnership up beside Mum and Peter's marriage, the marriage would be the one that was deemed 'right' by society.

That was what I'd always run from: the possibility that falling in love and getting married would result in a marriage like that of my parents, or that of my mother and her friends. The idea that all of the hope and possibility of new love could degenerate into something stale and lopsided filled me with fear. The idea of losing myself petrified me, but in doing as others thought I should, following the life that I was expected to follow, hadn't I lost myself anyway?

I'd heard friends say that they wouldn't leave their husbands because economically it didn't make sense. That they couldn't really complain too hard about his absences and the fact that they were left to raise the kids alone, because every so often he'd surprise her with a piece of jewellery or whisk her away on a flash holiday. 'My independence is a small price to pay for financial security,' they'd say. Sometimes, listening to their complaints about their husband's desire for them, I couldn't help but wonder if love had ever really played a part.

I had other friends who'd justified their infidelities through a curious range of complicated relationship equations: he was away too often, he didn't feel like sex any more, he'd played up after the last Christmas party, things had got boring … It was really no wonder that my accountant-trained brain had reduced it all to a series of equations. How did you put a price on independence, or loyalty, or self-respect?

I'd seen good marriages too, lots of them, so why was I so sure that the institution wasn't for me? Why was I so sure that I'd bring the worst of my parents into mine? Because that's what it boiled down to – a fear that the minute I stepped into the meringue dress and drank the champagne, the handcuffs would snap on and the negotiations would start. I didn't want that to happen to Brad and me.

Instead, in many ways I'd done the bad marriage thing when I hopped on the partner treadmill. I'd signed the contract, accepted a price for checking my personal opinions at the door, and spent the next however many years negotiating and compromising, giving away little pieces of my soul with every promotion, every pay rise and every bonus. The more money I made and the more senior I got, the less control I had. There was really very little difference between that and the should-I-stay-or-should-I-go considerations that so many unhappy couples went through. Whatever happened, in my next job I'd be looking for respect and partnership of a different sort. The money and the title were no longer sufficient compensation.

Sitting there in that Balinese hospital, holding the hand of my father and opposite the woman he belonged with more than he could ever have belonged with my mother, I wondered whether Brad and I would somehow be different – if we'd get the opportunity to be different. Brad wasn't the type of man to ask for my submission; we'd always been a partnership. We'd also always respected each other's space. What if we had that magical something that could stand the test of time? What if I'd destroyed that? Or, through my irrational fear, pushed him past the point where persisting was worth more than surrendering?

Why did I need to do this on my own? Why did I need to do anything on my own when I had Brad to help me do it? To help me through it. I'd told him I needed him, and then I'd told him I had to do this on my own and I'd left. I might as well have told him that I only needed him for the fun parts, not for the important things.

Before I could talk myself out of it, I reached for

my phone. The battery was dangerously low, and in the rush to leave I'd forgotten to pack a charger.

I tapped out a text to Brad: *I was wrong. I can't do this without you. I can't do anything without you. I need you – for the good, the bad and the ugly. I need you for everything.*

Then I sent another: *I know that I said it was unfair to ask you to wait, but now I'm begging. Please wait for me. Pour me a glass of red – I'll be home as soon as I can to drink it with you.*

Then I sent another: *I love you.*

As I typed, a nurse came in to check the machines that Roger was hooked up to. She wrote something on the clipboard hanging from the end of the bed, then turned to me. 'Please switch your phone off in here.'

I smiled an apology and complied. Later in the morning, a series of doctors wandered in, consulted test results and clipboards, and took Kate out of the room to talk to her. I sat by the bed with a heavy weight somewhere in the middle of my chest, and held the hand of the man she loved with all her heart.

As she walked back in, I looked up expectantly. 'Well?'

'They say he's stabilised enough to be operated on. There's still a way to go, and a lot more tests before he gets the all clear, but he's no longer critical. Abby, they say that if he pulls through the surgery, he's probably going to be okay.'

I held her and we both cried – tears of relief. Neither of us was ready to lose him forever.

•

I'd booked us into a hotel nearby for a few days, just until we were sure that Roger was out of the woods. The plan was that Kate and I would take it in turns to sleep there and sit with him in the hospital. I'd insisted that Kate go first, but before she left we grabbed a quick bite to eat in the hospital cafeteria.

As we ate, I caught her up with what had been happening – it was amazing how fast time flew when shit was hitting the fan. She listened without comment, and eventually I ran out of words. My father was lying in a hospital bed, and all I could think about was how much I wished that Brad were here.

'You've gone very quiet,' Kate remarked.

'Sorry, wasn't I listening?'

'No, love, you weren't.'

I sipped at my instant coffee and screwed up my face at the taste. 'Eeeeuw, this is dreadful … I'm just very tired.'

'Are you sure that's all it is?'

I smiled gratefully at her. 'I'm wondering, Kate, how do you do it?'

She looked confused.

'How do you stay in love?'

She smiled that gentle smile that I'd already learnt to adore. 'That's easy. We stay in love because we are in love. Your father is my best friend, my lover and my partner. Nothing else matters. There are no deals to be made or contracts to be agreed. It just is. We share everything that we have and everything that we are, unreservedly. Oh, and a good healthy sex life helps too.'

'I feel like I should be putting my fingers in my ears and going lalalalalala,' I said.

She laughed. 'No one wants to think about their parents having sex.'

'Brad's always been my best friend, but somehow I've managed to forget the rest and concentrate instead on being scared that it'll all blow up in my face.'

'You know, Roger always spoke of you as if you were the bravest and most special little girl that walked the earth, although he said you rarely slowed to a walk.' She looked hard at me. 'You can't calculate the risks of falling in love and staying together. You just grit your teeth, jump over the edge into the rapids and hope that you both end up on the same side of the bank.'

I laughed. 'An interesting choice of analogy given the circumstances.'

She giggled and put her hand over her mouth. 'Oh, I just realised what I said! Too funny.'

We were both silent for a minute.

Then she said, 'I know I'm not your mother, Abby, but over the years as I've listened to Roger talk about you, I knew that I'd love you if we ever met.'

My throat choked up again. I might have been relatively new to this emotional drama caper, but I was learning quickly.

She put her hand over mine. 'You don't need to say anything. Roger and I are so grateful that you've given us the opportunity to get to know you. I can't imagine how hard it must have been for you to do that.'

She reached into her bag and pulled out a wad of envelopes tied together with a purple ribbon. She handed them to me.

'What are they?' I asked.

'Every year on your birthday and at Christmas, Roger wrote you a letter and a card. Naturally he never sent them. This ribbon was yours – he had it in his pocket when he flew out of Sydney, and has kept it ever since. He always said that if anything ever happened to him, I was to find you and give them to you. I brought them with me, just in case, but Rog wants you to have them now.'

My tummy flipped and my heart skipped a beat. 'Does that mean …?'

She guessed at the path my mind had wandered down. 'No, don't worry, Rog will be alright, but he wants you to have these now. Take them, and read them in your own time. He might never be able to make it up to you, but don't ever think that he didn't love you – because he never stopped. He said good morning and good night to you across the ocean every single day.'

I swallowed hard.

Kate's eyes were gentle. 'Ab, what happened when

you were a girl was terrible. But please don't let that define your life. The past belongs in yesterday, and you have a chance now to start afresh – with your father, with Brad, with your career. Don't let it all have been for nothing.'

While Kate slept, I stayed with Roger, watching his face for any sign of change. Ignoring the nurses' orders, I checked my phone for a reply from Brad, but the battery was completely dead.

By early evening, Kate had returned. She'd showered, changed and had obviously managed some sleep. I was running on empty.

'Go, sweetie,' she urged. 'You've been in those clothes since yesterday.'

It was only yesterday. So much had happened, that surely it had been longer?

At the hotel I managed a shower, but, as I'd suspected, wasn't able to sleep. Although it was now almost midnight, I'd gone past being tired. Instead, I sat cross-legged on the hotel bed in my sleep shorts and singlet and opened the pack of letters Kate had given me.

She hadn't exaggerated. There was a letter for every birthday and every Christmas since Dad had left. There were also photos: of the beach, the house under construction, him and Kate, the various dogs they'd owned over the years, the bar, the staff at their annual

Christmas and other festival parties. He'd written about everything he'd been doing as if he'd just gone on a holiday and was sending me a postcard, except of course he wasn't on holiday and he'd never sent the cards. I got to know, through his words, the people in the village, the tourists who visited the bar, the fish that he'd caught and the meals that Kate had prepared with them.

I read them all, every letter my father had written to me. And, in shedding more tears than I'd thought I had in me, I finally said goodbye to the lonely, emotionally damaged little girl I had been for so many years. As Kate had said, nothing could change the past, but now I knew for sure that during all those years I felt so alone, someone sitting on a beach just outside Candidasa thought I was the most special person in the world. Through the letters, I began the process of not only understanding him, but also forgiving him.

And, once the tears had dried, I began to forgive myself for the way I'd treated Brad.

Kate was right. I'd let what had happened when I was a little girl influence every decision I'd made in the years since, but there was no reason why it had to influence my future … whatever it was that future looked like.

CHAPTER THIRTY

After the heat and humidity of Bali, Melbourne seemed cold, wet and dark. At the airport I'd changed from my Bali sundress and flip-flops into jeans, boots, a striped long-sleeved T-shirt and a long cream trench coat.

All too soon, and not soon enough, the taxi pulled up outside Brad's house. I lifted my bag out of the gutter and dragged it up the path. The rain was belting down and my boots slipped on the wet pavers.

And there he was. A glass of red wine in his hand, dressed in jeans with frayed bottoms, an old cable-knit jumper pushed up at the sleeves, the same thongs that he wore all year round – regardless of the temperature – on his feet. I could smell the fire from his living room and hear the faint crackle of the flames. It was all so familiar.

Bert had heard my voice and came running down the hall, skidding on the timber floor. He smelt of wood smoke, and I squatted down to bury my face in his fur.

Brad raised his eyebrows at me, but there was no smile on his face or hello kiss. I straightened, and pushed my hands into the opposite sleeves of my coat, doing this strange swaying movement, side to side and back again, my head tilted against one shoulder and smiling at him.

'You look tired,' he said.

'I am. I'm not sure I can remember when I last slept. Not properly. Maybe some time back in March?'

I looked at him hopefully, but his face still showed no reaction.

'How's your form, Ab? You text me and then don't answer your phone.'

'My battery ran out and I'd forgotten a charger.'

He continued to look at me and I continued with the swaying thing.

'I needed you,' I said.

'Do you still need me?'

'I think I always will. Maybe I can do this on my own, but I don't want to any more.'

He smiled then. 'Are you going to come in?'

He moved out of the doorway and motioned for me to enter, closing the front door behind me. I left my luggage at the front door and followed him in. Bert went back to flop on his mat in front of the fire, in a position where he could see us both.

My hands moved to the belt of my trench coat. I loosened it and then tied it tighter. I was still looking everywhere but at him.

'Do you want to get rid of that coat before you cut

off your circulation?' he asked.

'I guess.'

He raised his eyebrows when I made no move to unbelt.

'Oh,' I said, finally putting my bag down on the floor near the sofa where my bag always used to go, and hanging the coat over the back of it.

'How's your father? Wow, it seems weird to say that word … Did he …?'

I laughed a little nervously. 'I know, I'm still not used to it either. No, he didn't die. He was critical for a while, but he's a healthy old surfer – actually, he's not even really that old, I suppose. We think he's out of danger. There are still some tests that they want to do, but then he'll go back to Candidasa to recover. I needed to come home.' I paused and looked into his eyes. 'I needed to come home to you.'

His smile grew warmer and he indicated the glass of red wine at the end of the kitchen counter, in the place where I usually sat.

'You said you'd be home soon and to pour you one.'

My eyes welled and he moved to take me in his arms.

I stopped him. 'Not yet. I need you to see these.' I pulled the stack of letters from my bag. I'd reread them on the plane, waving the cabin crew away each time one showed concern at my tears. 'Kate gave them to me. They're letters that he wrote but didn't send to me over the years.'

'May I?'

'Sure.'

He settled at the kitchen counter to read. I leaned against the bench and looked out of the glass doors into the darkness, sipping my wine.

'Oh, Ab, these are tough to read.'

'I know. I cried a lot. It was almost as if he'd died all over again.'

I put my wine down and let out the sigh I'd been holding onto, before allowing my hands to drop to my sides. I drew one more breath before speaking, but didn't dare look at him.

'Here's the thing,' I said. 'I missed that life lesson where they teach you how to do this stuff.'

'How to do what?'

'This stuff. This grow up and be a partner and share a life and make compromises with someone stuff. I don't know how to do it. I'm fine with the sex, but I don't know how to do relationship well. In fact, I don't know how to do anything properly except work, and now that's gone too.'

I looked to the ceiling for inspiration. 'It was so easy for us at the start. You knew most of the things about me that I don't like to talk about, so we were able to skip those bits.'

I pinched my lips together as I thought about my

next words. 'Do you remember when we went to Luna Park, when we were kids?'

'Yeah, sure.'

I could see the 'what the fuck does this have to do with anything' look flitting across his face. 'Do you remember the Gravitron?'

'Yeah … it's the only time I've seen you scared.'

'I don't think I've ever told you, but that first night out with you, that's how I felt – as terrified as I did that day on the Gravitron. Like the bottom had fallen out of my world and I had no control over anything.'

'You never said …'

'Don't you see? There's so much that I never said. So much that I didn't trust you with – I hung on to everything that I could, so tightly. And you didn't. You gave me everything.' I shook my head. 'Maybe it's too late for me, for us. Maybe it's always been too late. Maybe I'm too damaged. I don't know. I hope it's not. You deserve more – you deserve someone who doesn't have my hang-ups.'

'Abby –'

'No, Brad, this is who I am. I'm not good at this. I don't know how to be. But I want to be – good at it, that is … with you. Nothing else really matters.'

I watched him carefully for a reaction, any reaction.

'You're right,' he finally said. 'You're shit at it. Definite performance counselling required.'

'What the fuck? That's not funny.'

'Sorry.' He was smiling.

'You're not at all sorry. See, this is exactly what I'm talking about.'

'Abby, I was joking.'

'I'm no good at it, Brad. I want to be, but I don't know how to, and I'm scared I'll fail.'

'That's why you have me. We'll get good at this together.'

'You don't know that.'

'I do.'

'How can you know?'

'Easy. We didn't find each other again to lose each other for good. I have to believe we'll figure it out as we go.'

The letters were still spread over the kitchen bench. I started to pile them up. 'What if we can't? What if it all goes wrong and you leave me and our kids and run off to Bali and pretend to die in a rafting accident? What if that happens? I don't even know if I want kids – I think I'd be a shitty mother.'

I had tears pouring down my face … again.

'Babe, you're not your parents. I don't want to go anywhere without you, and I happen to think you'd be a great mother – if you decided that's what you want to do. If you don't, that's okay too. Bert loves you.'

I let out the breath I was holding.

'Abby, I know you're scared, but if you walk out of here tonight and away from us because you're scared, you'll wake up one morning not long from now and regret it with every single cell in your body. As will I.'

He was right, I knew he was, so why couldn't I stop crying?

'So what do I do first?'

'Take a breath would be good, and maybe a sip of this wine. It's a good drop. Then have about twenty-four hours sleep.'

'No, I mean what do I do for work now? Do I –'

'How about we talk about what you want, rather than what you think you should be doing? Let's work this out like partners. You work, you don't work – I don't care. I think you owe it to yourself to give doing not a lot at least half a shot for a few months. Follow your dreams. You are your father's daughter. He wouldn't want to see you chained to a career path just because you think you should be. Then, if you really want to, take the role that Warner have offered you. Who knows, you might decide that you want to come and work with me ...'

'You're serious?'

'Sure I am. We'd make a hell of a team – your business experience, my designs. Clients wouldn't be game to say no after one of your pitches. Think of the ideas I could bring back from trips to see your father – I have a feeling coloured glass lanterns and buddhas are about to make a comeback in the rooftop bar scene.'

He was smiling, and I was beginning to think that

I should be smiling back.

'What if I turn out to have his lack of responsibility as well?'

'You won't. In any case, he proved himself to be faithful, not irresponsible – and he runs his own bar. It's every man's dream to have a relative with a bar. Besides, I'm not your mum – I'm prepared to give you whatever room you need to move. You have to know that I'd never try to pin you down. At least, not unless you ask me to … or beg me to.'

I looked properly at him now. His smile had turned a little wicked and he held his hand out to me.

'Zoe and Clinton have run away together to Los Angeles,' I said as I took his hand and leant beside the counter next to him.

He laughed, that great, fuzzy belly laugh that he did. The same laugh that I'd missed so much. The laugh I was terrified I'd never hear again.

That's when I started sobbing. Full-on, noisy, uncontrollable, blubbering sobbing. And that's when he pulled me close and held me so tight that I felt like I was cocooned within him. He let me cry, without saying a word until the noise stopped.

'I'm sorry, Abby. I shouldn't have laughed, I know it hurts.'

I scrabbled in my pocket for a tissue. He drew one from his pocket and I looked at it suspiciously.

'It's not been used,' he said.

'I'm not upset about Clinton and Zoe,' I explained. 'They deserve each other, and I seriously don't care if I never see either of them again. It's just that I realised how close I came to losing you.'

'I thought that with you and Clinton –' he started.

'No. I told you that was nothing. You left. He was there, but it never really started from my side. Anyway, he cost me my job, and could have cost me a lot more besides.' I dipped my head towards my right shoulder and risked a smile. 'Besides, it turns out that I really love you and I really, really need you. I didn't think I needed anyone to rescue me, but apparently I do.'

'That's good,' he said. 'Because I really love you and need you back.'

And that's when it happened. He went down on one knee.

'Abigail Brentnall, I've loved you my whole life –'

I didn't let him finish. Instead, I knelt on the floor in front of him and put three fingers to his lips.

'Bradley Ingram, I've loved you my whole life … Please, will you marry me?'

'Yes.'

It was a special moment.

ACKNOWLEDGEMENTS

Where to start?

Firstly, to my editor, Nicola O'Shea, for helping me tell Abby's and Brad's story; and Keith Stevenson at ebookedit for getting it out there. You guys rock.

A special shout-out to Grant for forcing yourself to follow me and my camera to Bali. You might call it a holiday, but for me it's about scouting out new locations. After all these years, you're still my favourite person to travel with.

While on the subject, my endless gratitude goes to the island of Bali. I was first fascinated by you in a cold classroom in southern New South Wales in 1981, and continue to be inspired and surprised by you today.

As always, this book wouldn't exist if it weren't for the support of my family: Grant, Sarah and Kali … love you guys … xxx.

•

If you enjoyed *Big Girls Don't Cry* I'd love it if you left a review in the usual places. If you'd like to stay up to date with my next happy ending, you can sign up for my newsletter at my website: https://joannetracey.com

You can also drop by and see me – virtually speaking, of course – at any of these places:

My blog: https://andanyways.com
Facebook: https://facebook.com/joannetraceywriter
Instagram: https://instagram/jotracey
Twitter: @jotracey_

ABOUT THE AUTHOR

Joanne Tracey would like to say that she's a thirty-something, perky-pony-tailed marathon runner. Sadly, it wouldn't be true. What is true is that she's sometimes a corporate warrior, sometimes a domestic diva, and absolutely always a believer in happy endings. Jo's novels are inspired by her travels and when she isn't writing words, she's procrastibaking, planning her next adventure or taking way too many photos of sunrises for Instagram.

Also by Joanne Tracey

Baby It's You

Wish You Were Here

Happy Ever After